# The Enlightened

*Mind Dimensions: Book 3*

## Dima Zales

♠ Mozaika Publications ♠

This is a work of fiction. Names, characters, places, and incidents are either the product of the author's imagination or are used fictitiously, and any resemblance to actual persons, living or dead, business establishments, events, or locales is purely coincidental.

*Copyright © 2014 Dima Zales*
www.dimazales.com

Published by Mozaika Publications, an imprint of Mozaika LLC.
www.mozaikallc.com

Edited by Elizabeth from
arrowheadediting.wordpress.com

Cover by Najla Qamber Designs
www.najlaqamberdesigns.com

e-ISBN: 9781631420474
Print ISBN: 9781631420559

# DESCRIPTION

Kidnapped. Consciousness expanded. And that was just the start of my day.

I always thought I was a nice enough guy. The kind who'd never want to commit murder.

Turns out I simply lacked incentive.

Some crimes can never be forgiven.

# CHAPTER ONE

"I can't believe how much life sucks without the Quiet. The last two weeks have been a total nightmare," I say to Mira as I put a final layer of sunblock on her long, perfect legs. The warm Florida sun is shining on my back, its relaxing effect mingling with the pleasant buzz from my piña colada.

"Yes, horrible." She snorts lazily. "We Russians had it wrong by sending all those people to Siberia as punishment. We should've sent them to South Beach instead."

I look around at the blue ocean and the beautiful girls, the hottest among them sitting right next to me. Maybe she's right to be sarcastic. Maybe things aren't so bad after all.

"You know what I mean. Your company and the locale are what make it bearable," I say, the details of all our wining, dining, chilling at the beach, and, most notably, our sleeping together—daily—flashing before my eyes. "But I just don't like the feeling that I'm not in control of my destiny."

"You want illusions, is that it? You're old enough to know we're never in control of anything," she says, raising the sunglasses off her nose. "Your best bet is to enjoy things when life brings you something good, and tough it out as best you can when it brings you the usual shit storm."

I know better than to argue against her bleak philosophy. We've had a version of this conversation before. If I keep it up, she'll remind me that most Readers spend the majority of their time unable to phase into the Quiet due to their shallow Depth, and that most people can't do it at all. She might then call me ungrateful and/or spoiled. Of course, keeping quiet doesn't mean I agree with her. Even as a kid, when Sara used the 'there are people starving somewhere' argument to make me feel guilty, it would never work.

So instead of doing the same dance, I try to strategically change the subject. "Are you hungry? I'll walk over to the bar and get us something."

"Sure," she says in a warmer tone. She's gracefully accepting my defeat. "Get me one of those cheese quesadillas. I'll be in the water when you come back."

I watch her walk down the beach, toward the ocean. The sight of Mira in a tiny bikini lifts my mood.

Okay, so maybe I've exaggerated my situation. Our efforts to spend all the cash that Jacob had in his briefcase—the briefcase that Mira had the presence of mind to appropriate while escaping a gunfight— had been pretty fun. That is, until I made a whopping two mil on the bank stock I shorted thanks to my fortuitous Read of Jason Spades, the bank's CEO. What I saw in his mind that time in the gym played out even better than I'd expected; the government actually had to bail the bank out, and the stock hit rock bottom, enabling me to cash in on my trades. The downside of being a multimillionaire, though, is that it takes some fun out of our frivolous spending—or at least, it does for me.

Once Mira is out of sight, I get up, brush the sand off my legs, and head for the Tiki bar. As I approach the bar, I'm reminded of another mitigating factor for these hellish weeks: my best friend Bert and my aunt Hillary are sitting at the bar, together, sipping fruity umbrella drinks. Bert arrived in town four days ago, while Hillary flew in at the end of last week.

"No, I'm not talking about black holes," Bert is telling her. "*This* Singularity is a point in history when the speed of technological advancements will go through the roof. It might be brought on by artificial intelligence or trans-humans—people who merge with technology. The AI, or the enhanced humans, will quickly learn how to build a more intelligent next generation, and that generation will do the same, and the generation after that, which will create a chain reaction of sorts. It'll be an intelligence explosion, beyond which we can't predict what will happen. And this is where it's a little bit like the singularity of physics."

"And these alleged technological Luddites are trying to prevent this Armageddon scenario?" Hillary asks, apparently fascinated.

"Yes. Except it's only an Armageddon scenario in their shortsighted worldview. In mine, if you were so determined to use a term from Scripture to describe it, the singularity is more like the Rapture—a hugely positive event where all the world's problems, such as death, might get resolved. But yes, that's what I think they're trying to prevent. That and any change in general."

"Hello," I say, interrupting Bert's favorite conspiracy theory.

"Oh, Darren." Hillary grins at me. "Bert was just telling me this really fascinating story."

She actually means it, which reminds me why Bert will be in my debt for the rest of his life. When they both arrived in Miami, I introduced them without any matchmaking ideas in mind. I was thinking that my aunt and my best friend should know each other. It would've never occurred to me, not in a million years, that Hillary would actually *like* Bert. The reverse is not a surprise; my aunt is very cute, in the way that all small things are cute, like puppies and kittens. Then again, her size might be what gave Bert the boldness to approach her in *that* way; she's that super-rare girl who looks small next to him. Bert's so-called courting of Hillary has been a huge source of entertainment during these dark times. That she said yes to dating him is an event as close to a miracle as I'll ever witness, and thus the debt. I am totally taking credit for this. He asked to be hooked up with a girl, and I started a chain of events that ended with Bert getting the woman of his dreams— cause and (accidental) effect.

"I'm just here to get some food," I say to stop Bert from launching into his conspiracy spiel.

"Okay, but at some point we should definitely discuss it," Hillary says with a small pout. "The idea of some very *traditional* people killing scientists because they don't want progress is very interesting."

Now she has my attention. Does she mean to say that either the Traditionalists of the Guide community or the Purists of the Reader community have something to do with Bert's Luddite conspiracy theory about the killings of scientists? No, can't be. It's more plausible that she's had too much of Bert's Kool-Aid. Yep, that would explain a lot.

Still, I say, "It does sound like we should chat. But now isn't the best time."

"In that case"—Bert smirks—"I take it you're also too busy to hear about my progress with the USB drive you gave me."

Bastard. This is blackmail at its finest. "I guess I could find a *little* time in my super-busy schedule to hear about *that*," I say, waving at the bartender— who ignores me in favor of a hot blonde.

"Well, that would get us back on the same topic," Bert says triumphantly, "because the first three names on the list you gave me belong to prominent scientists."

Oh shit. Sounds like these things might actually be connected. This will also complicate the story, or more precisely, the lack of an explanation I gave Bert regarding this drive. I can't exactly tell him that Jacob, a Purist Reader, wanted the Russian mob to kill these people, can I? That's a serious question. The only person who gave me the whole 'don't tell regular people about us' speech was Jacob—not someone to be posthumously trusted.

For a moment, Hillary looks as though she's concentrating.

Bert looks confused before saying, "We'll talk about that later. What I really wanted to ask you was whether you and Mira wanted to go on a double date tonight. There's this raw vegan place Hillary found on Yelp."

Okay, that is weird. I'm convinced Hillary just Guided him—though in this context, it's perhaps more accurate to say she Pushed him—and she did it to change the topic. The irony is that, unbeknownst to Bert, he's in the middle of the biggest conspiracy theory of all. His new love interest can *literally* make him do anything she wants. He's living the 'my girlfriend can control my mind' conspiracy, which even a tinfoil hat can't prevent. Hillary wasn't subtle about it either. Bert asking to go to a vegan restaurant? I had a hard time convincing the guy to try sushi, and that's yummy raw fish. He's a meat-and-potatoes guy to the core. Or maybe she included that little touch to make it clear to *me* that she had

Guided him? Her willingness to Guide him makes it even stranger that she didn't stop him from nerding out just a moment ago. If I weren't Inert—incapable of entering the Quiet after dying there—I probably would have. This convinces me that despite all logic, she really enjoys hearing Bert's conspiracy theories.

"Yeah, sure, I'll ask her," I say, wondering what Mira would think of this vegan food idea. Though she gets along with Hillary surprisingly well, all things considered, vegan food might be a problem for her. Mira is definitely a carnivore. If she were an animal, she'd be a panther—unlike Hillary, who'd be a hamster.

Finally getting the bartender's attention, I place our food order.

"Please come back in fifteen minutes, sir," the bartender says.

"Okay, guys. Mira's waiting for me in the ocean," I say. "I'll be back in a few to get the food."

I walk toward the ocean, looking forward to a swim. For the thousandth time, I try to phase into the Quiet. The fear of it failing is what I use as a catalyst, only I hit the usual mental brick wall.

Halfway to the water, I notice something strange: a big man wearing military-style clothing, on a beach. Startled, I look at him more closely . . . and my heart rate jumps.

I recognize the man.

It's Caleb, who's clearly looking for me. As soon as his eyes lock onto mine, his gaze sharpens, and he heads my way.

In a green blur, he cuts through the remaining distance between us.

Panicking, I turn around, intent on running the hell away, but he's already next to me. Before I can take a step, I feel the cold barrel of his gun pressed against my naked ribs.

"We're taking a walk, kid," he says harshly. "Don't make a sound."

"What's this about?" I try to keep my voice even despite the fear spreading through my veins. "I'm in the middle of something."

"Shut up and keep walking," he says, shepherding me away from the ocean.

We walk in silence down the stretch of beach that belongs to our hotel and exit onto the street, heading toward *Collins Avenue*. My bare feet hurt from the hot asphalt, but I'm too worried about my situation to focus on the pain.

After a couple of minutes, we approach a red Honda that's parked by the sidewalk. "Get in." Caleb jabs the gun into my side.

"Let me at least grab some clothes," I say, realizing I'm about to take a drive dressed in nothing but swim trunks.

Instead of answering me, Caleb pulls out a syringe, and before I get the chance to scream, he jams it into my upper arm.

"Are you fucking kidding me?" I manage to say, my speech slurring, and then I'm out.

# CHAPTER TWO

I'm aware of movement. I'm in a car, and it's driving very fast. That's all I'm feeling. I can't see for some reason, and I'm not sure how I got here—wherever 'here' is. I'm also freezing. Then it slowly comes back to me.

Caleb drugged me. This is his car. Where is he taking me? What the hell is going on?

I'm overflowing with adrenaline at this point, and even though I know it's futile, I try phasing into the Quiet.

When it works, I'm so surprised I can't believe it's real. But it must be. I'm in the backseat. The car is no longer moving. The roar of the engine is gone, and I'm not cold anymore. Frozen Caleb is sitting in the driver's seat. Next to him I see a black bag covering my frozen self's head. That explains why I couldn't see. I find it interesting that the bag did not join me in the Quiet. Clothes usually do, but I guess whatever it is that decides 'what to bring' into the Quiet decided that the bag wasn't part of my clothes. Good call, and another small piece of evidence in support of Eugene's theory that all this Quiet stuff is really something that just happens in our heads.

So after all the time I spent worrying about it, I'm finally back in the Quiet. However, I can't enjoy it. Not without knowing what the hell Caleb has gotten me into.

Opening the door, I leave the car. I'm no longer cold, though I wish I were wearing more than swim trunks. I look in the back of the car. In Brooklyn, Caleb's Hummer had all sorts of guns and knives in the back. This car, which I'm guessing is a rental, has nothing of the kind. Disappointed, I look around.

We're in the middle of a highway going through what looks like a forest. A dense wall of trees stretches for miles on either side of the road. There's no way for me to tell where we are. It certainly doesn't look like Miami.

I try walking into the forest, but after a few scratches and splinters, I decide that aimlessly hiking through the hostile woodland is a dumb idea, especially as a means to figuring out where Caleb is taking me. Wandering down the road proves just as pointless. Despite walking for miles, I find no sign of our current location.

Getting back to the car, I try to explore the front of it. I get my frozen self out of the seat, unceremoniously letting the black-bagged body fall to the ground, and look inside the glove compartment.

Finally, I find something useful.

True to himself, on top of whatever armament he probably has on his person, Caleb has a gun stashed there.

I take the gun and use it to push open Caleb's vest. I don't want to touch him; the last thing I want is to have him in the Quiet with me. I was right, though. He has a gun, and the huge knife he likes to carry with him is attached to the inside of his vest.

Okay. What now?

I decide to go back and pretend to be unconscious. Now that I'm no longer Inert, I can phase in once in a while to look around. Maybe after another couple of miles, I can figure out where we're going.

I touch my frozen self and phase out of the Quiet.

The noise instantly returns, as does the cold from the air conditioner. More importantly, I'm nauseous again from either Caleb's driving or the effects of whatever drug he used to knock me out. Or maybe a combination of both. The last thing I want is to throw up, especially with a bag over my head, so I employ a trick I've used since I was a kid and breathe in deeply. In. Out. In. Out.

The nausea slowly subsides.

Suddenly, the car comes to a screeching halt, undoing all my work. I almost puke.

In a blinding flash, the bag is off my head. I keep my eyes closed, pretending to be unconscious. I wish Caleb would kill the engine now that we've stopped; the cold of the air conditioner is making me shiver, which is a dead giveaway to my being awake.

Then the world goes eerily silent. Caleb has pulled me into the Quiet. I keep my eyes closed.

"Stop that bullshit, kid. I know you're faking it," Caleb says. "I pulled you in, which means even if you were unconscious before, you *are* conscious now. It also proves you're no longer Inert. So why don't we have a little chat?"

Shit.

He's right. The process of pulling someone into the Quiet wakes them; that's what happened with Mira that time when I pulled her out of her beauty sleep, and got a gun pointed at my head for it. Before I can dwell any longer on that fond memory, powerful hands grab me by the hair and trunks. In one swift motion, I fly out of the car, scrape my elbows, and land in an explosion of pain.

"Fuck, Caleb." Coughing, I attempt to get to my knees. "What the hell are you doing?"

"Ah, so you are conscious," he says and kicks me in the ribs.

The air rushes out of my lungs, and I struggle to take a breath.

He kicks me again. And again.

I gasp for air, nearly gagging from the pain as he finally steps away. I wonder if he's going to get a gun to finish the job. At least this time I know I'll survive getting killed in the Quiet, though I'll be Inert again and for who knows how long. With all my remaining strength, I start crawling away, though my shattered ribs scream in protest.

All of a sudden, I'm back in the car in real time, with the noise of the engine roaring and the cold of the air conditioner blanketing me. I'm blissfully *not* in pain, but then everything goes quiet again.

I stare at Caleb, who's now in the back seat with me. What the hell is he doing? He took me out of the Quiet only to pull me back in.

"Get. Out," he says through clenched teeth.

With a sinking feeling, I realize I've never really seen Caleb pissed before. Not until now, if pissed is indeed what he is.

My heart hammering, I scramble out of the car. He climbs out too and takes off his vest with the weapons, dropping it on the ground.

It seems like he wants to fight.

Ignoring the hopelessness of the situation, I focus and brace myself.

My right hand moves to block his first punch without my brain really telling it to. My left tries to hit him in the jaw. He manages to block my hook, and in the next moment, I'm seeing stars.

My nose is the epicenter of unspeakable pain. I feel something warm running down my chin, and as I try to inhale, something obstructs the air from entering. My nose must be broken. As that realization hits me, I block a punch to my solar plexus.

Then Caleb does a move I can only describe as a football tackle. He rushes me, and since I didn't expect it, I lose my balance and fall to the ground.

He kicks me in the head. The crack that accompanies the strike sounds as though the universe split open. *Must be a skull fracture*, I think vaguely as painful white light fills my vision.

Caleb seems to pause, and my consciousness ebbs.

I'm in the cold car again. The pain is gone, but my confusion is multiplied a hundredfold. What the—?

And then I'm pulled into the Quiet again.

"Do you want to keep playing, or are you ready to talk?" Caleb asks after I get out of the car, my legs wobbly.

This is what it's about? Some kind of a creative torture he invented? Kick the shit out of me in the Quiet, reset the injuries by phasing out, and then pull the restored me back in, beat me up, rinse and repeat?

"What the fuck do you want?" I say with more bravado than I feel.

"You can start by explaining how Jacob was killed by the gun I gave you," he says, and I know I'm in *really* deep shit.

"Jacob was killed?" I ask, trying my best to sound surprised, which is easy because I *am* surprised— surprised that Caleb found out about the gun. Thomas—my new friend and the only other adopted Guide I know—was so convinced we were in the clear. But I forgot that the gun I used was the one Caleb had personally given me. He must've gotten access to the ballistics report from Jacob's murder case and realized it was his revolver that had killed Jacob.

"You know he was." Caleb crosses his arms over his chest. "Do you really want to resume my game?"

I think quickly, knowing full well a delay in response will be interpreted as a sign of lying. If I come clean about everything, including being a hybrid, he'll likely kill me outright, like in the memory I experienced where he killed a Pusher bomber. If I give him a half-truth—yes, I killed Jacob, but he was the bad guy responsible for killing Mira and Eugene's parents—he might believe Jacob's guilt, or, again, he might kill me for murdering his boss. This leaves me with the weakest response of all, but I proceed anyway, feeling as if I have as many choices as a person being Pushed.

"Wait," I say. "I genuinely don't know anything about Jacob getting killed—"

Caleb takes a threatening step toward me.

I start speaking faster. "Look. I got shot after you dropped me off at Mira's house. You can check the hospital's records. When I was in the hospital, someone took the gun."

It's somewhat plausible, and given the circumstances, not the worst thing I could've come up with. Unfortunately, Caleb doesn't even dignify my quick thinking with criticism. Instead, he walks up to me and throws the first punch, which I manage to block with my left hand. At the same time, my right elbow connects with his jaw.

He raises an eyebrow in surprise and retaliates— how, I'm not entirely sure, as it looks like a blur of movement—and then pain explodes in my chest. Like before, I fall to the ground, and he kicks me repeatedly. The beating hurts like hell. And just like before, when I'm barely alive, he phases us out of the Quiet.

I'm cold, and this time it's not just from the air conditioning. The adrenaline is pushing me into a fight or flight response. I'm dreading another beating. I don't think I can take it. But he doesn't pull me into the Quiet. Instead, he puts the damned bag over my head again.

"They're going to find out exactly what happened anyway," Caleb tells me.

Before I can ask what the hell that means or who 'they' are, I feel a pinprick of what I assume is a needle, and the familiar nothingness spreads through my brain as I go under.

# CHAPTER THREE

A slap to the face wakes me.

It's the least fun way to wake up, followed closely by loud alarm clocks and cold water.

Before I am even done coming back to consciousness, I phase into the Quiet.

In the Quiet, I become much more alert—especially when I look around.

Caleb and I are no longer alone.

There is an older man staring at my frozen self through the car's side window. He looks to be in his sixties or maybe even seventies. I can't tell because I'm terrible at gauging the age of anyone over forty. I exit the car to take a closer look.

He looks completely out of place here, in the middle of the road, though the guy might look out of place pretty much anywhere with the white toga-like robe he's wearing—anywhere except possibly ancient Greece. Yep, the strange outfit makes him look the way I imagine Socrates would look—minus the beard, as this guy is clean-shaven.

Had he walked here on foot? If so, from where, given that we're in the middle of nowhere? More importantly, why did he come here? His dress puts only weird theories into my head. Weren't they into younger men back in ancient Greece? I nervously chuckle as I picture Caleb calling this guy on his cell and saying, "Hey Grandpa. I'm taking a nearly naked twenty-one-year-old out into the woods for you. I'll text you the GPS coordinates. The guy is still unconscious from the drug I gave him, so come quickly. It's molesting time."

I decide the only way I'm going to get answers is if I phase out and let things unfold as they may.

I touch my frozen self on the forehead, careful not to touch Caleb's hand, which is making its way through the air, coming back from slapping my frozen self on the cheek.

The sounds and the sting from the slap come back. I open my eyes, but before I can say anything, everything goes silent again, and the pain is gone.

I find myself in the backseat of Caleb's Honda, pulled into the Quiet yet again. I note that the strange old dude is now in duplicate, the animated version removing his hand from my frozen self's neck—meaning I'm in his Quiet, not Caleb's, at the moment. So the guy is one of us, most likely some kind of a Reader, given Caleb's presence. I also note that Caleb is sitting next to me in the backseat. He must've been pulled into this Quiet session before me. He's ominously holding another black bag.

"Don't move," the old guy says in a raspy voice. My snide remark that was about to graphically explain what Caleb and Grandpa can do to each other is interrupted when Caleb puts the cursed black bag over my head and jabs a gun into my ribs.

"Get out of the car and follow me," the old guy instructs.

"I can't see you," I say. "How can I follow you?"

"Here, hold on to this piece of rope," Caleb says. "And if you try anything, I'll make our prior conversations seem like a fun warm-up."

"Where are you taking me?" I ask no one in particular. "What the fuck is going on?"

"I'll explain when we get there," says the stranger in a tone that implies the conversation is now over. He sounds like someone who's used to giving orders.

My attempts at starting a conversation to gain information are ignored as we walk. This is probably the most terrifying walk of my life, by the way—also, the most uncomfortable. We walk across gravel roads, grass, a forested area, and hot asphalt, just to name a few of the horrid terrains. None of these surfaces are exactly friendly to my bare feet.

After what feels like a day or more of walking, we stop.

"Take that awful thing off his head," says the older man.

Caleb grabs the black hood and roughly rips it off.

"You nearly broke my neck," I complain, feeling something akin to whiplash, but no one deigns to give me a response.

The bright light hurts my eyes but only for a second. Recovery time is definitely quicker in the Quiet than in real time. My feet are already healing. It's odd. I've never stuck around in the Quiet long enough to recover from an injury, not when phasing out is so much easier. I was derelict in my science, apparently. This is useful information and adds more credibility to Eugene's theory that only our consciousness enters the Quiet and that these bodies aren't exactly real bodies, but manifestations of the mind. Or something along those lines.

I examine the old man again. His light blue eyes are looking me up and down with cold curiosity. For someone his age, he's in okay shape, and his white, slicked-back hair is nearly all there, which is rare, I imagine. Perhaps he's on the younger end of my age estimation after all? That aside, I still feel justified in mentally calling him 'Grandpa' for now.

I look behind him. We're standing near grassy plains, the forest we walked through visible in the distance. It's a scenic landscape, for sure, but what catches my attention is the huge temple right behind Caleb and Grandpa.

The temple is intricate and seems completely out of place here, in the middle of the United States. The architecture is definitely Asian-inspired. I'm no expert on the subject, so I can't say whether the style is Tibetan, Chinese, or Japanese, but I can say with certainty that it isn't American. Fear forms in the back of my mind. Could Caleb have knocked me out long enough to transport me to Asia? But that makes no sense. How would he get a comatose passenger onto a plane? He wouldn't. We drove here, so we must be somewhere in North America.

"What is this place?" I ask, trying not to sound too impressed. "Where are we?"

"It's our home," says Grandpa. "Follow me. I'll get you some clothes."

We enter through the large golden gates, with Caleb trailing behind us. It seems the theme of the day is breathtaking beauty. And it's not just the cherry blossom leaves frozen in the air or the gorgeous landscaping. It's everything. A deep sense of serenity is woven into every strategically placed little pagoda, into the very essence of the giant rock gardens. If I weren't convinced that I'm in the deepest trouble of my life, I'd probably relax and enjoy it all. As is, the landscape and peace of this Quiet slows my heart rate—slightly.

I'm not surprised to see monk-like people when we enter the Temple. They have shaved heads and are wearing orange robes. Maybe they're Buddhists? Everything points to that, though I don't recall seeing one of those iconic, chubby statues with serene smiles and big earlobes. According to my mom Lucy, that fat guy isn't even the original Buddha from India, but a Chinese version that came about much later.

We take an intricate set of stairs up to what looks like some kind of barracks.

"Here, put these on," Grandpa says, handing me a robe and plain sandals that match those of the monks.

I put on the robe, feeling silly about the resultant look.

"Now that you're more presentable, there are people I want you to meet," Grandpa says and unceremoniously heads out of the room, preventing me from asking any questions.

Annoyed, I follow, wondering whether he would've ordered Caleb to drag me out of the room had I decided not to cooperate. I'm guessing the answer is yes.

The three of us enter a large amphitheater located on the top floor. Around the perimeter of the massive round room is a large circle of orange-clad monks all frozen in the lotus pose. Their faces are serene and blank. Rows and rows of candles and incense surround them. The motionless fire and smoke look like the result of high-speed, three-dimensional photography. In the center of the room, surrounded by the monks, are over a dozen figures sitting in a large circle with a foot or so between them. Their white robes match that of Grandpa's, and like him, they all appear older. I see white hair on all but a few of the men, and those few are bald. As we approach, I notice a gray-haired, orange-robed person sitting at the very center of this strange arrangement. There is a lot of space between him and the circle of white-robed people, almost as if another, smaller circle belongs in the middle.

Navigating through the seated meditators, Grandpa approaches the white circle and touches an older woman on the back of her neck. In an instant, a lively version of this woman is looking at Grandpa intently.

"You should have a look at him," Grandpa says, gesturing toward me. "I now have little doubt."

The woman looks me up and down, her eyes settling on my face. Her kind, round face seems to be smiling without outwardly doing so, like the Mona Lisa.

"Hello, Darren," she says. "It's nice to finally meet you."

She knows my name. Is that good or bad? Probably bad.

"Hi," I say uncomfortably. "Who are you?"

"I am Rose," she says, breaking into a genuine smile.

"Nice to meet you, Rose." I try to keep my tone polite. "Can you please tell me where I am?"

"Didn't Paul explain it already?" she asks, looking at Grandpa.

"There was no time," Paul says. "We had to make sure everything went according to plan."

"Sure," she says, prolonging the word to make it sound placating. I catch a hint of eye rolling. "Do we tell him now, or do we pull Edward and Marsha in?"

"Your call," Paul says, his face even. If he noticed her reaction, he's hiding it well.

"All right, Darren, let me start by telling you who we are," she says, turning toward me. "You might've heard others refer to us as the Enlightened, though I personally think the term is a bit posh."

The Enlightened? I can hardly believe my ears. She's claiming they're the legendary Readers who, according to Eugene, can stay in the Quiet for record times—like me. I glance at Caleb, seeking verification, but he's not paying attention to me. Instead, he's looking at the older woman, his expression that of deep respect.

Okay then.

I take a steadying breath. "I've heard the term mentioned," I tell the woman. "But I'm not sure what it really means."

"Nor am I," she says, chuckling. "It's just what Readers call us."

"Okay." I decide to give up on that line of questioning for now. "Can you tell me where this is, and more importantly, why I'm here?"

"In due time," Paul interjects. "First, you have to tell us a few things."

"Sure," I say cautiously. "Like what?"

"Tell them why you asked me about Mark Robinson," Caleb butts in.

Paul nods. "That would be a good start."

I am so busted. If I tell them the truth, they'll figure out my mixed heritage. But I have no idea what lie I can concoct to explain why I was asking about Mark, a long-dead Reader.

"Jacob mentioned him when we spoke, the day I got shot," I say, deciding to start with the truth. "Naturally, I was curious."

At the mention of Jacob's name, Caleb's face darkens, and I realize that wasn't the most strategic response on my part.

"You know more," Paul says calmly. He isn't accusing me of lying so much as he's simply stating a fact.

"I might," I allow. "But why don't you tell me something next? Quid pro quo."

"He's scared," Rose says, her kind face turning serious. "Why is he scared?"

This turn in the conversation is completely unexpected. Rose sounds as though she's defending me. Is this some kind of strange bad cop (Grandpa) / good cop (Rose, the nice old lady) game?

"Why are you looking at me like it's my fault? Why not ask this oaf?" Paul says defensively, pointing to Caleb.

"Young man," Rose says, her full attention on Caleb. "What did you tell him?"

"Nothing," Caleb answers, and his voice takes on a note I haven't heard from him before. If it were someone else, I'd swear he sounded deferential. "I just asked him a few important questions about the business with Jacob."

I shudder, remembering how he'd chosen to ask those 'few important questions.'

"You were explicitly instructed to bring him in unharmed," Paul says, apparently noticing my reaction. His eyes narrow at Caleb. "Which part of that instruction was left open to interpretation?"

"Is he harmed?" Caleb says, and now he's the one sounding defensive.

"Darren," Rose says in an overly soothing tone, the kind a mother takes with a tantrum-throwing child. "Whatever happened with Jacob will not get you into trouble. Whatever Caleb told you was because he was mad about his mission going awry."

Caleb gives an angry grunt but says nothing.

"What mission?" I ask suspiciously.

"Jacob was part of a group that Readers call the Purists. The Purists are part of another group, a bigger group, called the Orthodoxy," she explains patiently. "Caleb has been working with us to penetrate the Orthodoxy, and Jacob was an important lead."

"What is the Orthodoxy?" I ask, my head spinning. Caleb was an undercover agent of some kind? Actually, when I think about it, it doesn't require a stretch of the imagination to picture Caleb in such a role. He's certainly well versed in fighting.

"It's complicated," Rose says. "We believe there is an alliance between the Purists and their traditional counterparts among the Pushers."

"There's a whole organization of these people? It wasn't just Jacob and a Pusher?" I blurt out before I can stop myself, and realize I might've admitted to knowing too much.

"So Jacob did have a Pusher ally?" Caleb asks, his face managing to darken even more.

"Yes," I say. At this point, lying probably won't help matters. "In fact, that's who I was really going after when this thing happened with Jacob."

"Tell us everything," Caleb says.

"Young man," Paul says to Caleb. "Remember your place."

"We'll find out what happened when we perform the Joining," Rose says gently. "For now, we just want to make sure you, Darren, are who we think you are."

"Wait, I want to learn about the Orthodoxy," I say, keeping to my original subject. I don't want to be at the center of their interest. I don't want them confirming their suspicions about who they think I am, especially if those suspicions include me being part Guide. It's a big break as is that they're apparently not angry with me for offing Jacob. At least the Enlightened aren't; Caleb clearly is.

"We don't know much about them. They're religiously secretive. People like him"—she nods at Caleb—"are trying to uncover more information about this sect. From what little we've learned, we know they're responsible for many actions we don't approve of."

"What kind of actions?" I ask, staring at her.

"They're too numerous to list," she says, frowning, "but their biggest mistake is their desire to get rid of *us*. They want to return to the days when Readers of our magnitude didn't exist. Our power scares them. Our practices scare them. Anything new scares them, really, which is why they intentionally stifle human progress of any kind. They want to make sure the world remains within certain parameters that are comfortable for them. We suspect they're behind most of the fundamentalist groups in the world, be it Islamic extremists or—"

"Enough," Paul says. "I'm sorry to interrupt, Rose, but we can cover this at another time. Darren, let's cut to the chase. Was Mark your father?"

I look at them. Rose gives me an entreating look. Caleb's eyebrow rises slightly, but his expression otherwise remains blank. Paul waits expectantly.

"Why would you ask that?" I ask, searching for a way to dodge this subject.

"We ask because we're almost certain that you are his son," Rose says. "We want to know without a shadow of doubt before we proceed with the next part of our plan."

I rattle questions at them as quickly as I can. "What plan? Why do you think I'm this person's son? And why does it matter?"

"We believe you're Mark's son because we looked you up before asking Caleb to bring you here. When we saw you, we noticed the familial resemblance. Combined with your questions about the man, the likelihood seems great, but given whom Mark married, we just didn't think it was possible," Rose explains.

"You know whom he married?" I give them a surprised look.

"We do," Rose says, cautiously looking toward Caleb. "No point in going into that right this moment."

"Indeed," Paul says. "But I am beginning to understand the source of your reluctance on this issue."

"Yes, now I get it, too." Rose smiles at me. "You have nothing to worry about, though. Not from us two, that's for sure."

"Oh?" I say noncommittally. "Why is that?"

"Because, child, Mark was our son," she says, gesturing toward Paul. "You're our grandson."

# CHAPTER FOUR

Rose is my grandma? Paul, the guy I nicknamed 'Grandpa,' actually *is* my grandpa? That's just too much to take in. Since I learned Sara isn't my biological mom, I knew I'd eventually come across new family—and it's logical that my family would be from the Reader and Guide communities—but knowing this and actually having it happen are two different things. I'm more surprised by Paul and Rose being my grandparents than I was to learn that Hillary is my aunt.

Studying their features more closely, I notice the resemblance: Paul has my eye color, and Rose has my chin. Or rather, I have theirs. My heart starts beating even faster. I hate that we're in the Quiet, because that means I can't phase out to take a breather, as I usually would in similar situations.

"As soon as I saw your pictures online, I suspected you were my grandson," Rose says, pulling me out of my shock. "I hoped. You look just like Mark did when he was your age, and even more like Paul."

"Why didn't you tell me this?" Caleb asks, looking at Paul. Apparently, this is a surprise to him, too. "It would've been nice to be in the loop."

"Did you need to know?" Paul retorts coldly.

"I guess not," Caleb says, deflating. "But it would've helped. I thought—"

"It doesn't matter," Paul says. "Rose, I think we should bring in a few of the others."

I have to say, in contrast to Rose, who is beaming at me, I'm not getting any warm and fuzzy feelings from Grandpa. Not one bit. Maybe he's one of those crankier older gentlemen.

"You may go," Rose tells Caleb. "But do stick around in this Mind Dimension for the time being."

"You got it," Caleb says and walks off. If it's possible to express anger through one's gait, he's doing an extremely good job of it. It sounds as though he misunderstood their reason for having me brought here, and I wonder what the actual reason is.

Rose and Paul walk over to two other white-robed figures. She touches a bald man on the head, and Paul goes for the neck of a heavyset woman who's sitting on the other side of the circle.

The moving versions of the two new people appear. I'm still digesting having grandparents—grandparents who are among the Enlightened, no less.

"Darren, this is Edward, my husband," Rose says, introducing the bald man.

"And this is my wife, Marsha," Paul says.

Both newcomers look at me with varying levels of fascination.

"I can see it," the bald one, Edward, says.

The chubby lady, Marsha, nods.

When the introductions sink in—and though it's not the weirdest thing I've heard today—I can't help but say, "Wait, you two aren't married?"

"No," Rose says, giving her husband a reassuring squeeze on the arm. "Paul and I had Mark because it was genetically advantageous, but when it came to choosing life partners, each of us married for love."

Okay, so fact one: I have grandparents. Fact two: they're swingers. It just gets better and better.

"Rose and I are the most powerful of our kind," Paul says. He must've interpreted the expression on my face as incredulity about the 'genetically advantageous' reference, when my astonishment was in regards to their sex life.

"Yes," Rose chimes in. "We were bred, through generations, for our Depth. Our ancestors have been trying to—"

"I'm sorry to interrupt, hon," Edward says to her, "but shouldn't we do the Joining first? Before we tell him everything?"

"That's a great idea," Paul says. "We can only fully confide in him after the Joining."

"Joining?" I ask, slowly regaining my scattered wits. "Like when I joined my mind with Caleb's to read the fighter's thoughts?"

"Something like that, yes," Rose says, "but on a bigger scale."

"Caleb gave us the report on your experience," Paul says. "He gleaned your guilt about your Pusher nature without fully understanding the situation. Since you obviously can Read and all."

"He did? I was so afraid he'd find out I was a Pusher and kill me like he did that guy in his memories," I blurt out. "I can't believe he saw my biggest fear and didn't confront me about it."

"The man Caleb killed was one of the Pushers allied with the Orthodoxy," Paul says. "You witnessed the event out of context. The explosion Caleb prevented was meant to put a deeper wedge between Readers and Pushers. It was also how we began suspecting Jacob of being in league with the Orthodoxy. He wasn't at the community when the explosion was supposed to happen." His voice hardens. "Believe me, he won't be missed."

"You mean to tell me that Readers don't kill Pushers just for being what they are?" I give him a dubious look. "What about the genocides?"

"That's in the past. Modern Readers don't kill Pushers for being born as they are. Or better to say, anyone we have influence over doesn't, not since we've learned of the good that Pushers have done in the world," Rose says.

"Good?" I blink at her. "What kind of good?"

"Well, for starters, during the Cold War, we know a powerful Pusher prevented nuclear war," Rose says.

"Possibly more than once, hon," Edward corrects.

"Wow." I'm surprised Hillary and the others never told me about such a feat.

"Yes. We have been fascinated by our Pusher cousins for some time now, and any enmity between us is a direct result of the Orthodoxy's efforts," Rose says with a touch of regret. "They want things to be like they were in antiquity, and their strategies are succeeding so far. In Russia, our people are still at each other's throats."

I nod, thinking about some of the stuff I heard from Eugene. "But something about the Orthodoxy doesn't make sense to me," I say after a moment. "If they don't want Readers and Pushers to be friendly, they're sure not acting like it. After all, they're cooperating with each other, like Jacob and that Pusher Caleb killed."

"Yes, it's a hypocrisy of the tallest order," Edward says, looking disgusted. "But cooperation is their only chance of taking us on. They know if we allied ourselves with the Pushers, everything would change, and change in the world is what they fear most."

"Bear in mind that we have no idea how the Orthodoxy is structured," Marsha says. "There is a chance that the alliance is tenuous. We certainly hope so. There is also a chance that they plan to eliminate each other as soon as they've achieved their goals."

"And truthfully," Rose says, "though we're not out to kill Pushers, this age-old hatred is very hard to overcome, despite everything we've learned. It happens to be the focus of my 'loving kindness' meditation."

"So, with those things out of the way, you should proceed to Joining with us," Paul says, giving Rose a strange look.

"Why?" I ask. "I didn't like it when I Joined with Caleb, so I'm not all that eager to do it again."

"You will do it so we can trust you," Paul says, furrowing his white eyebrows.

"Right, but don't we have a Catch-22 here? I don't want to do it because I'm not sure *I* trust *you*," I say, trying not to sound petulant.

"Your view on the matter is irrelevant." Paul's face reddens. "You're going to do as you're told."

He sounds like my uncle Kyle, and that pushes all sorts of buttons for me, so I tell him, "Listen, Grandpa, go fuck yourself."

"You little—"

"If I may," Rose says, interrupting whatever insults Paul was about to throw at me. "Darren, let me show you around the Temple some more. I think we should have a nice chat."

"Please bring me into your Mind Dimension when he's ready," Marsha says and walks over to her body. She says it as though it's a forgone conclusion, and that pisses me off too. Marsha touches her own neck and is gone before I can say anything about it.

As a side note, what Marsha just did is a very cool way to pass the time in this sort of situation. When she's pulled back in, she won't have experienced the time during which I was hypothetically being convinced to do the Joining, so to her, even if it takes a year, it will feel instantaneous. In that way, it's almost like time travelling. Of course, she won't be pulled in, period, because I have no intentions of letting them convince me.

"I'll do the same," Edward says and walks over to his own body.

"I'll be here," Paul says through clenched teeth and walks over to what I assume is his place in the circle. "Ask Caleb to keep guard when you see him."

Without saying anything else, he takes his position in front of an empty spot. It must be where his frozen body would be were it not near the car by the road. He's now an arm's length away from the bearded monk at the center of the circles. He settles into the lotus pose, closes his eyes, and, I guess, starts meditating.

Rose takes me by my elbow, and we leave the amphitheater in silence. I see Caleb on the right side of the corridor that runs around the big room we just exited. We turn left and start walking. From the corner of my eye, I take in the stunning view of the intricate stairway that leads to the amphitheater.

"We are *very* patient people, Darren," Rose says softly. "So we will get what we want."

"What is that supposed to mean?"

"It's simple. What choice do you have but to cooperate?"

"Plenty. I can get the hell out of this weird place and go back to Miami to enjoy the rest of my vacation."

"All right, walk me through that," she says, her eyes gleaming mischievously. "Step by step, how are you going to get to Miami?"

"Well," I start, thinking it through for the first time, "I need to phase out—"

"Is that what you call Splitting? I like it," she says. "To *phase out*, what do you need to do?"

"I need to touch myself," I say, my heart skipping a beat. I'm beginning to understand my predicament.

"Please don't do that here," she says, the gleam in her eyes turning into full-fledged amusement. "That's one part of your growing up I don't mind having missed."

Realizing what I said, I start laughing. The laugh is partly hysterical, though.

"Looks like you have my sense of humor," Rose says. "You wouldn't have gotten it from Paul, that's for sure."

I stop laughing. "The bag over my head wasn't to hide the location of this place, but to hide the location of my body, right?" I say, looking at her. "I can't initiate phasing out without touching my body, so I'm stuck here, in Paul's Quiet."

"Another term you invented?" she says approvingly. "You're as smart as I thought. The situation is exactly as you described, with two extra bits of information that should persuade you to cooperate. One—Paul is extremely stubborn, and I hope you didn't get *that* from him. And two—he can keep up this session for many, many subjective years, and he will. So you see, all we have to do is wait you out—something we have a lot more practice with than you do."

"I could kill myself," I suggest. "That would get me out."

"And become Inert? You wouldn't," she says, but her forehead wrinkles at the thought. "Besides, Paul and Caleb would only bring you to the Temple and we would wait for your Depth to return."

She's right, of course, but that gives me a more desperate idea. Without saying a word, I turn and head back for the amphitheater.

"Caleb," Rose yells. "Guard the Hall, *now*."

She must've guessed my intentions.

I start running up the stairs, but by the time I get to the Hall, Caleb is already there, arms crossed. Fuck. My idea of how to get out of this Mind Dimension involved killing my newfound grandpa. Since I'm in his Quiet, killing him would've kicked me out of it and made him Inert—a sacrifice I'm quite willing to make given the situation the old man put me in.

"You realize if something happens to Paul, you'll end up in the car with me, right?" Caleb's smile resembles that of a shark. "And I would be *very* unappreciative."

Okay, that plan is no good. I'm not even sure I could've gone through with it anyway. I probably just wanted to scare the old coot with the possibility of being Inert and blackmail my way out of here. But what Caleb says is true. In or out of the Quiet, I'm still in a precarious situation.

"Are you ready to continue our tour?" Rose asks from the bottom of the stairs. "Are we done with this foolishness?"

I don't answer. Instead, I run again, down the giant staircase.

In mere minutes, I pass all the frozen monks and race through the gardens until I find myself outside the Temple. The forest surrounds the entire perimeter of the valley where the Temple is located, so I can't be sure from which direction we came when I was blindfolded. On a hunch, I run toward the trees in the distance, hoping that's the right way.

I run and run at a pace where it's actually kind of fun at first, and reminds me of the excursions I took as a kid. The sandals make it easier to run, too, and my feet are very grateful for them. Unfortunately, after hours of running, all I achieve is getting as tired as a dog. I don't find the road, let alone the car. Stubbornly, I run some more. The fun of this is long gone, slowly turning into agonizing weariness. When I feel as if running another step will make me sick, I have no choice but to admit defeat. I was hoping I'd find my body if I searched long enough, and from there, I'd work on a plan for when I phased out. However, it seems like I might as well be looking for a person without a cell phone in the middle of Times Square—an impossible task.

With my proverbial tail tucked tightly between my legs, I return to the Temple, my slow pace making the trip back mind-numbingly boring. On my way, I decide that Joining with the Enlightened won't be the end of the world. I wanted to refuse them out of principle, because I didn't like the way Paul was ordering me to Join. However, I have to admit, a part of me is rather curious about the Joining. When I shared Caleb's mind—which, let's face it, was not the friendliest of places—it was less than pleasant. This experience, however, could be very different—perhaps *enlightening* in some way?

When I get back to the Temple, I make my way up the stairs decisively.

Caleb sees me coming and gets up from his lounging position next to the Hall. Was he just meditating? Though I guess this place would drive anyone to try it, Caleb doesn't strike me as the meditative type at all.

"I'm not here to hurt anyone," I tell him and raise my hands. "I'm ready for the stupid Joining they want to do."

"You're such a fucking idiot," Caleb says, and before I can respond, he enters the Hall and slams the door behind him.

Belatedly, I realize I should've nicknamed Caleb 'Mr. Personality.' As I wait, the thought of entering that moniker into my phone and one day ordering it to 'call Mr. Personality' helps me deal with my jitters.

Rose peeks her head around the door. "Thank you for coming back."

I enter the room. I have to hand it to Rose—she doesn't gloat or say, "I told you so." Neither does Paul, really. Instead, they methodically bring their spouses back into the Quiet.

"So we're doing the Joining now?" Edward asks when he appears in the room.

"And if so, how many of us?" adds Marsha, who appeared in time to hear Edward's question.

"Might as well be everyone," Paul says. "We only need to look back a few weeks. I can handle that much."

Everyone looks at one another excitedly. I ponder over the 'handle that much' comment.

"Let's get the others," Edward says and walks over to another old man frozen in meditation.

My newfound grandparents, their spouses, and the people they bring in all touch more of the white-clad figures—a ritual they seem to have performed many times before.

When everyone is in, I realize this is the largest crowd of live people I've ever witnessed in the Quiet. The 'handle that' comment makes sense now. I recall Eugene telling me how, when you bring people into the Quiet, you share your Depth with them. That means Paul's depth is split with everyone here, yet he doesn't seem concerned. But I guess even he has limits, and it sounds as though the Joining will have to be limited to 'a few weeks,' which I'm guessing means those weeks of my memories are what they're most worried about.

I'm mesmerized as each of the Enlightened sits in front of his or her own frozen self, Grandpa being the only exception. They end up forming an inner circle—the very circle I thought was potentially missing earlier. Rose and her husband leave a bit of extra space between them.

"Sit next to me, please," Rose says, pointing to the empty spot.

I walk over and take my designated place, mimicking the dignified lotus pose everyone is sitting in.

"Place your hand on the Abbot," she says, pointing to the white-haired man in the middle.

I reach out and gingerly touch his shaved head with the tip of my index finger. As I do this, I notice each person in the circle does the same. Together, we make a strange bicycle-wheel-looking circle—our hands and arms serving as the spokes, our bodies forming the rim, and the Abbot guy being the hub in the middle.

Once everyone is touching the monk, Rose says, "Read him and then let us in, the way you did with Caleb."

I close my eyes and slow my breathing. And then I'm in the head of the monk.

# CHAPTER FIVE

Omm.

Breathe in, breathe out. Breathe in, breathe out. Omm.

Our mind is incredibly blank. We are completely in the moment, one with our breath, one with nature, one with the universe. Omm.

Our lungs are not pulling air; the universe is breathing life, breathing air into our lungs. Omm.

A mundane thought in the form of a recollection surfaces. It's trivial, really. A memory of that verbal disagreement the two acolytes had earlier today, a disagreement we had to mediate. We experienced a rare moment of anger and frustration. Now, we treat this intrusion on our meditation as we always do when intruding thoughts arise. We don't feel guilty or upset about them. We let it go. Thoughts will always come. We need to put our attention firmly and gently back on our breath. Thoughts are like soap bubbles or clouds in our mind. They float in, they float out. They cause no disturbance. Omm.

We delight in our breath, focusing on the exact moment the 'in' breath is over and the 'out' breath begins. We note how our body subtly moves with our heartbeat and breath. We do not feel our body at all—not the strain on the back, which is straight without any support, and not the ankles that are crossed in the lotus pose. We are overcome with a sense of calm that is building, slowly reaching new heights. Omm.

I, Darren, reluctantly disassociate. I have never experienced the kind of inner peace and quiet that is the Abbot's mind. Nothing has ever come close. The feeling of not thinking, not worrying, not analyzing was incredible. I never realized how my mind is like a beehive with all the thoughts and ideas buzzing around in it. I never imagined how awesome it would be to have those distractions dissipate, the way they do for the Abbot.

And what's really frustrating is how I thought I'd meditated before through the simple breathing exercise Mom had taught me, the one that helps me reach Coherence when I need to Read. I recall how this technique was something she said her partner, Mark—my dad—introduced her to. He could've learned it here, in this very temple. Of course, comparing the breathing stuff I do to what I just witnessed is like comparing the effects of Tylenol to that of morphine.

I'm distracted from my reflections by a sense of vertigo. I recognize it as the same feeling I had when Caleb and I Joined, which now feels like ages ago. I don't fight the feeling but welcome it. At first, it feels like floating in water, but soon, it's more like the complete and utter loss of the concept of being embodied. It's like both my consciousness and my disembodied brain are floating in space.

And then another wave of strangeness comes, and another. This feeling intensifies for each of the Enlightened participating in the Joining. It hits me again and again. I can't imagine the potency of this incorporeal feeling increasing, yet each time it does—exponentially so.

I lose count of how many people I've Joined with, but it must be all of them. The feeling of being nonphysical gets mingled with a sense of wonderment of such intensity that what I experienced with Caleb pales in comparison. It's a bliss unlike anything I've ever felt. Even that time when I got an overdose of morphine at the Coney Island Hospital can't come close, and I suspect that if I took all the orgasms I've ever had, combined them, and then experienced them all at once in a single millisecond, it would still fall short. The pleasure is so intense that I wonder if it will turn to pain—but it doesn't. Instead, it intensifies some more.

Now I experience a sense of oneness with the universe, a feeling of meaning and belonging. Strange thoughts enter my mind. I wonder whether the universe can think for itself. What if every star in every galaxy, every subatomic particle and the atoms they make up, every black hole, supernova, and even dark matter developed the ability to think together and became self-aware? Is this what such a being would feel like—the way I'm feeling?

And then I feel my memories spew outward. It doesn't feel like a violation of privacy, even though it probably should. Instead, it feels as if I'm sharing myself, like I'm being understood on an intensely deep level. Through some remnants of my rational mind, I realize this sort of thing already happened during my Joining with Caleb, but this time, the Joining is different. The Enlightened are reading weeks of my life with laser-sharp focus.

You know those stories where people's lives flash before their eyes before they pass away? Well, the recent weeks of my life flash in front of mine. And not just the big events like the trip to Atlantic City, the search for Mira, her rescue, my getting shot, our going on a date, and my killing Jacob. I see every tiny detail, from the sizzling hot nights with Mira in Miami to the relaxing days on the beach. I relive the science talks with Eugene and the brunches with Bert and Hillary. All our conversations, all the times we goofed around—it all floods my brain in a single moment.

As this is happening, I feel for the minds of the people with whom I'm Joining. If my privacy is being violated, I might as well try to learn a few secrets from my grandparents and their colleagues in turn. But instead of seeing any of their memories, all I feel is a kind of meditative calm, a state very similar to the Abbot's mind—just peace, serenity, and calmness, but no specific memories.

Are they blocking their memories from me through some form of meditation? The thought should disappoint or upset me, but feeling as rapturous as I do, I can't seem to understand or experience those negative emotions.

As my memories near the end of the process of being drained out, I feel something new: a tsunami of thoughts, an avalanche of something I can only describe as 'sacredness,' even though I know it has nothing to do with religion or any belief system. I feel my intellect, *our* intellects, increasing and permeating everything, and suddenly, I'm drawn somewhere, plummeting to some destination at the speed of light, and I see a bright light flash before my eyes.

When my eyes recover, I see a vision—or what I assume to be a vision.

First, I'm aware of being in some place. Until this point, I was feeling as though I wasn't inhabiting my body; therefore, I was not in any specific place, as that would require being corporeal. Now I'm definitely feeling like myself, feet planted on some kind of gray surface, eyes looking out into a vague, hard-to-describe landscape. My surroundings lack color and depth. They remind me of those green rooms where the weather people shoot their forecasts; only instead of green, everything is a washed-out gray. Out of the corner of my eye, I catch flickering gray shadows, but I can't make out what they are.

The only thing I can see clearly is a figure.

It's floating in the middle of the strange gray room. Based on its broad shoulders and shaved head, I believe it's a man—though I can't be sure of the person's gender, since all I can see is his white-robed back. His legs are folded in that now-all-too-familiar lotus pose. He seems to be radiating some kind of light, which is the best way I can describe his halo-like effect. The light isn't bright and has that same gray, washed-out quality as the rest of this place. And why am I not more surprised to see someone floating in the air like a helium balloon? It's probably because I know, deep down, that this is just a vision.

Suddenly, without turning around or seeming to move in any way, the man is facing me. My mind reels at the sight. It's almost painful to look at him because he's blindingly, incredibly beautiful. I know it's an odd thing for me to think about a guy, but he doesn't look like an everyday, real-world person; he looks like something else entirely. If angels or deities were real, I imagine this is how they would look.

"Hi, Darren," he says. His voice is the most melodic and harmonious sound I've ever heard and does to my ears what his visage does to my eyes.

"Hello," I manage to say, unable to blink from all the staring.

I can't exactly describe him. The beauty and perfection of his face are leaps and bounds beyond simple symmetry. It's like every skin cell, every molecule on the right side of the face matches an exact one on the left. But even that doesn't really explain it.

"You have to stop worshipping me like this," he says. "I look the way I look and sound the way I sound because I am not encumbered by the mundane limitations of physics. I am more of an abstract construct in your mind than a real person. You didn't actually see me when you first saw me. The sight of me didn't *really* register in your brain the way you were thinking of it a second ago. I explain this only because we have very little time, and I need you to get over your shock."

"You're a what?" I can't stop staring at him. "And little time for what?"

"I'm you, Darren," he says, "and Rose and Edward. I am also Paul and Marsha and all the other Enlightened with whom you are currently Joined. And the Joining is coming to an end, thus we have little time."

"I can sort of understand the time limit, but I don't understand how you can be me."

"You don't give yourself enough credit," he says, still floating in the air. "I see you already know, on some level, that I am a manifestation of the combined intellects of all of you, but you are going through the motions reminiscent of denial, which we have no time for."

"You're like a hive mind composed of all of us?" I ask incredulously. "Including me?"

"Yes. Though without the negative connotation the term 'hive' carries."

"Wow." I blink. "I'm not sure what to say to you."

"We're not here for you to say anything to *me*," he says calmly. "That would be pointless, since I know everything you know, as well some things you know but don't realize you know. I am here because I have an important message for you."

"Isn't this a lot like talking to myself?" I ask, and for the first time, a disturbing thought occurs to me. Did the Joining make me go insane?

"You're not crazy," he says. "But I don't have time to convince you of your sanity. We've already used up too much time as is."

*Wouldn't an imaginary friend say something along those lines?* I think at him, testing the theory that he can read my thoughts.

"Perhaps," he admits out loud, confirming my suspicions. "If it helps, you can think of me as a creative way your mind processes the information that's already there, like clues in your memories that are crunched after accessing some extra brain hardware."

"You sound like Liz, my shrink." A smile tugs at my lips. "And a little bit like Bert, my best friend."

"That's intentional," he says patiently. "I want to make sure you don't think of me as a trick the others are trying to play on you."

"Oh," I say, realizing he just voiced a fear that had been lurking around the edges of my awareness—a feat that is extremely creepy.

"My message will be counterproductive to the plans your Joining companions have for you, which should convince you that they have nothing to gain from this," he says, floating a bit closer.

"What plans?" I ask warily.

"That will be made clear to you after we're done here. I really should get to the point. We have but moments left."

"Wait. What will happen to you after the Joining?" I don't know why this matters to me, but it does. "Will you die?"

"Great question, and I wish we had time to discuss it," he says. "I am touched that you even care enough to ask about my fate. The short version is: I will, as you say, phase into the Quiet."

"What? What do you mean? How does that work?"

"This is exactly why I didn't want to get on this topic. In a nutshell, I will be in a different dimension. My Depth is unlimited, meaning that in a fraction of a millisecond, before the Joining ends, I can live forever."

"What do I call you?" I ask, my mind reeling from what he's just told me. The idea of a god-like being like him, originating from some old farts and me and living forever isn't easy to digest.

"We have no time, Darren. Call me Mimir, if you must. This whole conversation is so that I can tell you something, and you must forgive my rudeness, but I have to come out and say it." He seems to take a deep breath. "You need to go back to New York. Lucy is in danger. Big danger."

"What?" My insides twist with fear. "My mom's in danger? How do you know that?"

"The question is: how do *you* know that?" Mimir says. "And the answer is, as I said, clues. You know more than you realize, but you haven't properly processed the information. You lack focus. You lack the experience in deductive reasoning."

"What will happen to her? What can I do?" For some reason, I believe him. I have complete and utter conviction that Lucy is in trouble.

"Go to her. Tell her not to investigate *anything* until you get there. When you see her, tell her everything about what you can do and what happened. Don't leave anything out," he says urgently.

"But who is she in danger from?"

"It's your—"

And before he finishes the sentence, I'm in my body, staring dumbly at my finger that's touching the Abbot's bald head. The Enlightened in the circle look more animated.

The Joining is over.

# CHAPTER SIX

Dazed, I overhear bits and pieces of conversation as the old people murmur to one another.

"So it's true," someone says.

"Unbelievable," someone else whispers.

Their discussions would've riveted me had I not been overcome by dread.

*Mom is in trouble.* I can't think of anything but that. Lucy's tough, but she does have a dangerous job. Could the threat be coming from some scumbag she put away during her long career as a detective? From someone who just got out of jail and is hell-bent on revenge? Mimir mentioned clues. Could one of them be some case she told me about at some point?

The idea that it's a case she investigated sticks in my mind. Even if I've consciously forgotten about it, Mimir was able to access the information and use it to warn me. But for the life of me, I can't recall Lucy ever saying anything about a dangerous case or a criminal getting released. Sure, she worked in Organized Crime for years, but she never told Sara or me anything about it. No 'such and such crime boss went to jail thanks to me,' and no 'I shot such and such mobster.' She's too professional to gossip. Besides, for the past few years, she's been in White-Collar Crime, a department that doesn't deal with violent criminals.

I take a deep breath. As urgent as the situation is, I can let myself relax a little. I'm currently in the Quiet, so whatever the threat is, it's not getting any closer. Along with the rest of the outside world, it's on hold. So long as I stay in the Quiet my grandpa created, I have time to contemplate my next move.

I need an exit strategy. After that, I need to organize an urgent trip to New York.

"See, that wasn't so bad, was it?" Rose says, breaking my concentration.

"Not so bad?" I give her an incredulous look. "Did you not hear what Mimir had to say?"

The room goes quiet.

"Who?" Paul asks, his eyes widening. "What did you just say?"

"Mimir? The good-looking guy in the vision?" As I say this, I realize I've made a blunder. "Weren't you there when that being spoke to me? I figured you heard it too since we were of one mind and all that."

"Incredible," Edward says, putting his hand on Rose's wrist. "Your grandson attained Enlightenment on his first Joining."

"It was his second Joining," Paul corrects, his tone pedantic. "But that doesn't make it any less impressive."

For the first time, something warm shows on his face. Is Grandpa proud of me? I wish I understood what he was proud *of*.

"It sounds as if you experienced what we consider to be the most important effect of the Joining," Marsha says in a solemn tone. "Seeing what you saw is a prerequisite for becoming part of our community."

"Yes. Enlightenment requires meditation, wisdom, and a great Depth," Paul says. "Which means, since you lack the first two—"

"We're incredibly proud, regardless of how it was made possible," Rose says, interrupting Paul's backhanded compliment.

"Your grandparents are thus far the youngest people to ever reach this state," says the oldest-looking guy, who is sitting across from me.

"Okay, great," I say, trying to digest it all. "What does this mean in practical terms? Am I, like, one of you?"

The man looks at me, confused, and says, "You must be joking—"

"Now, now, Sean. The boy asked a reasonable question," Rose says. "Listen, Darren. First and foremost, there is that delicate matter we need to discuss. A matter of duty made more critical by what we've just learned."

"And that would be?" I ask, straining to keep my voice free of any skepticism. 'Duty' is a word that triggers my rebellious side, especially when it's used as an excuse to make very unreasonable demands, and particularly when the motives for those demands are pompous and irrational. In general, logic is rarely part of the equation when someone appeals to your sense of duty. To make matters worse—or to highlight my stance on that word—I always think of 'doody' when I hear it.

"That things are as we thought and you are, indeed, Mark's child and the first hybrid to exist in recorded history. Also, your Depth is so great that we underestimated it," she says, answering the wrong question.

"Indeed. I'm glad we made the necessary preparations," Paul says, running with what Rose said without explaining the actual 'what' that they want from me. "Shall we head to the visitors' lounge?"

"That's a great idea," Rose says. "Best get that business over with. Your Depth might—"

"Yes," Paul says curtly. "You should accompany us, Rose." He looks around the room, closely examining his peers. "The invitation extends to anyone who's interested."

"I think I'd rather stay back and discuss the implications of all this with the others, dear," says Marsha before kissing him on the cheek. "You go."

"I'll stay behind too, hon," Edward says, letting go of Rose's hand. "Wouldn't want to crowd you."

Paul gets up, then Rose, and I follow their lead. Their spouses sure are trusting. I always thought that if you let people who had sex with each other hang out, they might hook up again. And my grandparents must've done it out of wedlock at least once. Not that I'm certain sex is part of their lives

66

now. Nor am I sure that it's safe for my sanity or libido to ponder this any further.

"You still didn't answer my question about this *duty* thing," I say as we walk out.

"We'll discuss that in a moment," Paul says as he slows his pace to let Rose catch up.

"Fine. Then can you at least tell me what the vision actually means?" I ask. "Since all of you seem to have had yours . . ."

"It's different for everyone," Rose answers. "But the common thread is that when we each received our visions, we received the most important piece of wisdom of our lives."

"Wisdom?" I ask carefully, unsure whether I want to tell them what I saw. If I tell them, they'll realize I have a very good reason for wanting to get out of the Quiet as soon as possible, and they might take some precautionary measures to stop me. "What about warnings or premonitions? Did anyone ever get those?"

"Is that what you received?" Paul asks, looking over his shoulder. "If you were given a warning, you should heed it. What is revealed during the Enlightenment always proves to be true."

"Always? These things are never, ever wrong?" I don't try to hide my disappointment. I hoped he'd say the visions were all metaphorical and up to interpretation, like dreams, and shouldn't be taken literally.

"If the beings in those visions are to be believed," Rose says, "they're just *us*. Since *we* can be wrong, they can also be wrong. It just so happens that we've never witnessed a vision that has proven to be incorrect. Some of us believe these beings are divine and simply lie about being *us* to conceal their true nature. Others think it makes sense that the combined intellects of so many wise people would produce—"

"So what did you see?" Paul asks.

I don't have a lie on hand, and I don't want to tell them the truth, so I decide to annoy Paul by asking a question of my own. "What do you plan on having me do?"

He continues walking in somber silence. Rose winks at me, I guess to show she's not angry. I don't trust her. Not fully, not yet. I think they're still playing good cop / bad cop with me.

We walk through the Temple, allowing me to get a better look at the monks. I notice that they're not all men. The women are harder to spot due to them having the same shaved heads as the men. Their bare faces and shapeless robes also serve to conceal their gender. Despite this androgyny, I find that one of the lady monks we pass looks pretty.

The diversity of this place doesn't end with the presence of women. The monks are also a good mix of ages and races. The latter is in contrast to the Enlightened, who, like nearly all Readers and Guides I've met, are white. My friend Thomas, who's half-Asian, is the only non-white Guide I've encountered thus far.

Paul leads us through a smaller side door to the outside of the Temple. This must be a sort of backyard. Unlike the beauty-packed front, with its rock gardens and cherry blossoms, this area is more practical and plain. We're walking on a field of green grass, with blue forget-me-nots scattered here and there.

As we walk, something on my left catches my attention. In this part of the yard, a bunch of monks stand frozen in poses that look like either kung fu or tai chi. Whatever they're doing, it's different from the other sorts of meditation their brethren inside the Temple are practicing. When I see Caleb performing some type of martial art on his own, I realize they probably are practicing kung fu. Though his moves aren't the same as the frozen figures', it puts this open space into context; it's some kind of outdoor dojo. Now that I'm paying attention, I spot tall, wooden poles in the distance, each with a monk standing atop them on one leg, with the other foot held in their right hand. The pose looks like a combination between a stretching and a balancing exercise. In another part of the dojo, someone is crouched, deep in concentration, about to break a slab of stone with his bare hands.

"Here we are," Rose says as we reach the end of the yard.

Paul opens the door to let us into another large structure, saying, "This is the guesthouse."

The 'guesthouse' is the size of a mansion. The Temple dwarfs it from the outside, but once we're inside, the grandness of the house feels comparable. When my attention settles onto two women sitting near the entrance, frozen, my awe of the place is extinguished, replaced by shock.

Because while one looks vaguely familiar, the other woman I know very well.

It's Julia, the Reader woman I usually think of as 'Eugene's girl,' even if they aren't currently together—a situation that's due in large part to her late father, Jacob.

Fuck. My heart starts beating faster.

I shot Jacob and was present when Mira finished him off. I can't think of a good reason as to why I'm being reunited with Julia, other than for some kind of reckoning. The woman accompanying Julia must be her mother, Jacob's widow.

What is going on? I can see a very logical chain of events: the Enlightened who Joined with me learned the truth, and now they want that truth to come out. After all, Caleb knew it was me, so they might have decided to bring Julia in ahead of time and do the whole Joining just to confirm the situation.

"What the hell are they doing here?" I ask evenly.

Caleb is outside, so if I had to, I could utilize a few desperate measures, such as killing Paul to phase out of the Quiet. But I remind myself that if I killed him, I'd only end up back in the car, next to Inert Paul and angry Caleb—not to mention that killing my newfound grandpa would feel wrong, or disrespectful, or something.

"You know Julia and her mother," Paul says calmly.

"Is that a question?" I'm starting to get annoyed. "You just poked around in my head, so you know what I know."

"Allow me, Paul," Rose says, putting her hand on my elbow. "Your friend and her mother think they're here to get our clarification on who will be the new leader of their Reader community."

"And the real reason?" I brace myself for the answer.

"The real reason is a bit more complicated," she says.

DIMA ZALES

"Simplify it for me."

"Okay. Let's start with this. You've probably already gathered that you're unique," she says tentatively.

"Well, yeah. Because of my mother."

"No," she says. "Well, yes. But aside from your mother being a Pusher, *you* are different."

"Oh?" That definitely gets my attention. "What else is there? Something to do with you and him"—I point to Paul—"being bred for your Depth?"

"Exactly," she says. "You see, our people have been trying to accomplish something for some time, something that requires a tremendous amount of Depth. Paul, do you want to explain this part, since it's your area of expertise?"

"I can try," he says with a sigh. "The short version is that it's possible to Split after you're in the Mind Dimension."

"What?" My mind is reeling. "Of all the things I expected to hear . . ." I take a breath, considering it. "Is it really feasible? Phasing into the Quiet, from the Quiet? What would that even be like?"

"We don't know," Paul says. "It's all rather theoretical. One thing we do suspect is that this feat would allow you to Read *anyone*."

"Read a fellow Reader?"

He nods.

Wow. Reading a Reader would be like the Holy Grail for these people, who can Read the minds of anyone but the people who matter most—the people in their own community.

"I think I understand," I say, "and it does sound impressive."

"It does present some very exciting possibilities," Paul says. "The big problem is: the Depth required to Split in that way would have to be enormous."

"So you've been breeding people to create more Depth?" I think I'm catching up.

"Yes. And if your father had had a child with the woman he was supposed to, with *her*"—he points to Julia's mom—"our grandchild might've possessed the required Depth, and if not that child, then our great-grandchild."

My head is spinning. "Julia's mom was supposed to 'breed' with my dad? Is she especially powerful?"

Since I never met my dad, it's not all that weird to think that he could've done it with Julia's mom. What do I care? The thing I do care about, however, is the glimmer of suspicion forming in the back of my mind. No, I tell myself. They wouldn't be *that* crude.

"She is indeed," Paul says. "Her parents are the most powerful of our kind from Ontario. Unfortunately, she's post-menopausal, so we can't use her anymore. But her daughter . . ."

"You have got to be kidding me." Unfortunately, my sneaking suspicion was right. "You want me to fuck Julia?" My voice rises in pitch. "No, sorry, you want me to fucking have a kid with Julia?"

"You make it sound like such a horrible thing," Rose says, the corners of her eyes crinkling as she smiles. "She's a rosebud. It's not like we're asking you to do something you wouldn't enjoy."

"She's my friend's girl," I say weakly. I could've made a million other, more obvious objections, but this one was the first to come to mind.

"We're not asking you to marry her," Paul says nonchalantly. "We just want you to perform your duty."

All my reasons against this proposition swirl and overwhelm my mind until I blurt out my main objection: "I'm too young to have kids." As I say it, I realize it's probably not even in the top ten cons that *they* would've taken seriously.

"We'd take care of the child," Rose says. "Of course you're too young for that."

I can't believe we're actually carrying on with this conversation. Breeding *me?* For some trait? The idea is beyond ridiculous. All this talk of breeding people hadn't fully registered until this very moment—until it got personal. The choice my parents made, the choice Eugene and Mira's father made—not to have kids with the 'right' person—was all very theoretical, until now.

"I also have a girlfriend," I say, realizing that in their eyes, I probably sound like a five-year-old justifying why he won't eat his broccoli.

"We're not asking you to leave your little girlfriend either," Rose says. "Look at us. Paul and I married the people we love dearly. Giving birth to Mark never changed that. In fact, it's the opposite. Marsha and I are best friends. So are Edward and Paul."

I feel like I'm in a strange dream version of the *Twilight Zone* mixed with a 'I had a child with my twin sister's husband' Jerry Springer episode. Inadvertently, I look at Julia. Blond hair, blue eyes, curves in all the right places. She's as hot as ever, and I can't stop an erotic image—or two—from slipping into my consciousness, confirming what Rose said. This *could* be something I, or any other red-blooded guy, would enjoy, on a purely mechanical, execution-of-task kind of level.

"So what's the timeline?" I ask uncomfortably. "When did you want this . . . act . . . to occur?"

"Caleb and Paul can drive you here as soon as you're ready," Rose replies.

"Wait. Did Julia already agree to this?" I ask. Even if I wanted to agree to this crazy plan, there's one huge problem: my mom's in trouble and I don't have the time to be, literally, fucking around.

"She will agree," Paul says. "Same as you."

I never thought I'd be this tempted to punch an old guy in the face. I resist, barely, and try a different approach.

"Is there any way I can leave this place and do this with Julia in New York? Or come back in a little while?"

"No," Rose says, and for the first time, the good-grandma act slips. "We're not taking the risk of you disappearing on us for good."

"Can I think about it?"

"Sure," she replies. "Just like with the Joining, we'll wait until you make the right decision."

Translation: I'm trapped in the Quiet, and in this stupid temple, and I'm not going anywhere until I agree to impregnate Julia.

# CHAPTER SEVEN

"I'm taking a walk," I say. "I need some air."

"I'll be in the Hall," Paul says and heads for the door.

"I'll join you," Rose says to Paul.

We exit together and walk for a few moments in silence until I stop, deciding to stay here, on the frozen exercise field.

"Come get us when you're ready," Paul says over his shoulder.

"You're bound to get tired of playing here sooner or later," Rose adds.

The bitch is rubbing it in. In general, their confidence is infuriating. And in no small part, it solidifies my answer.

Fuck, no.

Could they be bluffing when they say they're willing to 'wait as long as it takes'? I recall Rose inadvertently saying something about Paul running out of Depth, which would make sense given how he brought over a dozen people into the Quiet and used his Depth for the Joining. But I have no idea how much Depth he has left, which means I have no idea how much time I'll have to kill.

"Hey, Caleb," I yell and walk toward the big guy. I have a half-formed idea on how I can pass the time until Paul hopefully runs out of Depth, and if that turns out to be unbearable, I also have a contingency plan.

Caleb acts as if he didn't hear me, so I get up close and cough.

"I heard you, kid," he says without facing me. "I was ignoring you."

Usually I don't talk to people when they're behaving so rudely, but since I need something from him, I ask, "Are you still mad about Jacob?"

"Mad? I'm fucking furious," he says. "Was there a good reason for you to undo years' worth of painstaking undercover work?"

"There was," I say. "He was going to shoot Mira. I had no choice but to pull that trigger."

Caleb stops his exercise and gives me a serious look. "Why was he going to shoot her?"

"Because she was going to kill *him*."

Caleb looks thoughtful. "Looks like she figured out who killed her parents after all. Clever girl."

"You knew?" I ask, unable to believe my ears. I bet if Mira knew that Caleb had been aware of her parents' killer all along, she would want to shoot him right about now.

"I wasn't certain, but I figured it was likely him," Caleb says. "But it could've been his Pusher partner or someone higher up the food chain."

"Do you know who his partner was?" I ask with little hope. I suspect if he did, he wouldn't be here; he'd be wherever that person is, killing him.

"No, and thanks to you, I don't have a lead on him either," Caleb says bitterly. "I didn't tell the girl because she was conducting her own investigation, and one way or another, she would've led me to the right people."

"Wait a minute," I say. "You used Mira's quest for revenge for your own means?"

"And her as bait, yes," he says.

"I thought you were friends." I'm actually relieved. At one point, I thought there might've been deeper history between the two.

"We weren't friends." Was there some defensiveness in his tone? "When I showed interest in her little vendetta, she thought there was more to it than that and tried to flirt with me. Of course, you don't need to worry," he says with mock concern, *after* he sees I'm ignoring the ribbing. "I turned her down, gently. She wasn't even eighteen at the time. Much too young for me and jailbait to boot."

I recall how he pretended not to know why Pushers would be after her when she got kidnapped and Eugene came asking the Reader community for help, and how he then easily agreed to partake in the rescue mission. He wanted to see whether the Pusher he'd been stalking would take the Mira bait. He must've also been interested in seeing how Jacob would refuse to help, revealing a small clue as to his allegiance to the mystery Pusher.

These thoughts remind me of why I came over to talk to Caleb in the first place. I want to learn how to fight better. If I were a better fighter, I would have, for example, given in to my strong urge to punch him in his smug face. Today seems to be the day for violent urges.

"I've gotten into a couple of fights since we did that Joining," I begin, changing the sensitive topic. "I noticed I can fight much better than before, but I still don't really understand what I'm doing, or how."

"Yeah. You aren't that bad, all things considered." Caleb actually looks serious. "I know from experience."

This is as close to an olive branch as anyone has probably gotten from Caleb, so I say, "Thanks. How do I improve?"

"The best way, as with anything, is practice. Tons and tons of practice. I can help you with that, if you're interested, for a small price."

"Depends on what the price is," I say, remembering our Joining with Haim, the Israeli fighter. That's how I got my fighting skills, but it was a scary experience that I don't care to repeat.

"It's nothing, really. I just want to know what the fuck is going on here. Why did they have me bring you here? I thought it had something to do with Jacob, but now I suspect something else is going on."

"You mean they didn't even tell you? I thought you guys were working together."

"Certain things are on a need-to-know basis," he says. "But if *you* tell me, I'll spar with you for a while. I can use the practice anyway."

"Throw in some shooting lessons, and you've got a deal."

"Fine. I've got some guns up in my room, and lots of bullets."

"Okay then." I look in the direction of the guesthouse. "You know Julia is here, right?"

"I do." He narrows his eyes at me.

"Well, she isn't here because she or her mom is about to take Jacob's place. Or at least, not only because of that." I shift my weight from one foot to the other. "There's another reason."

His eyes widen, and then he starts laughing. His laugh is odd-sounding, like Santa getting tickled.

I wait, arms crossed over my chest.

"This is rich," he says between bouts of laughter. "You're in deep shit, kid."

"It's not *that* funny." Though truth be told, if I were in his place, I'd probably find this fairly amusing.

"Oh, I don't know about that," he says, catching his breath. "It's funny if you know Julia."

"What do you mean?" Maybe I've been looking at this from a very self-centered perspective.

"Let's just say I'd rather be celibate, like these monks, than marry that one." He points to the guesthouse. "Very high maintenance and way too much attitude."

"They didn't exactly ask me to *marry* Julia." I look over my shoulder, as though paranoid about Julia overhearing me.

"Oh." And the laughter is back. "They just want the stud service then?"

"Yes," I say, realizing I'll have to tread more carefully here, for the sake of my contingency plan. "They want us to have a kid."

"That's it? That doesn't sound like a big dilemma to me."

I resist the urge to say, "Then you go fuck her, or better yet, yourself," and instead ask, "What do you mean?"

"They'd raise the kid here, so you wouldn't have to worry about diapers and sleepless nights. All you'll have to do is fuck Julia, who, all her bitchiness aside, is, let's face it, a looker," he says.

"I didn't think of it like that," I lie. My own grandma laid it out to me in almost the exact same way. "Maybe it's not so bad."

"You don't have to tell Mira, you know." This is more than just Caleb being friendly. He's being loyal to my grandparents by pushing their agenda, even though they didn't bother to tell him what it was—

which is fine with me. Let him think I'm getting convinced.

"I'll make my own decision," I say. "Is that all you wanted to know?"

"One more quick question. What was Joining with *them* like?" Caleb cracks his knuckles.

"You mean you've never done it? You work for them."

"No, they never deemed me worthy, with my measly Depth and lack of memories they would find useful." Caleb looks toward the Temple. "Why would they resort to Joining when I tell them anything they need to know anyway?"

Maybe that's why he was in Florida when I called to get his help to deal with the guy who I thought was a Pusher but turned out to be Jacob. Caleb could've been giving my grandparents a report on me about the things he'd learned during our Joining. Does that mean I'm still in Florida? That would be good to know.

"You're not missing much," I lie in response to Caleb's statement. Then I tell him a variation of what happened during the Joining. Nothing about Mimir's message, but I highlight my inability to glean information from the Enlightened minds.

"They're tough bastards." He smirks.

"So what do you get out of working for them?"

"Time," he says. "They let me spend crazy amounts of time in their Mind Dimensions. That, and well, they're the highest authority Readers have."

I suspect it's more the former than the latter, but I hold my tongue. "Speaking of payment," I say instead. "Now that you know what's going on and about the Joining, why don't you teach me what you promised? A deal's a deal."

"I will, but first tell me why you had those thoughts. Why did you think you were a Pusher?" He gives me a hard look. "I mean, if you're their son's kid."

"You said you only wanted to know what happened here," I say. "And I got a very strong impression this was something the grandparents didn't want you to know."

"I won't kill you, if that's what you're worried—"

"Why don't you ask Paul?" I figure I might need another favor from Caleb some day, and if he doesn't figure it out by then, I can trade this info for it. Then again, if we're about to fight, do I really want to antagonize him?

"Maybe I will," he says and stands in a semi-familiar stance. "A deal's a deal. I'll hold my punches, but you don't have to." As he says this, he punches me in the shoulder, lightning-fast. He definitely isn't using his full strength, but it still hurts when his fist connects with my body. "You were about to block that with your right elbow, but walking out of it would've been more effective," he instructs.

He throws more punches and gives me feedback on my responses to them. He claims I'm getting the hang of it, and maybe I am, but if I ever needed to fight Caleb for real, I'd still be pretty hopeless. I rarely manage to block his punches and land few of my own.

"You ready for the shooting part?" he asks after I'm barely moving from fatigue. We've been practicing hand-to-hand combat for what feels like a number of hours. "I'll give you some more combat tips after. It's good to take a break now and then."

Pushing aside my exhaustion, I follow him and help carry the guns and ammo from his room and out of the Temple, as Caleb insists on shooting in the forest.

"You see that frozen-in-time bird?" He points to a hawk in the far distance. "I want you to hit it."

I point the gun, a revolver he handed to me, and take careful aim.

Then I take the shot. The bird remains untouched.

"Don't feel bad for the bird," he teases. "You won't really kill it."

"Being an asshole wasn't part of the deal," I tell him. Truth be told, I've always had an aversion to hunting. His reminder that no animals will be harmed actually does help.

"You have to pull the trigger on your exhale," he says. "Place the front sight blade on the target, and then place the front blade in between the valley back sights."

"Next you'll be telling me to pull the trigger," I say, but do as he instructed. The exhale thing must've helped, because the bird falls to the ground.

"Now try shooting that squirrel," he says, and then spends a few minutes explaining how to spot my new target between all the branches.

Many bullets and forest creatures later, I tire of the lessons. My shooting has improved, but of course it would, after so many subjective hours of practice.

A different problem becomes apparent now: patience is not my virtue. There's only so much shooting and fighting I can do before going crazy. My plan to kill time until Paul runs out of Depth has been revealed as the pleasant delusion it was. No matter how much of his Depth is depleted, Paul still has plenty left to outwait me in my worried-about-Mom state.

"All right," I say after the last shot. "I'm ready to head back."

"Why don't you run and try shooting a few things along the way?" Caleb suggests.

I perform the final exercise as he said, shooting, among other things, a couple of barely noticeable beetles and a bat. I'm definitely getting better at this.

"Do you want to spar some more?" Caleb asks once we've returned to the dojo field by the guesthouse.

"Sure," I say, deciding to give Paul one last chance to run out of Depth. Might as well take advantage of Caleb thinking he owes me.

We go at it until I actually lose track of time. Caleb's feedback gets progressively less snarky and more genuine. I must be improving.

"Okay. I've had enough. Time to face the music," I say when he throws me to the ground for the millionth time. "I think I'll go tell them that I'll do this thing with Julia."

"Let me give you one piece of advice," Caleb says, giving me his hand to help me to my feet—the first time that's happened.

"Please do," I say. "Unless it's of the 'how to' variety."

He laughs. "No, though I'm sure I could teach a mini person like you a thing or two in that department." He chuckles. "I was going to say, you should let Julia hear about this shit from *you*. Better chance it all goes smoothly later."

This is probably good advice, though it'll be one super-uncomfortable conversation. "Thanks," I say.

"Sure. If you need me, I'll be reading in my room. Thanks to you, I've had enough exercise."

As I watch Caleb walk away, I think about his advice some more. Talking to Julia—there is something to it. What if my contingency plan doesn't work? It might be worth having a backup, and she might be of help in that regard. Also, my contingency relies on me looking as though I'm going through with this breeding thing, and if I'm being monitored, talking to Julia would show my good will.

On a whim, cognizant that I'm just delaying my weird confrontation with Julia, I approach one of the monks doing kung fu.

He seems to be the most capable of the bunch, his frozen movements reminiscent of a lion or a cobra about to strike. I put my hand on his wrist and enter the Coherence state.

\* \* \*

Strike. Breathe. Strike. Breathe.

Our mind is blank, like a pond on a windless day. There are no ripples on the lake, no movement of any kind, only stillness and serenity.

I, Darren, find this very odd. I came here in an attempt to sample this monk's fighting style, but that's not what I'm getting. Like the Abbot's, this mind is in an altered state, as though the monk is meditating, despite the fact that he's moving around. What's stranger is that when I try to feel light and rewind the monk's memories, I get a similar result: some nirvana bullshit but no actual memories. That's really odd.

Frustrated, I exit his head.

\* \* \*

My self-esteem has taken a serious dive today. First, I lose all those fights with Caleb. Then I miss all those targets. And now I just screwed up a Reading. Still, I suspect all this stuff is small potatoes compared to Julia's reaction when I tell her why she's here.

# CHAPTER EIGHT

Determined, I walk into the mansion-like guesthouse and approach Julia. She's wearing a sleeveless dress. Without giving myself a chance to flake out, I touch her exposed elbow.

An animated version of Julia appears next to me, her blue eyes filled with shock. "Darren? What are *you* doing here?"

I look at her uncomfortably, unsure what to say.

"Is something wrong?" she asks, her surprise turning into worry. "You look pale."

"I . . . sort of have something strange to tell you."

"Okay." She blinks. "I'm not sure I like the sound of that."

"You're not here for the reason you were told," I say, looking at her.

"I'm not here for any reason at all." She frowns. "They're giving the reins to my mom."

"Right. That succession thing? It's a ruse to get *you* to come here," I say, watching her closely. "The real reason is different."

"Okay, and are you planning on telling me this reason you're building up so much?" she asks almost teasingly. She has no idea what's coming.

"It kind of involves me," I say. "Or, rather, us . . ."

She stares at me for a moment as I search for the most delicate way to proceed. Then her eyes widen.

"You. Have. Got. To. Be. Kidding." Her joviality forgotten, her perfectly manicured hands tense. "These old farts want us to marry each other? Or are they liberal enough nowadays to just breed us like fucking livestock?"

"The latter," I say, glad she guessed it for herself, sparing me the need to explain.

"How could you, Darren?" she says with disappointment. "I thought Eugene was your friend."

"What? He is. I said no." Realizing that might have sounded insulting, I explain, "I'm not here to talk you into it. I'm here to see if you can help us get out of it."

She looks a tiny bit calmer and takes a breath, letting it out with an audible sigh.

"Fuck," she finally says.

"They didn't call it that," I say, attempting to lighten the mood.

"It's not funny," she says, but the corners of her eyes crinkle. "What are we going to do?"

"When I said no, they basically decided to bore me to the point of agreeing to do it."

"What do you mean?"

I explain to her how I have no idea where my body is, and how because of that, I can't phase out of the Quiet.

"What I don't know," I say, "is how they're planning to convince *you* to do it."

Her lips tighten. "Sadly, they have many ways. For starters, they can threaten to ostracize me if I don't cooperate. Perhaps that's why they brought my mom here. They might tell me the only way she'll get what she wants is if I play ball. But what makes you think they would have to convince me at all?"

"What do you mean?"

"Well, if you were willing, all they'd have to do is tie me up—"

"Oh, come on. You can't be serious." I shudder from the images in my mind. "If it goes that way, then they can wait as long as they want. I will fucking travel the world on foot before I stoop to raping for them."

"They might not have presented you with their most persuasive arguments yet," she says. "These old people are ruthless."

"I was thinking it'd be easier to 'go along with it,'" I say, making air quotes. "We can just pretend to do it. We could sleep in the same room but do nothing. I'll sleep on the floor or something."

"Gentlemanly, but extremely naïve." She gives the door a worried look. "The Enlightened know what they're doing. If they don't watch us do it in person, they'll install a camera in our room for sure. And I doubt they'd let us out of here until I passed a pregnancy test."

"Shit." I begin to pace around her. "I didn't realize they'd be so thorough."

"Yeah, that they are," she says, watching me.

I stop after a minute. "So what do we do?"

Instead of responding, Julia steps closer to me, making me uncomfortably aware of her rather ample breasts. In a daze, I wonder whether she decided to see if she might want to go along with what the Enlightened want by first giving me a kiss or something, like a little test to see how bad the situation is. But instead, she whispers in my ear, "We try to escape. Though I'm not sure how yet."

Now I understand. If she thinks these people are paranoid enough to put cameras in the hypothetical bedroom where we'd do it, she also sees them as capable of eavesdropping on us right now. Even if they have cameras in this room in the real world, they wouldn't work in the Quiet, but it's all too plausible that my grandma is putting her ear to the wall, waiting for us to reveal our plans.

"I have an idea," I whisper. "But if it fails, I don't have a backup plan."

"If your idea fails, we'll still have time," she responds quietly. "I had a birth control implant put into my arm two years ago. So, for another year, I can't get knocked up."

"But that would mean we'd—" I cut myself off, shaking my head before I can complete that thought. "No, no way. And besides, I need to get out of here fast." At her questioning look, I say, "It's a long story."

"We can say yes and play it by ear after," she whispers.

It doesn't sound like too good of a plan to me. I also really don't like the idea of them not yet having used their 'most persuasive arguments' on me. I don't even want to know what that would entail.

"So the plan is we both say yes to this?" I ask. "That's a prerequisite for my idea too."

"We don't have much choice," she whispers. "If your plan works and you get out, can you tell Eugene to call me, please?"

"Sure," I whisper back, glad she can't see my face. Her mention of Eugene reminds me of my guilt. "You guys haven't talked recently?"

I've been wondering how the events in New York affected Eugene's interactions with Julia, the girl whose father is dead because of us. In some stoic Russian tradition, Eugene has been avoiding the whole subject of Julia. Mira told me he's been avoiding Julia too, though she saw that as a positive, having never approved of the relationship. And now it looks like she was right about Eugene taking the avoidance route. I can't really blame him. I have no idea what I would've done in his place.

"No," Julia whispers, this time louder. "I haven't heard from him at all since—" She swallows audibly. "Since my father was killed."

"I heard," I say, trying to keep my voice expressionless. "I'm very sorry for your loss."

"Thank you," she says, her voice catching.

"I'll go announce my willingness to do my duty," I whisper to change the subject. "You might want to return to your body."

"Sure," she says. "No offense, but I hope I don't see you again."

"None taken. I feel the same way."

She doesn't even know how serious I am. I never want to feel this guilt again—the guilt I feel when the subject of her father comes up.

# CHAPTER NINE

I enter the Hall and find Rose and Paul sitting in that special spot in the middle of the meditation circles. Not surprisingly, they're meditating. The sound of my steps pulls them out of their concentration and they look up.

"I've thought about it," I say to Paul when I get close enough so I don't have to shout across the room. "If you're really going to take care of the child, I'll do what you want, but I have one extra condition."

"Which is?" Rose asks.

"I want you to answer a few questions."

"Sure," Paul says dismissively, getting up. "Let's talk on the way to my body. I'm sure I can answer whatever questions you might have."

"I'll walk with you," Rose adds, rising to her feet as well. "Whatever Paul can't answer, I'll try to."

"Okay," I say as we start walking. "For starters, what is the Mind Dimension? What actually happens when we Split, as everyone calls it?"

They don't answer for a bit. Finally, Rose says, "Well, Darren, despite everyone calling us the 'Enlightened,' there are many things we don't know, and this is one of them, unfortunately."

"But you must have some idea," I press. "For example, Eugene thinks it's an alternate universe."

"We're aware of that theory," Paul says, holding the Temple's big doors open for us. "We saw your memories, remember?"

"So do you think he's right?"

"The one thing we agree on with that boy is that we're not truly here in regular, physical form," Rose says. "In the old days, we called what we do 'Spirit Walking.'"

"That has a nice ring to it," I say, "but I don't believe in spirits."

"I don't either," Paul chimes in. "But you have to admit, this experience has a certain ethereal quality to it."

"I guess." It's disappointing that they know as little as I do. *Or that they're willing to share so little*, a skeptical part of me suggests.

I walk in silence for a few seconds, trying to decide what else I want to ask. Then it hits me. "What's up with the monks? Did you start a religion or something?"

"That is a long tale," Rose says. "It all started centuries ago, when the first of us, the Enlightened, realized that Joining works best when the host's mind is as clear from distractions as possible."

"So they sought out meditators?" I ask, fascinated.

"Sort of," Rose says. "They might've invented the practice or taken it further, but in a nutshell, yes. The rest fell into place. Once meditators started living side by side with our people, they created legends about us. It would be hard not to, since these 'wise people' knew their inner thoughts and probably showed off in other ways."

"With time, the whole thing evolved," Paul says, picking up the story. "It turned out that certain meditation regimes can make a mind more difficult to Read, and more importantly, to Push."

"The monks can't be Pushed?" I ask excitedly. I recall my attempt at Reading that one monk, and indeed, all I got was the serene-mind equivalent of white noise.

"We don't know for sure how immune they are," Paul says. "But our oral tradition claims they are, and this is why they were encouraged to learn martial arts over the years, to become our protectors of sorts."

"Maybe you can test how much influence you have over one of them?" Rose suggests. "Once the business at hand is over."

"I'd love to try," I say, and mean it. If I *were* to stick around, I'd do exactly that: try to Guide one of these monks. As is, though, I hope to be out of this mess long before such an interesting experiment can happen. A shame, as I find the idea that someone can resist us rather intriguing.

We talk about this some more. I learn how Buddhism actually branched off from the monks who lived with the Enlightened and not the other way around, as I assumed. Rose and Paul explain to me that they're not deified by the monks, but are seen as normal people who have achieved enlightenment. This belief is where the nickname 'the Enlightened' originated. Of course, once the nickname was given, the Enlightened appropriated it, making it their own and going as far as calling the visions inside the Joining 'Enlightenment.'

"What can you tell me about my dad?" I ask once my curiosity about the monks is satisfied. "What was he like?"

"A lot like you," Rose says, smiling, and proceeds to tell me about young Mark.

Like me, he was impatient and a big troublemaker as a kid. He was perhaps even more rebellious than I was as a teen—a difficult feat, I imagine. Through it all, I glean a lot of information between the lines. I picture someone like me growing up under the thumb of someone like Paul and can easily imagine that person running away from the Temple and doing everything to spite them. Hell, not only would I not have impregnated the girl of their choice, I likely would've burned the whole freaking Temple down on my way out. Mark showed some restraint, in my opinion, but obviously Rose and Paul don't see it that way.

"I'm tired," Rose says after we've been walking for a while. "I'll sit on this stump and wait to be pulled out, if you don't mind."

"Sure, Rose," Paul says. "We should be there in a few hours."

"I'll practice my meditation then," she says and takes up a comfortable position on her makeshift chair.

The rest of the way, Paul and I walk in silence. I don't have many questions left, nor am I sure I can talk to him without getting into a verbal fight.

My grandpa is about as far from my favorite person as it gets.

* * *

"We're here," Paul says when we finally reach the car.

I say nothing, doing my best to keep comments such as 'no shit, Grandpa' firmly in check.

Paul approaches his body. The frozen Paul is still staring at the frozen me through the window. The frozen Caleb is still where he was originally, behind the wheel.

I realize something at this point. When Paul phases out of the Quiet and causes us, in turn, to do the same, Caleb will be caught by surprise. He wasn't told about any of this. There's a small chance he'll be disoriented as a result.

Good. I'll take any advantage I can get, no matter how subtle.

Without much ado, Paul walks to his body and touches his frozen self on the neck.

I'm in the car again. With my robe gone, the cold hits me. It's been so long that I forgot about this cursed air conditioning.

"Caleb," Paul says imperiously, "untie him."

"So you finally went for it?" Caleb says, winking at me as he unties the rope around my wrists. If he was at all surprised to be back in the real world, he recovered annoyingly quickly.

"I talked to her," I say, giving him an ambiguous lift of my eyebrows. "That was good advice."

"I would've loved to see Julia's reaction," he mutters as he unlocks the car. "She must've freaked," he adds as he opens the door and exits.

"Yeah, it wasn't pretty," I mumble in case he's listening.

When he's completely out of the car, my whole body tenses.

This is my moment. This is when I make my move.

I turn as though to exit and hope I'm blocking Caleb's view with my back. Then, as fast as humanly possible, I reach into the glove compartment.

The gun is, of course, still there, just as it was in the Quiet when I did my clandestine snooping.

I grab the weapon and hold it tightly against my right hip as I open the car door and exit. I then proceed to shut the door in as casual a gesture as I can manage under the circumstances.

"There really ought to be a road leading to the Temple," I hear Caleb saying across the car to Grandpa, who's on my side, just a couple of feet away.

Paul replies with something along the lines of 'stop bitching.' I don't register the exact details of the conversation because of my heartbeat pounding in my ears.

As though in slow motion, I step toward Paul, who's looking at Caleb and not paying me any attention. At that moment, Caleb turns to look at something on the road, and I make my move, jamming the gun into Paul's back.

"Don't you dare move," I whisper in his ear.

"Darren," he says, clearly shocked.

"Shut up," I whisper. "Or I'll fucking shoot you."

His body sags against my gun, shoulders drooping. He doesn't say anything else, so I take it as a sign of capitulation and whisper, "Now tell Caleb to go lie on the ground where I can see him."

"Caleb," Paul says, his voice quivering more than I would've expected. "Go lie on the road. Now."

"What?" Caleb turns, frowning. "What are you talking about?"

"He's got a gun to my back," Paul says, and I jam the gun in harder, causing him to stop explaining.

Caleb's arm moves toward his vest. Shit. He's reaching for his gun.

"Drop it, Caleb," I order, moving my gun down to press against Paul's leg. "Or I'll show you how serious I am."

"Do as he says, and lie on the ground behind the car," Paul barks. He clearly doesn't think I'm bluffing, even though, to be honest, I might be. "Do it, Caleb. This is not a request."

Caleb's features darken. I see him fighting the urge to do something heroic. *Please don't,* I will him. Suddenly, Caleb reaches a decision and gingerly walks over to the middle of the road. I assume Paul phased into the Quiet and convinced him to play ball. I guess Grandpa doesn't doubt my determination.

When Caleb gets far enough away, he slowly, almost lazily, lies down on the ground a few feet away from the back of the car.

"Get that rope," I tell Paul, pointing to the back of the car where there's a bundle of rope. I think it's the very rope Caleb used to tie me with. Payback's a bitch.

As Paul gets the rope, I press the gun more firmly into his back and keep Caleb in my peripheral vision. The big guy isn't moving.

"Now tie his hands," I order Paul as we approach Caleb.

As Paul bends down, I see a blur of movement and realize my mistake.

I underestimated Caleb's reach.

As Caleb's fingers close around my ankle, I shift my balance in a desperate maneuver and push Paul at Caleb. The old man falls on the big guy with an undignified shriek.

*He'll be okay*, I tell my conscience to alleviate the pang of guilt. It's not like he fell from a height.

As Caleb deals with a sudden armful of wriggling Grandpa, I stomp on Caleb's right wrist to free myself. This part is completely guilt-free. I even savor it. When Caleb still doesn't let go, I stomp on his arm harder, like I would try to squash a huge spider.

His fingers finally release my leg.

I step back a few feet, aiming my gun at Paul's leg, and tell him in a ragged breath, "I'll count to ten. If Caleb's hands aren't firmly tied behind his back, I *will* put a bullet in your kneecap. One . . ."

Paul rolls away from Caleb, stands up on shaking legs, and fumbles to pick up the rope he dropped when I pushed him.

"If I hear you say anything, I will also shoot," I say to reestablish my authority. They could phase out at any moment and have long conversations without me knowing, but I doubt it would help them.

"Two," I say as the old man gets the rope. "Three . . . four . . ." I stretch out every second, trying to time it so I won't actually have to shoot anyone. "Ten," I finish when I'm convinced Caleb's hands have been thoroughly tied. "Good. Now give me his phone."

When Paul brings me the phone, I motion with the gun toward the car and tell him, "Get behind the wheel."

"Why do you need to take me?" Paul protests, giving me a disgruntled look. "Just tie me up and leave."

"Nice try, Grandpa," I say. "You might've already Split to alert the Temple. They could be on their way to stop me as we speak. No, thanks. If you're with me, any surprises we might come across will have consequences for us both."

I see a tiny glint in his eyes. Was it disappointment or something else? If I didn't know any better, I'd think it was pride. Was he impressed by me acting like a conniving bastard? Does the knowledge that he passed on one of his personality traits give him a warm, fuzzy feeling?

"Get in through the passenger side so I can keep the gun on you," I instruct him, and without complaining, the old man complies.

Climbing over the seats looks difficult for him, and I feel another slight pang of guilt. But I quickly squash the feeling. Paul got himself into this mess. I would've been happy to continue my vacation and not be dragged into all this. My abduction, carried out under his orders, created the chain of events that culminated in his current discomfort.

"You'll regret this," Caleb tells me as I climb into the car.

Instead of responding, I slam the passenger door with such force that some of the paint chips off the Honda. Paul cringes, having been startled by it.

"Drive," I tell him, planting the gun firmly in his side.

And he does. He drives in silence, which I don't mind. With my free hand, I put my Miami hotel address into the GPS app in Caleb's phone. It looks like we're about five hours away and moving in the right direction.

We ride in tense silence for about an hour before the forest gives way to a suburb.

When we pass by a blue sign, I tell him, "Stop the car and get out."

"You're just going to leave me here?" Paul asks once he's out of the car.

"Would you rather I shoot you?"

"No, but how will I—"

"Stop. Don't even try to play the feeble old man card on me. We just passed a sign that says there's a rest stop less than a mile away. You can walk it."

His face is unreadable for a moment, but then he says, "Caleb was right. You *will* regret this."

"I highly doubt it," I say and scoot over into the driver's seat. Then I close the door, missing Paul's nose by a hair, and slam my foot on the gas pedal, hoping the exhaust fumes hit that asshole in the face.

# CHAPTER TEN

When I get on the highway, I crack open the window to let the warm Florida air in and draw in a deep breath, reflecting on how lucky I was that my desperate 'grab a gun and kidnap Grandpa' plan actually worked.

Now I need to make sure my mom, Lucy, is all right. Pulling out Caleb's phone, I put in her number from memory. Her current cell number is what used to be our household's landline, back when my moms lived in the city. That's a number I'll never forget, and I'm grateful to her for keeping it. I'm terrible at remembering phone numbers these days.

The call goes straight to voicemail. I'm guessing that means she's on the phone and doesn't want to interrupt her conversation for an unknown caller. Or at least I'm hoping that's the case. I refuse to think of other possibilities. I'll have to try calling her again in a bit.

As I drive, I alternate between going the speed limit and doubling it. I decide against speeding on the fourth fluctuation. The last thing I want is for the police to stop me. The idea of being taken in, almost naked, for grand theft auto is not at all appealing. Though, on second thought, I could probably Guide my way out of it.

Pulling into a large rest stop, I waste a few minutes buying myself some clothes and flip-flops. Thankfully, I'm in Florida, so no one seems to think I'm crazy for driving around in my swimwear—else there'd be more people that I'd need to Guide. As is, they probably assume I'm a tourist. While I'm at it, I take a bathroom break and grab a bag of chips— something I would not normally consider food. Since I don't have any money, I have to Guide the cashier to put his own money into the register and allow me to pay him back via PayPal through Caleb's phone.

As soon as I'm back on the road, I call Lucy again.

To my relief, she picks up on the third ring.

"Hello, who is this?" she asks.

"Hi Mom, it's me, Darren. I had to borrow someone's phone. Can we talk?"

"Oh, Darren, hi. How's your vacation going?"

"Great, Mom. But this isn't just a 'how are you' call. I have something strange I need to talk to you about."

"Oh?" Had this been Sara, my worrywart mom, her voice would've sounded concerned by this point, but not Lucy. Ever the detective, she just sounds curious.

"What are you working on?" I ask. "And I know how random it sounds, but please just tell me."

"Hmm . . . not much, to be honest. Not work-wise, anyway. We just closed this high-profile embezzlement case . . ."

"What about any cases dealing with dangerous people?" I ask, two steps away from sounding crazy. "Or could this embezzlement case get someone who's dangerous in trouble?"

"What's this about, sweetie?" Now her voice sounds a tiny bit concerned. "Why are you asking me this?"

"I don't want to talk about it over the phone, but I need to know if you're working on a dangerous case," I insist. "Can you please tell me?"

"This makes no sense," she says. "Is this some kind of game, like when you were a kid?"

"Do you need me to beg you to answer?"

"Fine," she says, blowing out a breath. "But I have to say, you sound like your mother when she's had one of those bad dreams. And the answer is no. I don't have any cases that even Sara would consider dangerous, which should tell you a lot. Nor do I have many cases, period, even the boring kind. But I have been busy looking into the case file on your friend Mira's parents' murder. A case that was shelved long ago—"

"That," I say, my heartbeat picking up. "*That* sounds like it could involve dangerous people."

"True, but I'm not really working in the field. Just reviewing some old paperwork. It's a bit odd what happened with this case."

"What's odd about it?" I can't help being intrigued.

"It was dismissed as a mob hit. The file states that Mira's father worked for the mob, which is why no one looked into his death too closely. They don't bother when mobsters kill each other."

"But Mira's dad—"

"Wasn't with the mob," she cuts in. "I realize that. He was a scientist."

"Okay. This is what I was talking about. The people who killed Mira's family are obviously dangerous—"

"Actually, no," she says. "I mean, yes they *were* dangerous, but not anymore. Not given what I just found out. Once I started digging, I cracked the case. Most of the players involved turned up dead a few weeks ago. The only reason this is still on my mind is because of that misinformation about Mira's father . . ."

Shit. When I *do* tell her everything, it'll have to include the truth about what happened to those now-dead players and how I was involved in their deaths.

"You there?" she asks when I don't say anything for a couple of seconds.

"Yeah, sorry," I say. "So who's dead?"

"The Russian assassin who most likely planted the bomb in Mira's father's car," she says. "If it wasn't for the error about Mira's father being in the mob, I suspect even my less talented former colleagues in Organized Crime would've figured out who'd planted it. That tidbit about this being a mob hit ruined every chance for her parents to get justice. And I can't help but wonder about that. This misinformation makes it seem as though these people, this Russian crew, had someone on the inside, looking out for their best interests—"

"Mom," I interrupt, "as crazy as it sounds, I want you to stop working on this case and do nothing until I speak with you in person."

"Darren." She lets out a sigh. "Are you on drugs again?"

Damn it. She catches me smelling like weed one time, and for the rest of my life, she's worried about me being 'on drugs.' "Mom, I am not on drugs," I say patiently. "Have I ever asked you for something like this?"

"Well, no—"

"So now I'm asking you to do this, no matter how strange it sounds. I'm taking a red-eye to New York, and I'll tell you everything as soon as I get there. Everything will make sense, I promise. I need like six hours or so, if I get lucky with the tickets."

"This is nuts," she says, but her voice sounds uncertain. "Then again, it's not like I could've made much progress—"

"Watch the *Godfather* again," I suggest. "The whole trilogy."

I know how much she likes mafia movies, especially the ones set during the early history of the mob, long before Lucy's career began. They're more fun for her because she can't complain as much about how they got all the facts wrong about the 'real' underworld.

"Fine," she says. "You're lucky I can't do much with this internal breech theory anyway. It's a very delicate matter, as you can imagine."

I look at the phone. It's 4:00 p.m. The GPS estimates I'll arrive in Miami in about four hours. Add in a couple of hours to get to the airport and board the next available flight, and I'll probably arrive in NYC sometime during the middle of the night. "I'll do my best to be back tonight."

"Call me as soon as you land."

"It's a deal," I say.

"And Darren," she says as her goodbye, "you better have a good explanation for all this."

* * *

I park Caleb's car in our hotel's parking lot and make my way toward the hotel's entrance. As I approach, I see Mira standing there. As soon as she lays eyes on me, an expression of sheer outrage flits across her face.

"Darren!" she yells. "You fucking bastard."

She's shouting at me from across the main road. The passersby look uncomfortable and try to stay out of her way as she heads toward me. I can sympathize with them. How else would you react to hearing a young, attractive woman dropping the f-bomb this loudly in the middle of the street?

"Mira," I say once she's crossed the road, having ignored the loud honks coming from an asshole inside a red convertible. "I'm happy to see you too. I'm about to tell you the craziest story—"

She runs up to me and, standing up on her tiptoes, gives me a big hug. Her breathing is jerky and uneven. Whatever anger she felt has clearly been replaced by something else.

"You stupid shit," she says, pulling back after a moment. Her eyes look suspiciously moist. "Do you have any idea how worried we all were? Any fucking clue?"

"Not my fault," I say quickly. "I was taken."

"What?"

"I was kidnapped by my own grandparents. I know," I say in answer to her perplexed expression. "I told you, I've got a crazy story."

"We had the beachfront searched for your body," she says grimly.

I sense she didn't really hear my 'I was taken' and 'kidnapped' comments.

"Your aunt made them search, and we were about to file a missing person's report," she continues, her voice quavering.

"Listen." I cradle her face between my palms. "It was Caleb. He approached me as I was leaving the bar, and took me at gun point."

"Caleb?" she asks, my words finally registering. "What did *he* want with you? Is this about Jacob?"

"Not exactly. Well, Caleb was pretty pissed off about Jacob, but my grandparents had a different agenda. Do you mind if I tell everyone what happened at the same time, so I don't have to repeat myself?"

"Oh, right, the others," she says and takes out her phone. In a whirl, her delicate fingers type out a couple of texts. Almost as soon as she clicks send on the last text, her phone rings.

"Follow me," she says, ignoring the call. "We're getting pizza."

I think about objecting for a moment and trying to rush to the airport, but I need to explain what happened, and it might as well be at a pizza shop, since I'm starved. We walk to Winnie's New York Pizza, a place that's half a block away from the hotel. We've never been there for dinner, but we've frequently gotten lunch there. Though, for the record, it's nothing like the pizza in New York and has more in common with big chains (crappy, in other words).

Mira's phone doesn't stop ringing, so once we're seated, she angrily taps the receive button. "Yes, he's okay, Zhenya . . . That's what I said in the text . . . Just get here and bring the others." After a few angry words in Russian, she says, "That's what I also said in my text—"

Lowering the phone, she glares at it. My guess is that Eugene hung up on her after having had enough of her abuse. *Better him than me,* I think.

She shuts off her phone after it rings a few more times and sullenly studies the menu. I'm both flattered and frightened by how much she was worried about me. If that's what her reaction is about. But I do know one thing for sure: given that she's gotten the brick-oven thin crust pie with basil every time we've come here, she doesn't need to study the menu.

Thinking about Mira's favorite choice of pizza reminds me how hungry I am.

"Can I start you off with drinks?" our waiter asks.

"We're waiting for the rest—"

"We'll have the Sicilian-style pie with the works as an appetizer," I say, interrupting Mira as gently as I can. "And I understand that it's a large appetizer, but I still want it." When the guy leaves, I say to Mira, "That's actually for me. Though I guess I can share a little—"

"Darren, what the hell happened?" Hillary asks as she and Eugene approach the table.

"What the shit?" Eugene adds, his accent as thick as I've ever heard it.

"Hello to you too," I say to them.

"Can you now tell me what Caleb wanted?" Mira asks. "And where you've been?"

"Chill, people. Don't all talk at the same time." They look confused for a moment, so I tell them, "Please, sit. I'll tell you what happened."

"Shouldn't we wait for Bert?" Hillary asks. "He was just as worried as the rest of us."

"Actually, no," I say. "Quite the opposite. This involves Reader and Guide stuff."

"Well," Hillary says, looking at her phone, "you only have a few minutes before he gets here."

"I'll make it quick," I say and swiftly tell them everything, only stopping when my pizza arrives. Eugene's eyes look like they're about to pop out of their sockets when I get to the 'making a baby with Julia' part. Mira's expression is harder to interpret, but she does rudely cut off her brother's attempt to ask me how Julia is doing, as though Julia and I had the chance to bond on that level.

"So your grandparents on your father's side are just as fucked up as my mom and dad," Hillary concludes when I finish.

"I guess," I say between frantic bites of pizza.

"So you believe this Mimir being?" Eugene asks. "You think your mother is in trouble?"

"Yes. I found him very convincing. So I *have* to get back to New York, and I'll need Bert's help to get there. I'm getting this really bad feeling about my mom."

"Need my help with what?" Bert asks, startling me. I didn't notice he'd arrived. "What's wrong with your mom?"

I phase out and the bustling Miami street stops in its tracks. I pull Hillary and the others into my Quiet session.

"What do I tell him?" I ask, pointing to frozen Bert. "How do I spin it?"

"Just say you were on the phone this whole time, because your mom is sick and you need to go to New York," Hillary suggests.

"That makes no sense," I say. "He'll never believe that horseshit."

"I can make it so he does," Hillary says. "Since time is of the essence."

"Maybe, but he's my best friend. It feels wrong doing that to him. Does Pushing leave any permanent damage?"

"I don't think it does. But that's more his area of expertise." She nods toward Eugene.

"I doubt it causes brain damage," Eugene says in his most pedantic tone. "But I think we should tell him about us."

"What, why?" Mira gives her brother one of her most derisive looks.

"For starters, his girlfriend is a Push–I mean, Guide. I, his new friend, am a Reader. And more importantly, his oldest and best friend is both," he says. "On a more selfish note, I need someone with his skills to help with my research. And I could use someone without our abilities to act as a control group of sorts. There is only so much I can do with the neighbors without their cooperation."

Now I know why Eugene got all excited when I mentioned my friend is a hacker.

"It's tempting," Hillary says, a hint of a smile appearing on her face. "If he knew about us, going out with him would feel more honest."

"I can't believe this," Mira says. "Isn't telling *them* forbidden?"

"Good question," I say, finally getting a chance to speak.

"In *our* society, it's not forbidden so much as frowned upon," Hillary says. "When you tell them, you're responsible for making sure they don't blab."

"Oh, right," Eugene says. "I hadn't thought of that. You can prevent people from talking. This settles it, then. If you and I combine our efforts, we can be pretty secure in telling Bert everything. I can Read him from time to time to see whether he would expose us, and if he would, I'll tell you."

"Sounds lovely," Mira says sardonically.

"It's not as sinister as it sounds," Hillary says defensively. "If things go that way, he'll only find that he keeps forgetting to talk about this subject."

"Bert wouldn't talk," I say, tired of the back and forth. "Not if we deliver this to him with proper finesse, that is. And by *we*, I mean *me*."

"All right, *we* can let Bert into our little circle later," Hillary says. "For now, just tell him you were on the phone with your mom, and I'll make sure he doesn't ask too many questions. We'll have plenty of time for the whole story once we're not in a hurry."

She walks over to Bert and kisses him deeply. When I catch a glimpse of her tiny tongue in my friend's mouth, I take it as my cue to avert my gaze.

"I don't need to see that," Mira says and touches her frozen self on the neck. With that, she's gone.

"I'm out too," Eugene says and grabs his other self's wrist.

I can't phase out because that would take Hillary out of the Quiet with me, and she's not done with her odd, French-style Guiding technique.

"All set," Hillary says after releasing Bert. "Hold on," she says as I reach for my pizza-holding doppelganger. "I wanted to talk to you about something."

"What's up?" I ask, deciding I can stay in the Quiet for a moment longer, since no time is passing on the outside.

"It's about this new ability your grandparents mentioned. The one they're trying to 'breed' you for." She wrinkles her tiny nose at the word. "I've heard about something like this before."

"You have?"

She nods. "There have always been rumors about some of our Elders being able to Split while in the Mind Dimension, into a sort of extra level of alternate reality that's accessible only to them."

I'm taken aback for a moment. "Do you think those rumors are true?"

"I wouldn't rule it out. And what's even more interesting is that these same rumors claim it requires a Reach of incredible proportion. The kind of Reach only the most powerful Elders possess."

"Really?"

"That's what I heard growing up," she says. "You've got to remember that my family was essentially a breeding farm to replenish the Elders' ranks. In fact, the reason I never met my grandmother is, I think, because she is—or was—an Elder."

"That would make her my great-grandmother," I say.

"If she's alive. But here's my point. My sister's children were supposed to join the ranks of the Elders if she had, you know, mated with the 'right' person." She makes another face as she says the word 'right.' "My children too. Though that's also not going to happen."

"Okay," I say. "So what's the point?"

"Don't you see? Your father had to breed with someone with great Depth, and my sister was someone with big Reach, which are, at the core, one in the same, as they both relate to how long you can stay in the Mind Dimension," she says, looking at me expectantly.

"So what are you saying?" I ask, my heart skipping a beat.

"What if your Depth, or Reach, or whatever we'd call *your* thing, is already powerful enough to access a dimension beyond this one?" Her eyes gleam with excitement. "Have you considered the possibility?"

I blink a few times. Could she be right? How do I know I can't do what my Enlightened grandparents are hoping to achieve by breeding Julia and me? How do I know I'm not on par with Hillary's rumored Elders? After all, it's true that my Depth, when it comes to Reading, is formidable. I can measure my Depth by recalling the furthest I've ever gone with it, which has to be when I Read my mom's memories from before I was born—on the day I learned my biological parents had given me up for adoption before they were murdered. I never connected the dots before, but according to that one Reading experience, I can conclude that my Depth is truly insane.

Given that Readers split their Depth with the person they're Reading, my Depth must at least be double my age, or a little over forty years. And who knows, it could be greater, as I've never tried to go further into someone's memories yet. To put these forty years into perspective, Mira and Eugene's

Depths allows them to be in the Mind Dimension for mere minutes.

"I understand what you're saying, but it's still hard to believe," I say slowly. "If I could do something like that, something so big, wouldn't I know it by now?"

"I have no idea," Hillary says. "But I think your grandparents were fools to dismiss you and focus on your future offspring."

"They're fools for many reasons."

She smiles. "Agreed."

"So if true, then what?" I ask. "What do your rumors say about the practical aspect of it for a Guide? My grandfather said the ability would allow a Reader to Read another Reader."

"I'm not too sure," she says thoughtfully. "The rumors don't reveal much, but everyone fears the Elders who can do this. Some of the rumors echo what your grandfather said, though. They say these special Elders can actually Guide anyone, even a Reader or a Guide, which is why my parents said this kind of power was 'abominable.'" She sighs. "Then again, they found a lot of things abominable."

"It would certainly explain their fears. Who would want their mind manipulated?" I glance at frozen Bert as I say this.

"Exactly," she says, ignoring my hint. "And who would be more afraid of it than the people who know the full extent of that power?"

"Especially anyone who's ever abused what they can do."

"Have you ever tried to Split while in the Mind Dimension?" When I shake my head, she asks, "Can you try?"

I examine myself. I'm so excited that, were this the real world, I could've easily phased into the Quiet. But this is the Quiet, and I'm not sure how phasing works here. I try to phase in, though 'try' isn't the best word to describe it. I can't pinpoint what it is that I actually *do* to phase in. I consciously control it only to a very small degree. Phasing is more of an instinctual process, like blocking a punch became after Reading Haim. Yes, I knew how to block a punch before, but while practicing with Caleb, I was relying on instinct rather than conscious thought. And because I was relying on instinct, there were many times when I couldn't block his punches. This is similar to the result I'm getting now as I try to phase into an alternate level of the Quiet. Because I don't consciously know how phasing works, I hit a mental wall and nothing happens.

"No luck," I say.

"Are you sufficiently stressed?" Hillary asks.

"Well, no." Then I remember something. "You know that time on the bridge, when Sam was basically murdering us all? I did feel *something*."

She looks excited. "What did you feel, Darren?"

"Well, it was a lot like what I feel before I phase out, or Split as you call it. Time slowed down, but then it felt as though I was hitting a brick wall."

"I've never experienced anything like that," she says. "So that has to be good news."

"But it still didn't work."

"Have you ever tried the Bellows Breath technique?"

"The what?" I stare at her.

"It's a breathing exercise that puts your mind in an excited state. We teach it to our young people to aid in the Splitting process," she explains.

"I never learned anything like that. I learned to Split the old-fashioned way, by nearly dying a few times."

"Damn," Hillary says. "I'm still amazed by your story. That you managed to tap into your power on your own is incredible."

"You flatter me," I say. "But didn't Thomas do the same thing?"

"I'm just as impressed with Thomas. I had a lot of trouble with Splitting in the beginning, even when I was told about it explicitly and taught how to bring it about."

"Oh, I didn't realize."

"Yeah, so that's actually good news for you. Just because you haven't already Split from the Mind Dimension—and we need to call that something else, by the way—doesn't mean you never will. And the breathing technique is how I learned, so it's worth a shot."

"Okay, tell me what to do," I say. "And what do you think of 'Level 2' for phasing in a second time?"

"I hate it," Hillary says. "But we can come back to that later. For now, let me show you how to do the Bellows Breath."

She proceeds to teach me the technique, which derives from yoga, though she made it sound as if the ancient yogis learned it from the Guides. The short version is that it's a lot like purposefully hyperventilating by pretending to have a panic attack. You're supposed to take very quick 'in' breaths and release them just as quickly. This is how I imagine the big bad wolf exercised his lungs before he confronted the three little pigs.

When I think I have the hang of it, I say, "Okay, let me try."

I start breathing, in-out, in-out, as quickly as my diaphragm will allow. It's an odd thing to do and reminds me of how I'd breathe after getting chased around the schoolyard by bullies.

"Is it working?" Hillary asks.

"I feel a little more awake and energized, but no, nothing. Not even that almost-phasing-in feeling I got on the bridge."

"Oh well. Maybe I'll need to scare you shitless one day while we're in the Mind Dimension."

"Please don't," I say, unsure whether she's kidding.

"Let's continue this later," she says, and I notice how she completely skirted around my request for her to not 'scare me shitless' one day. "There are a couple of other things I can teach you. Like I said, Splitting didn't come easy to me at all, which now has the benefit of making me an expert on different techniques we can try with you."

"Deal. But later, after I sort out this thing with my mom."

"Sure," she says. "Though strictly speaking, you might be more conducive to phasing while worried about your mom and all."

"I hear ya, and as much as I want to figure out how to phase while in the Quiet, I first want to get to New York and make sure my mom is okay."

"It must be nice having a mom who's not a nutcase," she says and reaches for her frozen body.

"Wait," I say. "I just remembered. On the subject of weird powers, can Guides control where they—I mean, we—appear in the Quiet? I've seen someone do it in Caleb's memory."

"Many rumors about this also exist. Someone always knows someone whose cousin can choose where he or she appears in the Quiet. I can't do it myself, nor do I personally know anyone who can, but my parents claimed to know a number of people who could. I thought it was an urban myth, to be honest."

"Oh well," I say. "Would've been cool to be in New York and then appear in the Quiet on some Caribbean island."

"Even in the tales I heard, I've never heard of anyone having such a long range," she says. "But who knows? Ready to talk to Bert?"

"Let's do it," I say, walking over to my body to phase out.

When the sounds of the streets are back, I look at Bert and say, "Dude, my mom isn't feeling well. I've been on the phone with her doctors this whole time." I give him a onceover. He looks as if he's buying it, which can only mean that Hillary's juju is working.

"I need your help getting back to New York. Do you think you can get us on the next flight out?"

A confused expression flashes across Bert's face. I guess he's switching from a 'believe any bullshit' mode to using his brain.

"Sure, Darren," he says. "Let me go do my thing."

He turns on his heels and walks in the direction of the hotel.

"You overdid it," I say to Hillary.

"You might be right," she admits.

"At least get him some food to go," I say.

"Of course," Hillary says. "What kind of monster do you think I am?"

Instead of answering, I, Twix-commercial-style, stuff my mouth with pizza.

# CHAPTER ELEVEN

"Why are we here so early?" Mira asks after we've gone through Miami airport security. We were the first to go through, but the rest of the gang isn't far behind.

"I needed to be somewhere that wasn't our hotel," I tell her. "Since Caleb abducted me from the beach right next to our hotel, it's safe to say if he tries to find me again, that'll be the first place he looks."

"There are nicer places to hide," Mira says. "Especially in Miami."

"I didn't know the cab ride and check-in would be so quick. They say you have to arrive at the airport a couple of hours early anyway. According to that logic, we're right on schedule." I try not to sound too defensive, wanting to stay on Mira's good side.

She's upset about my kidnapping, and her way of handling it is to blame me for it. Or to pick a fight. Anything to create a grievance to match her emotional state without actually dealing with her feelings. Then again, it's feasible that I am overthinking Mira's current prickliness. She doesn't have the sunniest of personalities, even on good days. It's just that sometimes my inner shrink starts talking with a voice that sounds suspiciously like my therapist, Liz.

"Of course it's quick," Bert says, joining us after having just cleared security. "You didn't even let us take any luggage. Dude, having the hotel ship us all our stuff is going to be very expensive."

"I'm good for it." I tap my pocket. "Getting to my mom is my top priority and if paying to have our shit shipped speeds things up—which it clearly did—it'll be more than worth it."

"Sure, leaving our stuff behind helped, but not as much as I did," Bert says. "If I hadn't gotten us those last-minute tickets, there's no way—"

"Listen, Bert. We should take a walk. I need to talk to you about something," I say. "Mira, you mind if we meet you guys by the gate?"

"You're going to tell him *now*?" she says incredulously.

"Tell me what?" Bert looks puzzled.

"You said it yourself." I ignore Bert to focus on Mira. "We're early, so we have some time to kill." What I leave unsaid is that I'd rather reveal the world of Readers and Guides to Bert than deal with Mira in her current mood.

"What do you need to tell me?" Bert repeats.

"Let's walk," I say and head in a random direction. Once we're out of Mira's earshot, I stop walking and say, "Okay, dude. I'm about to tell you the craziest thing you've ever heard. In fact, I doubt you'll even believe me, seeing that if I were in your shoes, *I* wouldn't believe me."

"Let me guess," he says excitedly. "You and Mira are getting married?"

"What?" I say, taken off-guard. "When I said it was crazy, I didn't mean it *that* literally. I meant in the sense that you'll think I'm crazy, which I guess I would be if I were getting married—"

"So out with it then."

I draw in a deep breath, unsure how to proceed. "You know how I sort of know things sometimes? Things I shouldn't know?"

"Sometimes?" Bert snorts. "You mean all the time, don't you?"

"Yes, well, there's an explanation for how I do this stuff, but it's hard to believe," I say.

"And you're going to take as long as you can, building it up before you tell me, aren't you? Because you're sadistic like that."

"Fine. Here goes. I can stop time. Sort of."

"Huh?" Bert looks at me like I grew a second head. "What?"

"I can make it so that the world is frozen, and I can walk around and look at things that I otherwise wouldn't be allowed to see. And more importantly, I can do this without people knowing, since they're frozen in time."

"You're right. That does sound crazy."

"I know, which is why I'll prove it to you," I say.

I walk over to a store redundantly called Books & Books, with Bert following behind.

"There's no way you can prove something like that to me," Bert says. "But I'm curious to see how you'd even try."

"I can and I will," I say. "And if this doesn't work, there's some even crazier stuff I plan on telling you about, which, ironically, might be easier to prove."

"Crazier? Like you're *the* Napoleon, or Mother Teresa maybe?"

"Just play along." I buy a pad of paper and pencil and hand it to Bert. "Here. Write something I wouldn't have any idea about and then put the paper, or even the entire pad if you want, in your pocket. I'll turn around."

"This is stupid," Bert mumbles, but I hear the sound of pencil on paper.

"Don't write so loudly. I don't want you to think I deduced what you wrote by the sound of the pencil," I say. "Let me know when you're done."

"Done," he says.

I phase into the Quiet, walk over to frozen Bert, and gingerly reach into his pocket, trying not to touch anything other than the paper. I take out his note and read it: 42. I walk over to my body and phase out.

"Very funny," I say without turning around. "You wrote forty-two, the answer to life, the universe, and everything."

"Oh, that's a good one," Bert says. "Even better than the card thing you do. But that whole patter about stopping time—"

"This wasn't a fucking magic trick," I say, turning around. "Nor was the card thing, actually, but—"

"Oh, come on. If you know me well enough—and you do—you could've just guessed."

"You know what? I'll move on to something that might sound harder to believe, but will be easier for me to prove. I'll read your mind."

Before Bert can say anything skeptical, I phase out again. I walk up to him and put my hand on his forehead. Then I even out my breathing. I didn't realize how annoyed I was by failing to convince him, or by his stubbornness. The Coherence state comes very quickly and with it, entry into Bert's mind. As I fall in, I make sure to fall deep. Best to learn something that happened before we met, or else he'll just say I have a good memory and keen observational skills.

* * *

We're sitting alone at a dingy, gray cafeteria table, looking at the big greasy clock hanging on the white wall. Another half hour before the bell rings, signaling the end of our lunch break. Our bladder will explode if we wait that long, so we decide, unfortunately, to go to the dreaded bathroom.

We get up and walk, doing our best not to drag our feet. All the while, we mentally curse the principal or whoever came up with the idea of not letting kids out of the cafeteria during lunch.

*Maybe it'll be okay today,* we think as we walk. It doesn't happen all the time. Just sometimes. And besides, at least we already had our lunch.

We open the door and see a shadow. Our heart sinks, and we back out of the room. Hands grab our shirt and pull us in.

*Fuck.* It's him.

Roger.

"You know the drill, Dookie," Roger says. "Give me the cash."

Rationally, we know the guy is not as giant as he seems. But at five-eleven and one-hundred-and-eighty pounds, he seems truly enormous to us, whose weight is only in the double digits.

"I've spent it," we say, trying to keep our voice steady.

Roger's response comes in the form of a punch to our stomach. Air escapes our lungs, and we fall to the floor, glad about one thing—we didn't empty our bladder.

He goes through our pockets and finds the leftover five bucks from our lunch. He usually takes the ten Mom gives us.

"Tomorrow, you owe me double," the guy says and spits on the floor, missing us by a hair.

To keep from crying, we run some numbers through our head. He's taken a total of $465 from us. Some part of our mind is keeping count. Who knows, maybe one day we'll get every dollar back. Maybe with interest.

I, Darren, disassociate.

Poor Bert. I've had my own run-ins with bullies, but never this bad. For starters, no one could ambush me since I always scouted things out in the Quiet. Plus, there was no way the school could've kept me in the cafeteria during the entire lunch break. I always had a way of weaseling my way out of this type of situation. I would've gotten my doctor to give me a note of some kind, or I would have convinced my shrink, Liz, that I had the first known case of cafeteria anxiety. Still, I totally relate and sympathize with my friend's experience. Bullying is a hazard that even befalls kids who haven't skipped grades like Bert and I did. For kids who do skip grades, the chances of being preyed upon increase drastically, since they're likely to be much smaller than the would-be bullies.

Did Bert deal with this fucker at some point? If he didn't, I will, as soon as this thing with my mom blows over. This Roger guy might find himself naked and using his boss's office as a bathroom, or something worse.

I focus on Bert's recollections that deal with revenge. As I do, I feel the heaviness I associate with fast-forwarding through memories.

We get an invitation to our high school reunion in our inbox, and it reminds us of that scum, Roger Blistro. It's funny how memory works sometimes. We haven't thought of that fucker in years. Now that we have thought of him, though, Roger's luck has just run out. We're getting a very strong urge for some payback.

We look around. Everyone is at lunch. We wonder whether our work computer at the FBI is the best place to do this. Then again, why not? It's unlikely anyone is tracking our computer, and besides, we've taken a number of counter measures, which the FBI would require an expert of our caliber to defeat. Good luck with that.

It takes us only a few dozen keystrokes to look up the creep, and a few more to find some useful details.

Interesting. Looks like someone has expensed a trip to Aspen, claiming it was a professional conference. Given the honeymoon suite, the flower deliveries, and the room service for two, it sure looks more like someone took his mistress on a getaway. If true, this is borderline embezzlement, or at least that's how his employer will see it. Furthermore, he wrote off that same trip on his taxes, claiming, in this case, that it was for his consulting firm, which has nothing to do with his day job. We know these things are probably lies. We wonder what the IRS would think of double-dip accounting. Yes, the IRS might indeed be interested in this. We see this trip is just the tip of the iceberg when it comes to our old pal Roger's tax-dodging activities.

The keyboard sings its little song as our fingers dance around it. We get into the IRS's system and flag Roger for an audit. That should be plenty of fun for him, but we're just getting started.

After a few more keystrokes, we locate his wife's email and anonymously inform her of the trip, making it clear that if she wasn't with Roger on his Aspen vacation, he was cheating on her. We try to sound like a disgruntled mistress. We'd bet good money that the wife wasn't on the trip.

Next, we hack into his employer's intranet. Aha! His secretary was away during that same week. Bingo. We'd now put double the money on his wife being upset. We look around some more and locate a nifty 'see something, report anonymously' program on the HR part of the website. We write a memo about the Aspen trip and how Roger is having indecent relations with his secretary (even if the second part is false, the first one will get him in deep shit).

That was mere karma. Now for the real payback. This last part would be harder to pull off if Roger hadn't trusted his banking needs to Citibank. It just so happens that Citibank is the very bank we found a back door into a year ago. We haven't used it, since we knew we'd be treading on extremely dangerous ground, but we decide to push aside our concern over such minor details for this important task.

We get in through Citibank's back door, and our fingers dance some more around the keyboard. We do some quick mental calculations along the way. Assuming a reasonable rate of twenty percent, and the starting principal of one grand (rounding up), with compounded interest (again, rounding up), Roger owes us five grand. No, that's not enough. We add a zero at the end for emotional damage and what not. That number turns out to be perfect, since fifty grand is about the amount he has in his account.

We decide against taking the money for ourselves. That could get us into trouble, and it's not like we're desperate for cash. Some more clicks of the keyboard, and we smile. How noble is it of Roger to give all his money to the Stop Bullying Now Foundation? How admirable, given how he's about to need this money quite desperately to hire a tax attorney.

I, Darren, feel proud of my friend and decide I don't need any more proof.

\* \* \*

"You worked for the FBI?" I ask as soon as I'm out of the Quiet.

"I mentioned that to you—"

"Did you ever tell me about that asshole from your high school? Roger?"

He looks taken aback. "No. I'm fairly sure I haven't. I don't like talking about that shit . . ."

I proceed to tell him what I just saw through his younger self's eyes, down to all the little details. When I recall it, I even mention the hacking techniques he used, saying terms that are foreign to me, such as 'SQL Injection' and 'buffer overflow.'

As I go on, Bert's expression becomes harder and harder to read. If I had to pinpoint what he was feeling, I'd say it was something between awe and terror.

"I never wrote any of this down," he mumbles softly. "And I never told anyone. No one." He shakes his head. "But you could've learned about him from someone who went to school with him—"

"Seriously?" I say. "Your denial is getting weak, my friend."

He rubs his nose. "Okay, but that personal stuff can be found out . . . somehow. What if I think of something completely random? You'd still know?"

"Go for it."

He grabs a book off the shelf, turns his back to me, and opens the book to a random page. I see where he's going with this and instantly phase out.

I approach frozen Bert from the front and follow his gaze. He's looking at the top of page 188. I memorize the line and walk back to my body.

"Page 188," I quickly say when the noise of the airport is back. "The line reads, 'Korum wasn't home at all, and she wondered where he—'"

"Shit," Bert interrupts. "I haven't even read the whole line yet . . . but that's what it says."

"I did the time-stopping thing and looked at the page while you were frozen," I say. "I didn't need to actually read your mind."

In stunned silence, Bert returns the book. His hands are shaking.

I decide to do another demo, something that should cinch the deal. I admit I'm probably showing off at this point. I phase in again and approach my friend. The Guiding only takes a moment and when I'm done, I phase back out.

As per the instructions I imbedded in his mind, Bert, eyes glazed, takes out the pen and paper and writes, "Oh yeah, Bert, buddy, I can also make you do shit. Why did I just write this? Notice how the handwriting is yours?"

Bert's eyes return to normal, and he reads the paper. Then he looks at me. Then at the paper. "Fucking fuck," he finally says. "You have to tell me *everything*."

"Let's walk over to Starbucks," I say. "This might take a while."

* * *

"Can we talk?" Bert says to Hillary when we get to the gate.

"I just told him everything, Aunty," I say playfully. "So you guys have some catching up to do."

Hillary gives me a seething look. It's as if she wasn't the one who okayed my bringing Bert up to speed. I'm guessing she's mad that I didn't let her talk to Bert first. Then she grabs Bert's arm and begins dragging him away.

"Just remember I have to make this flight," I remind them before they walk off. "With or without you guys, I'll be on it. I can't afford to wait till tomorrow."

They don't respond, already arguing as they walk. I'm sure they'll be fine. I don't need to get inside Bert's mind to know Hillary can get away with pretty much anything as far as he's concerned.

"Boarding is in twenty-five minutes," Eugene yells at them.

"Wow," I say. "Time flies when you're breaking taboos."

"Yeah," Eugene says. "I have to say, this is really exciting. Did you tell him about my work?"

"How could I, when I don't know much about it?"

"Well, since you bring it up—"

Eugene goes into detail about his work for about twenty minutes. Mira leaves as soon as he starts talking, giving me a 'you deserve this' kind of stare. She's still clearly in a bad mood.

I won't repeat much of what Eugene shared with me, because frankly, if he expected me to understand even half of it, he must think really highly of my background in neuroscience. However, there is one thing I do grasp when it comes up.

"You know," I say, grabbing on to a familiar subject, "when it comes to stimulating a specific region of the brain, instead of implanting electrodes, something no sane person would let you do, you can use TMS—Transcranial Magnetic Stimulation—"

"I know what that is," Eugene says. "The problem is that those machines are very pricey."

"And getting someone to drill a hole in their head is cheap?"

"I was thinking of finding someone who already—"

"Listen," I interrupt. "It just so happens that through work, I know of a company that's about to make those things very affordable. And more importantly, better and more portable. So you know what? I'll buy you one."

He looks as if I just handed him the world. "I don't know what to say." I hope he doesn't tear up, though it looks like he's considering it. "An assistant and a TMS machine," he says, his voice shaking with emotion. "I'm going to leapfrog years—no, decades—in my research."

"Glad to be of help, buddy." I don't remind Eugene that Bert hasn't agreed to help him yet.

Knowing Bert, he probably will. "If you don't mind, I've got to swing by the restroom before we board."

"Hurry up. We have mere minutes," he says. "If you see my sister or the lovebirds, tell them to come back too."

I walk briskly in the direction of the bathroom. He's right. I need to hurry. Getting us these tickets was a feat only Bert could've managed, as airlines don't usually hold five empty seats last minute. But through Bert's computer magic, four people got bumped from this flight so we could get on. Bert kindly made sure that the family that was affected got a nice compensation from the airline. That's Bert for you. He also made it clear that the 11:00 p.m. flight is the last one out today, which means I have to be on it, no matter what. If there's a line in the bathroom, I'll just have to hold it.

I'm almost ready to enter the men's restroom when something catches my attention. Something orange. Something that makes me do a double take.

There is a bald, orange-robed figure a few feet away, heading in my general direction.

It could just be a regular Buddhist monk, I tell myself as my heartbeat skyrockets. It's not necessarily one from the Enlightened Temple.

But then I spot another one behind the first monk I noticed. And a few feet away, I see yet another.

Worse, when the nearest one sees me looking at him and his friends, he drops his leisurely pace and starts running toward me.

I'm in deep shit.

# CHAPTER TWELVE

I phase in, and the ambient noise of the airport disappears. Something else is missing. It takes me a moment to realize my poor bladder isn't demanding anything from me anymore. Not until I phase back out, that is.

I walk over to Eugene and pull him into the Quiet.

"Darren," he says. "What are you doing? I'm like right here, mere feet away—"

"We've got a problem," I say. "Make that a *big* problem."

"What's going on?"

"The monks from the Temple are here. See that guy in the robe there, and the other ones?"

"Oh, shit," Eugene says. "What do you think they want?"

"To take me back, make me and Julia do what I refused . . ."

"*Tvari*," he says furiously, switching to Russian.

"Yeah, whatever you just said."

"But—"

"I can't miss my flight. Can you help me with this?"

"You insult me by even asking," he says. "Let's find the others."

We find Mira at the nearby grocery stand. She's holding an apple and is about to pay for it. I pull her in and give her the rundown.

"Let's Read them," she suggests. "That should tell us how many there are and whether Caleb is with them."

"Shit, I didn't think of him," I say. "He could be a real problem if he's here."

"Right, which is all the more reason to do as Mira suggests," Eugene says and walks toward the monks.

"I don't think we'll have any luck with this one," I say. "I recognize him. He's the very one I tried Reading before, but all I got was the white noise from his meditation."

"It's worth a shot," Eugene says. "Maybe one of us will have better luck?"

Mira walks up to the monk and touches him. She looks as if she's concentrating, and her expression becomes serene. Then she looks annoyed.

"No go," she says. "All I get is what Darren described, a sort of emptiness."

She then notices the piece of paper the monk is holding, grabs it from his hand, and reads it.

"Right. According to his boarding pass, he's flying to Detroit," she says. "And I'm the Pope."

"Let's try Reading those two." I look at the other two monks standing in the distance. Decision made, I approach the younger one, saying, "I'll try this one. You go for that one."

This monk is also holding a boarding pass. This one is to Houston. They must've bought random tickets just to get through security. I wonder why airport security doesn't flag people who say, "I'll take a ticket to anywhere please. Oh, and random tickets to I-don't-care-where for my brother monks." Asking these monks what they're up to would make a hell of a lot more sense than forcing old ladies to take off their shoes.

I put my hand on the monk's shaved head, noticing as I do that he's barely out of his teens. After a moment of concentration, I'm in.

\* \* \*

We're wondering what's so special about the guy we're following. The Master didn't say. He just said the excursion might do us some good, but we think this might be the rare case when the Master is wrong. Keeping centered is incredibly hard with all these people around. The noise, the smell of junk food and perfumes—it's all overpowering.

I, Darren, realize this monk is distracted from his unreadable state of mind by the day-to-day life of the airport. Or he's just not as good as the others at keeping his defenses up, being younger and less experienced. Whatever the reason, it works to my advantage, and I dig deeper.

"Let's split up," Caleb, the outsider whom the Master seems to respect for some reason, says. "Let's cover this whole airport. If you see him, stall him, and use this." He hands every one of the brothers a burner phone that's programmed to call him.

I, Darren, disassociate. Things are bad. First, the Master is the monk nearest me, and I get the impression that this monk is called 'Master' due to his fighting skills and not just his meditating prowess. What's worse is that Caleb *is* here. And just to top it off, many more monks, all from the Temple, are surrounding the airport.

I know I should get out of the monk's head and figure a way out of this mess, but curiosity overtakes me. Inside this young monk's mind is something useful.

These monks' fighting style.

I try to feel lighter, enough to go back just a few days.

We're sparring with our more experienced sister. We much prefer no-contact practice, but the Master frowns upon it. He calls no-contact 'flowery fists and embroidery kicks.' The Master says that no matter how pleasing it is to the eye of the spectator monks, or cleansing for the mind of the monk performing the movements, no-contact practice can never take the place of sparring.

The sister we're fighting is amazing. Being a woman of small frame, she's supposed to be weaker than us, but we can barely keep up with her. We know small bruises will appear tomorrow where her punches land. And what impresses us the most is that we know she's holding back the intensity of those punches.

I, Darren, eventually disassociate from the training, but not before I get a compressed month's worth of sparring sessions, and triple that of the stylistic, dance-like solo training. I don't bother remembering the fancy names for the stances, though I guess it would have been cool to show Bert a move and say, "Yup, that was the 'Fierce Tiger Descending from Mountain.'" My goal was to learn the strengths and weaknesses of the style in case I need to fight the Master, who's frozen in the process of running toward me.

Fighting lessons out of the way, I allow myself an indulgence. I try to zoom in on a very specific memory—that of the Reading-resistant meditative technique these monks possess. The young monk was thinking about it while sparring and practiced a version of it during his solo training, but I wasn't focused on it enough to really understand how it works.

I jump around in his head and come up empty. I don't see anything specifically relating to this mysterious technique. All the monks ever taught my host was a type of meditation, which I doubt is special in any way. None of the meditation techniques are qualitatively different from the focused concentration we all think of as meditation. No secret sauce that I could glimpse. These monks simply meditate a lot. Either this monk wasn't entrusted with the special technique, or blocking someone from entering your mind doesn't involve some kind of special trick.

Could it be that regular, vanilla meditation—with enough practice—can make you resistant to Reading and Guiding? Or is it more likely that these monks have special genetics? Like a breed of people who are naturally capable of resisting us? This last theory is flawed. It doesn't explain how I can Read this monk, which suggests blocking people like me is a skill he hasn't yet mastered. Or maybe there's another alternative that I'm not considering.

I file this away as something I can talk to Eugene about someday. I also make a mental note to Read the next 'regular' Buddhist monk I come across, which could prove or disprove my vanilla meditation theory. Not sure where I'd find such a monk, but one time, I did see the Dalai Lama near the United Nations Headquarters. He's a Buddhist.

Damn, I wish I'd known about Reading then. Reading the Dalai Lama would've been cool, but it could've ended with him joining me in the Quiet. How do I know he's not one of us?

Realizing I'm getting sidetracked, I mentally smack myself into focus and exit the young monk's head.

\* \* \*

"It's amazing," Eugene says as soon as I'm out. "I can't Read him. I wonder how—"

"Zhenya, focus," Mira interrupts. "Now's really not the time for your science."

"I had better luck Reading than the two of you, but the information I gleaned doesn't give me much hope," I say, preventing Eugene from arguing with his sister. "Caleb *is* here, as well as more of these monks."

"Damn it," Mira says. "Let's go find the tiny one and figure things out from there."

Finding Hillary is a great idea, so I lead the charge.

She and Bert are in the Starbucks where I told him our secrets. I can't help but smile when I see my friend holding another cup of coffee. He had two while we were chatting less than an hour ago, but he has an extremely high tolerance for caffeine. I think he can drink coffee all day long without getting even a little jittery. Or maybe it's hard to tell the difference between normal Bert and jittery Bert, given how keyed-up this kid normally is.

I pull Hillary in, and a moment later, she's looking up at me with concern written on her small face. Her eyebrows furrow even deeper as I explain the situation.

"Give me a second," she says.

She walks over to Bert and does that kissing thing to him again. Mira and Eugene look away while I just look off to the side, unsure what etiquette says to do in situations such as these.

"Ready," Hillary says when she's done with whatever it is she was doing to Bert.

"You Pushed him?" Mira asks.

"I *Guided* him to go straight to the plane and not look back or start any trouble," Hillary says.

"Good call," I say. "One less variable for us to worry about."

"My thoughts exactly. Now follow me," Hillary says and walks away. Mira and Eugene exchange questioning glances, then look at me. I shrug. I have no idea what my aunt has in mind, but since she looks as though she knows what she's doing, I decide to follow her for now.

She approaches a man in uniform. He appears to be a TSA agent. Without hesitation, Hillary frisks the guy.

"No weapons," she says with obvious disappointment.

"I don't think TSA agents carry," Eugene says. "They're not cops."

"I think I see where you're going with this," Mira says, looking at Hillary approvingly. "Let me have a look."

She places her hand on the shiny, bald head of the aging TSA agent and concentrates.

"How stereotypical," she says when she's done. Turning determinedly, she walks to the stairs and down a level. We all follow her.

As we walk, I notice Hillary is looking around thoughtfully. I wonder what she's planning. Whatever it is, it requires her to learn her surroundings.

"There," Mira says, pointing at the Dunkin Donuts.

I see two other men in uniforms. These two turn out to have 'Miami-Dade' written on their badges.

They're cops.

"MDPD," Mira says and takes the gun from the shorter of the two officers.

"Oh, I get it now," Eugene says. "Cops in a doughnut shop."

Mira slowly shakes her head but doesn't say anything snide. I wonder if that means her mood has improved.

"You should take his gun," Hillary says to Eugene, pointing at the taller cop.

"Shouldn't Darren take it?" Eugene asks. "He learned to shoot very recently, and ironically from Caleb, who—"

"You should take it," Hillary says again. "And here's why."

She tells us her plan.

"That's a good start," Mira says when Hillary is done. "But it won't be enough once we're out of the Mind Dimension."

"That's why I'm not coming with you," Hillary says. "I'll walk around, doing my part. Darren, can you describe the younger monk to me?"

I tell her what the younger monk looks like and where he is in reference to our departure gate.

"Do you think I could Guide him?" she asks. "Since you were able to Read him?"

"Probably," I say.

"I'll throw in an emergency plan, in case he doesn't cooperate," Hillary says. "You three go do your parts."

"Will you have enough time to do what you have to do?" Mira asks.

"It's not important," Hillary says. "I can Split and take as long as I need if I have to. I have more than enough Reach on my own."

"You're right," Mira says. "My nerves are making me stupid."

Hillary doesn't say anything and walks away, touching the first person near us.

It takes Eugene, Mira, and me only a few minutes to locate our target, Caleb.

"Here comes the weird part," I say.

"Everything that follows this will be weird," Eugene says. "Let's go get *you*, Darren."

Leaving Caleb's body behind, we walk through the airport, back to our gate, and back to where my body is on its perilous way to the bathroom.

"Alrighty then," Eugene says. "Do you want me to take the legs?"

"Sure," I say. "I'll take the arms."

"Hold on a second," Mira says and walks away.

She comes back with one of the luggage carts that travelers can rent for five bucks. Yes, five bucks for a glorified shopping cart with no electrical components (verified by the fact that this thing works in the Quiet). That's airport prices for you.

"That's genius," I say.

"Not really. You guys are idiots for planning to drag him—you—by arms and legs across half the airport," she says wryly.

I don't say anything, partly because she has a point. I should've thought of using a cart, but I'm also too wired about the next part of the plan to think straight.

Without much aplomb, I push my rigid body over and he falls onto the cart. It's really odd seeing my limp body lying there like that.

"I'll push it," I say. "It's my body, after all."

No one objects, and we make our way to where we found Caleb. I feel silly dragging myself out of the cart. I imagine this is how a celebrity would feel if they came across themselves in Madame Tussaud's wax museum and started messing around with their statue.

"Let's put him here," I say. "Behind this column."

And to the sound of Mira's disrespectful chuckling, Eugene and I unload the immobile version of me and prop him, as best as we can, behind the shiny metal column.

"Now for the fun part," I say.

"Listen, Darren. It's not too late to think of something else," Eugene says. "Something not so reckless."

"I'm fine," I say. "Just do your thing, both of you."

Without another word, Eugene and Mira walk away, and a minute later, I have no idea where they went. This is part of the plan. Now for the insane part—the part Hillary might've thought up as payback for the way I told Bert about her nature.

I walk over to Caleb and punch him in his immobile face. I know this will pull him in, just like any other physical contact would. This too, unfortunately, is part of the plan.

"You shouldn't have done that, kid," Caleb says as soon as he materializes.

In a whirlwind of motion, he's next to me, and pain erupts in my jaw.

# CHAPTER THIRTEEN

"Stop," I manage to say, proving my jaw isn't broken. "I just want to talk."

As I speak, I block a full-fledged roundhouse kick with my elbow. Caleb aimed the kick at my head. Had it landed, it would've knocked me out. Instead, as my arm meets his foot, I hear a cracking-like thud. The pain from my jaw suddenly feels like child's play. My jaw might be fine, but my elbow is definitively broken.

"No offense, kid, but this time, I *will* kill you," he says, and I'm forced to block a hit to my chest with that same broken elbow. The pain makes me see stars. Still, I get a good punch in, my right hand connecting with his ear.

"Nice one," he says. "So you did learn something." He goes to strike me with his right elbow, but I duck under the attack. "Like I was trying to say, it's not personal," he continues. "It's just that when you're Inert, you'll be much easier to catch." He follows those words up with a double-feint move—or I hope it was something that clever, because he lands a punch to my midsection, and while I'm distracted by the lack of air in my lungs, pushes me back, tripping me as I stumble.

I fall to the ground, and on my way down, I think how this is probably the way my frozen self felt when I pushed him into the cart. I must look just as ridiculous. Then I land and can't reflect on how I look or anything else. The impact manages to squeeze even more air out of me. My body feels cold. I must be going into shock. From about a foot away, Caleb approaches me. *Why is this taking so fucking long?* I wonder.

Caleb raises his foot, and my mind does that thing again, the thing it did when I was fighting Sam in the Quiet on the bridge. It feels a lot like when I'm about to phase into the Quiet. The 'I'm dying so my life is about to flash before my eyes' kind of feeling. Only I'm already in the Quiet. Through the pain, a still-rational part of my brain tries to encourage the feeling, to channel it. My hope is to phase in—to reach what I dubbed Level 2 of the Quiet. I remember how horrible the pain was when Caleb kicked me earlier today. I even try breathing faster, inspired by the technique Hillary taught me.

The kick connects with my ribs, and all I get is debilitating pain that becomes my only point of focus. I open my eyes and see Caleb's leg raised for another kick, this one aimed for my head. At least the pain will be over when I die, even though I'll wake up Inert. Instead of feeling the pain of impact, I hear a gunshot.

I open my eyes again. I didn't realize I closed them. Caleb's face is the epitome of surprise. He's holding his chest, blood seeping from between his fingers.

Then a second shot fires.

Caleb's head explodes. His lifeless body falls to the ground, not far from mine.

Some bits and pieces of him splatter onto my clothes. I even feel something on my face. I'm in too much pain and shock to feel disgust, or to even gloat. I just lie there, willing myself to get up but failing miserably.

"Come on, honey," Mira says as she grabs me gently under the armpits. I'm in too much pain to wonder whether my ears are deceiving me. Surely Mira didn't just use a term of endearment with me?

"Grab his feet," she says more gruffly. Must be talking to Eugene. "Careful, you graceless dimwit."

They drag me somewhere, and in a haze, I recall where.

"Why the fuck did you wait?" Mira says to Eugene. "Why didn't you shoot him immediately?"

"He was too close to Darren," Eugene says. "I didn't have a clean shot. Why didn't *you* shoot?

"Same fucking reason, but unlike you, my angle really was shitty," she says. "This is the last time I listen to that stupid little Pusher bitch. How many of her plans need to end in fucking disaster before I learn?"

"Darren is alive, and Caleb is dead. Hillary's plan wasn't so bad," Eugene objects.

"If we hadn't hid, we could've killed Caleb quicker," she says.

"Using Darren as a distraction was smart. If Caleb had seen us, with guns, he would've been rolling about like a maniac, the way Sam did, remember? And that didn't go so well."

"Whatever," she says and stops. "Roll up his jeans and help me put Darren's hand on his leg."

We brought my frozen self here so I could phase out quickly. I'm grateful to Hillary for thinking of this precaution. If they'd had to carry me through the whole airport, I think I might've died on the way. As my hand touches the hairy leg of my other self, we phase out.

Oh, the bliss of not having broken ribs, elbows, and other parts. As the noise of the airport returns, I relish not being in pain. Even the discomfort of my full bladder is a welcome contrast to the debilitating agony I experienced in the Quiet.

So the first part of the plan worked. Caleb is Inert. He's still very dangerous, but he can't see the next part coming by using the Quiet. The next part of the plan is where my friends and my aunt slow him down, the corollary to which being that it will slow the monks down, too.

My part is next, and it'll be tricky. I have to deal with the monks approaching me, starting with the Master, who's closest. I also need to do this as quickly as I can.

I watch as the Master closes the distance between us. The monk behind him is on his burner phone. *Crap.* Everyone will know where I am. I need to deal with the Master even more quickly if I'm to have a chance at getting out of this.

"Come with me, my son," the Master says once he's standing within striking distance of me. Is this some kind of kung-fu, violence-avoiding mumbo jumbo? He wants me to go peacefully so he won't have to fight? Not happening.

I assess the situation and formulate a makeshift plan. Since this isn't the Olympics, where sportsmanship matters, I kick the Master in the balls—no disagreeing to go with him, no warning, nothing. As I do, I recognize that the move is a standard Krav Maga groin kick.

To my utter amazement, the Master doesn't fall to the ground screaming, as any regular man would. He performs what looks like a tai-chi move with his hands, takes a deep breath, and settles into a defensive stance. Getting over my initial marvel at his lack of a reaction, I kick him in the shin. He moves out of my reach and then lunges forward and punches my exposed shoulder.

The shoulder hurts like hell, and what makes it worse is knowing I can't undo the damage by phasing out. This is the real world, and these are real injuries. Thinking of phasing gives me an idea, and I slip into the Quiet.

I'm standing beside the Master and myself. He's about to kick me behind my knee. I have an advantage here. I can phase in and out to observe his next move. This is the strategy that Caleb mentioned to me once.

A very promising strategy.

Phasing out, I move my foot out of the way, turning to face my opponent from a more opportune position. As soon as I do, I phase into the Quiet.

I examine my attacker. His shoulder and arm muscles are tensing in a way that suggests he's about to punch me with his right hand. With some confidence, I suspect the punch will be aimed at my shoulder that he already damaged.

I phase out and walk under the punch, placing one of my own into his midsection. His abs are like steel, and I doubt I hurt him at all.

I freeze everything again.

Aha! He wants to bring down his elbow on my arm. And his leg is getting ready for a kick.

I phase out and avoid both attacks, and then do an aikido-inspired throw, something that should be foreign to his style of fighting. The Master falls to the ground, and I give him the Caleb special—a kick to the ribs. Then, just in case, I phase into the Quiet—and I'm glad I did.

The other monk is almost on me. *Shit.* Even with the advantage of the Quiet, I'm not sure I can deal with two people at once. I need to knock the Master out so I can deal with this new guy.

I phase out and kick the Master in the jaw. He moves his head, and my kick's impact is drastically diminished.

I spare a glance at the other attacker and see the younger monk behind him; he's almost caught up to his companion.

I'm done. I can't deal with three of them at once.

I look at the younger monk, who's trying frantically to close the distance, and consider my rapidly dwindling options.

Then the younger monk grabs his brother monk by the shoulder.

"Darren," the young monk says, "run for the gate."

I get it. This is the monk we thought might be Guidable by Hillary. Looks like our theory was right.

"Last call for JFK-bound flight 2447," I hear over the intercom.

Oh no. I decide to follow Hillary's suggestion. I turn to run, but the Master's hand grabs my leg.

I phase in, and the noises around me fall silent.

I run through the frozen people, in the direction of the gate. I need to buy myself a little extra time. As I move, I notice Eugene in the distance. In the real world, he's running away from the gate. I contemplate pulling him in but decide against it. Let him focus on whatever he's doing.

It takes me a few seconds to locate the girl who made the announcement. I Read her and learn what I already know. There are only moments left before departure. I also learn who her boss is.

*No one is flying anywhere without me,* I say to the frozen girl and look for her boss. In her mind, he's in charge of ending the boarding process.

It takes me a few minutes to locate the guy—a thin, mousy individual. I Guide him to wait for me. Then I Read him and learn that despite what his subordinate thought, when it comes to boarding, not everything is up to him.

Armed with this new knowledge, I enter the jet bridge leading to the plane and locate the pilot. Reading him, I learn I can't stall things for too long, not without making a journey to Flight Control and visiting a bunch of other airport bureaucrats. I do the best I can and Guide the pilot not to take off for the next five minutes. He has that much leeway.

As I walk back to my body, I Guide any person I meet to make sure they get out of my way. I also instruct them to get in the way of any Buddhist monk they see following me. I wonder whether the monks will hurt these civilians. For some reason, I doubt it.

Regaining some of my hope, I look around. The young monk is keeping his brother busy, but it's clear he won't last long. The Master is bleeding, yet he's stubbornly holding on to my frozen self's foot. I see what I need to do. It won't be pretty, but it should free me.

I phase out.

I swing my leg back, giving it all my strength. As expected, the Master's wrist makes an unhealthy tearing sound. I'm glad when he lets go of me. I phase in again to see whether he's planning to pull some other stunt, but it doesn't look likely. I feel terrible when I see his wrist hanging at a weird angle. Whatever damage I inflicted, I remind myself, is on my grandparents' conscience, not mine.

*He'll heal*, I tell myself and phase out. As soon as the sounds of the airport are back, I run.

The young monk yelps in pain, meaning I probably have the older one on my tail.

The people I Guided behave as they should. Without knowing why, they step aside for me.

As I run, I phase in to see if the monk is pursuing me, and I find that he is. And it's not just him. A few other monks are right behind me too. The new ones must've arrived as I was dealing with the Master. Fortunately for me, the regular airport travelers have formed an impenetrable wall in their path.

I'm halfway to the gate when the people around me start speaking in unison. "Run faster, Darren. Caleb is right behind you." This cacophony of voices is eerie, and I instantly know it's Hillary warning me.

I phase out and look for Caleb to see how bad the situation is.

Eugene is holding on to Caleb's leg, not unlike the way the Master grabbed me. There's a black and blue shiner under my friend's eye where Caleb must have punched him.

I touch Eugene to bring him in.

"Buddy," I say as soon as he shows up. "What the hell are you doing?"

"I'm stalling him," he says, "to give you a chance."

"Look at that." I point to the people surrounding him and Caleb. They look like zombies zeroing in on yummy brains. "Hillary has these people under control, so Caleb isn't going anywhere. No reason to get yourself killed."

"Oh," he says. "I'll let go then."

We get back to our bodies, and as I phase out, I continue my desperate dash for the gates. I was never much of a sprinter, but I am today. My heart is pounding in my chest, and my breathing is shallow. As I run, I hope what I told Eugene is true.

After a few more feet, I unconsciously phase into the Quiet. My body must be confusing the effects of this run with a near-death experience.

In the Quiet, I make my way back to where I left Caleb. Eugene's released him. The zombie people have moved in on Caleb. But Caleb has managed something I've never seen before. He's basically climbing on top of the crowd surrounding him. He looks like a rock star doing a strange, upright stage dive. The crowd is trying to grab him, but he's dodging their arms. I Read a man who has a nice vantage and see Caleb moving surprisingly fast despite this strange mode of locomotion. I have to hurry.

I get back to my body, phase out, and sprint harder.

I'm approaching the door when I notice Caleb standing on someone's head and shoulders. He's planning to jump at me.

*No fucking way*, I think as he launches himself into the air.

At the last moment, I dodge.

Caleb lands next to me, but I'm already flying through the doorway.

I smack the door in his face—literally. I think I hit his nose. Not caring what happens to Caleb, I instantly lock the door.

I hear banging behind me as I run for the plane. When I find my seat, I feel real hope. Bert looks at me with no expression whatsoever. Ignoring my friend and my full bladder, I phase into the Quiet again.

I make my way to the pilots. I'm lucky the boarding isn't officially over as far as the pilots are concerned, or else this door would be locked. Once inside the cabin, I get inside their minds. My Guiding command is simplicity itself:

*Get in the air as soon as safely possible.*

# CHAPTER FOURTEEN

It's only when the plane is rolling down the runway that I allow myself a sigh of relief.

"What the hell?" Bert says in confusion when I sit down next to him. "How did I get here?"

Ignoring my friend, I phase in.

The plane stops moving, along with the rest of the world. I make my way to the door and exit the plane using the inflatable evacuation slide. Luckily, this thing seems to run off compressed air and not fancy electronics.

Monks aren't climbing up the wheels of the plane, action-movie style. Good. No one is running after us. Even better. I think I actually escaped them.

I just need to find out whether my friends are okay.

I find a way back into the airport. It's easy to navigate high-security places in the Quiet, since I don't have to worry about security guards and can take 'personnel only' pathways—at least the ones that are not important enough to require keycard entry.

I make my way to the closed gate. Caleb is frozen in the midst of a passionate argument with the mousy-looking boss.

"Good luck with that," I say to frozen Caleb. "There's no fucking way you're stopping a flight that's already en route."

Gloating done, I find Eugene. He got up from where he'd been holding Caleb and looks to be walking away. He actually got farther than I'd expect given what just happened to him. I take that as a good sign. His eye is swelling, but I don't see any other damage. I touch his forehead to bring him in.

"Darren," he says. "What the hell happened *now*?"

"Nothing," I say. "I made it. I'm on the plane."

"Good. Now come, let me show you something."

I follow Eugene as he leads me toward the gate. Two cops are heading in Caleb's direction.

"Hillary's work," Eugene says. "Caleb is about to be apprehended. Not sure how long it will last, but there's no way he can strong-arm his way onto your plane *now*."

"I doubt he had a chance to begin with."

"I guess we'll have to wait for another flight," Eugene says.

"Sorry about that. As soon as I land, if you haven't gotten onto another flight already, I'll get Bert to help you."

"Thanks.

"Where's your sister? I want to say goodbye."

Without another word, Eugene briskly walks to the opposite side of the floor.

Standing by the ice cream shop, Mira is making a makeshift splint for her arm. Hillary is standing a little to the side of her. Eugene touches them in turn.

"Darren," Mira says, concerned. "Your plane is already in motion."

"I came back to check on you guys. What happened?"

"She tried to stop Caleb before the people I controlled got the chance to help," Hillary says. "She's lucky her arm is not broken."

"That fucking bastard," I say. "To hit a girl . . ."

"Shut up," Mira says and walks over to me. Without warning, she kisses me with a ferocity that surprises me. She doesn't let go, and the kiss goes on for a while.

"Should we give you kids some privacy?" Hillary asks drily. "I can Split."

"No," Mira says, releasing me. "He needs to get to New York."

"That was some crazy Guiding, Aunt," I say. "As usual."

"She's dangerous," Mira says with begrudging respect. "I'm glad she's on our side."

We say our goodbyes, and I make my way back onto the plane, which is a hell of a lot harder than getting off was. The evacuation slide was not designed for somebody to go *up*. I manage, though, and returning to my seat, I phase out.

"You're here because your new girlfriend wished it," I say in response to Bert's earlier question. "She Pushed or Guided you. You can decide what term you prefer."

I let him think about it as I finally go to the bathroom. On my way, I have to Guide a stewardess to stop her from bugging me with her safety mumbo jumbo. Then, as the turbulence shakes me, I realize they have those rules for a reason. It doesn't matter, though; at this point, I'd gladly hit my head to relieve my poor bladder.

When I return to my seat, Bert still looks like he's processing data, not unlike those computers he's so good at abusing. Then he snaps out of it and says, "The last thing I remember is asking her to promise me she wouldn't use her powers to make me do things."

"That's pretty ironic," I say. "But trust me when I say she did it for your own good." And then I tell him what happened at the airport.

When I'm done, he says, "All right, I can see why she did it. I'm grateful even."

"Oh?" I buckle my seat belt. "I have to say, you're taking this whole 'my girlfriend can control my thoughts' thing surprisingly well."

"I guess so." Bert shrugs. "I learned a few things from watching my parents over the years. Women get men to do what they want anyway. This way, Hillary and I get to skip the unpleasant guilting, and pouting, and fighting, and screaming, and all the general manipulation people use to get their way. So in a way, this might make our relationship go smoother."

"Sure," I say, and resist adding, "Keep telling yourself that."

"I've been dying to ask you something," Bert says as the plane takes off. "What was it like the first time you 'phased into the Quiet'?"

"Remember how I told you I almost died falling off a bike?"

"Yeah, also from a roof and into a manhole." He smirks.

"Well, I didn't tell you the nitty-gritty details about those falls," I say, ignoring the jibe. "Like how time slowed down as I somersaulted through the air off my bike."

"Doesn't time always seem to slow down in situations like that?"

"Maybe. But I imagine my experience was different from most normal people's, because it got *really* slow. I'm talking like bullet mode from movies and video games. I was flying at an inch per second. It was terrifying."

"And then?"

"And then, after I imagined what would happen when I hit the ground—from dying to becoming paralyzed—and reached a threshold of sorts, everything stopped entirely. I was on the ground looking at a copy of me still sailing through the air. Had I known about the concept of having a soul then, I probably would've thought that mine had left my body. As it was, I thought I was having a strange dream. When I walked over and touched my flying self to make sure he was real, I was back in the air,

DIMA ZALES

and shortly after that, on the ground and in agonizing pain that proved I wasn't dreaming."

"There are always two of you?" he asks.

"Yep."

"And when Hillary does it, there's two of her?"

"Correct."

"Is that why she calls it Splitting?"

"I think it has more to do with the Split of reality, but hey, you have a point," I say. "In any case, the first few times were like that. I experienced a severe slowing of time before phasing into a time-stopped mode. Later, the slow-down stage happened less and less until it went away altogether and everything just instantly stopped when I phased in."

"Fascinating," he says, "but I have more questions."

For the next half hour, I tell Bert about the Quiet, trying to ignore my growing drowsiness. When I begin yawning after every other sentence, I stop, and we agree to try to sleep for the rest of the flight.

* * *

"Dude, wake up," a voice tells me from far away. "We've landed, and they're finally letting us off this plane. We've been stuck at the gate for a freaking hour."

"Let me fucking sleep," I mumble.

"We're in New York," the voice says. I vaguely recognize it as Bert's. "And you need to get to your mom, remember?"

The reminder wakes me up enough for me to exit the plane.

As we walk though JFK International Airport, I wake up some more and decide to call Mira.

"Darren, do you know what time it is?" her sleepy voice says from the other end.

I look at the top of my phone and hit myself on the forehead. "Sorry, Mira. I didn't realize it was three in the morning."

"Fuck," she says. "I didn't realize *that* either."

"I was just calling to check on you guys. Do you need Bert to do his magic and get you tickets?"

"No," she says. "Your aunt worked hers. We have first-class tickets on the first flight out. Now let me sleep."

"Wait. Caleb didn't give you any more shit, did he?"

"No," she says. "He was arrested, and the monks split incredibly fast. Your aunt didn't exactly create a friendly welcome for them."

"Okay, sorry again. Go back to sleep."

"Bye. And next time, text me." She hangs up.

Aware of my faux pas, I decide not to call Lucy this early. I have a set of keys to the house, so I think it would be better to let myself in and snooze in the guestroom than wake them so late at night. I'll just have to make sure not to accidentally spook my moms in the morning.

I feel reassured until we get outside. The weather is horrible, and not just compared to Miami's. It's raining and cold.

It takes us a horrendous half hour to get the first cab, which Bert graciously gives up for me.

"Stay in touch, dude," he says, closing the cab door almost in my face.

I give the cab driver two instructions: take me to Staten Island and do not wake me up for any reason.

That done, I fall asleep.

* * *

I wake up and look around. I'm still in the cab. We're on the highway. The red digital clock under the taxi meter reads 5:35.

"Sir," I say to get the cab driver's attention. "Are we far from Staten Island?"

"I'm sorry, friend," the driver says with an accent I can't place. "We're just entering Brooklyn. There's a big accident on the road ahead."

All remnants of sleep gone, I watch the road.

We're barely moving at five miles per hour. The accident must've shut down one or more of the lanes, driving traffic, like a current, into a tight funnel. Only unlike water molecules, cars have drivers inside them, and when in traffic jams like these, people shortsightedly make matters worse by switching lanes over and over. I know they're trying to pick the one that's moving faster, but all they're doing is slowing everyone down, more so than if they'd followed the path of least resistance like water does.

*Have you boarded yet?* I text Mira.

*In about an hour,* she replies. *But not a direct flight. Fucking Caleb and his fucking monks.*

*Don't get me started,* I type. *Hope you at least got a little sleep.*

*I tried. Did you get to your mom's?*

*Not yet. Stuck in traffic.*

*Okay. GTG. Eugene is hungry again.*

*Ttyl,* I send.

Having done the only thing I could to kill time, I'm ready for alternative ideas. With this in mind, I phase into the Quiet and exit the stopped cab.

The sounds of rain, traffic, and thunder are gone. Despite the early hour and the weather, the highway is fairly well lit, thanks to all the cars. In the bright light of the high beams from the car behind me, I observe the stuck-in-time rain droplets with awe. Then I walk through them, and my appreciation for the wonders of nature drastically declines as these same droplets soak my clothes. Every time my body connects with the floating raindrops, they react like regular liquid. I swear I get wetter in the Quiet than when the rain isn't frozen. The only consolation is that I'll be dry once I get back to reality.

I touch the idiot in a Honda who's about to switch into our lane. I make it so that for the next few miles, he'll be content with driving in his own lane. I provide the same Guidance to a few more nearby drivers, and then it hits me.

Instead of trying to improve the flow of traffic, I should take a more selfish approach. As soon as the idea comes, I begin executing it. I choose a few drivers who are in our lane, Read them, and if they're the asshole types who change lanes at every opportunity, I Guide them to do so *now*, even though I know it won't improve their progress at all.

I return to the cab and phase out. I'm dry and amused to see the cars in question get out of our way without anyone veering in to take their place, even though our lane is now moving faster. Despite this progress, all the work I did barely gains us a few extra feet.

"Is there any way to get us to Staten Island faster?" I ask. "I'll double the fare."

"I can take the next exit and go through city streets." The cabby makes eye contact with me in the rearview mirror. "But other people might have the same idea, and reaching the exit, with the traffic as it is, will be pretty difficult."

"Let's try it."

I phase into the Quiet and walk around in the frozen rain, making sure the other drivers around us don't get the same idea to take the next exit. I then clear our path toward it. When I return to the real world, I let the driver handle the rest.

"That was very strange," the cabby mumbles to himself as we turn off the highway after a half hour of driving at a snail's pace.

I know what he means. As slow as our progress was, it must've been strange for him to see so many cars making stupid decisions by switching lanes in front of us. And it must've been even weirder when everyone forgot about the exit. Thanks to my meddling, even those who live off this exit missed their turn. I wonder how much they'll be cursing themselves when this fact registers.

I pretend not to notice the cab driver's confusion and doze off. After about an hour of driving through Brooklyn side streets, we finally get back on the same highway. Only here, it's nearly empty as we're clearly past the accident.

The rest of the way takes fifteen minutes as the cabby goes double the speed limit. He must be determined to get his double fare.

"Here, by this townhouse," I instruct him. I give him three hundred, which is more than double the fare, but he earned it. "Keep the change."

Only Lucy's car is in the driveway, which makes sense. Sara would've already left for work. Which means Lucy is awake, since they always eat breakfast together.

Approaching the door, I ring the bell.

Nothing.

I ring it again.

Still no reply.

I try calling Lucy's phone. It goes to voicemail.

This is odd.

I search my pockets for my keys. Once I locate them, I grab the door handle—which, to my surprise, turns in my hand.

Okay, this is even weirder. The door was already unlocked. Did Sara forget to lock it when she left for work?

Walking in, I yell, "Mom? It's me. Don't shoot."

I don't hear a response. In general, the house is very quiet.

Shit.

I have a bad feeling about this.

# CHAPTER FIFTEEN

As I make my way to the second floor of their three-story townhouse, I try to dispel my sense of foreboding. Lucy must be taking a nap, or maybe she's in the shower.

When I get to the second floor, it's still quiet. This is where the living room and kitchen are. I smell coffee and bacon, so I was right. They must've eaten breakfast together, and it wasn't too long ago since the coffeemaker is still hot to the touch.

There's another smell, the smell that every former pyromaniac kid such as me recognizes with ease. The smell of burned paper. I look around and find the source. The usually decorative fireplace has just been used. Ash and little bits of burned paper are inside it. What's that about?

"Mom!" I yell as I run up to the third floor.

No response.

I approach the master bedroom and knock. "Mom, are you in here?"

Nothing.

I open the door.

Empty.

She can't be far, though. The bed isn't made, and Lucy's OCD wouldn't allow her to leave things in disarray for long. Leaving the bedroom, I go into the office across the hall.

No one here either. But there's a note on the desk.

*I am sorry*, it says in Lucy's super-neat handwriting.

My heart starts beating faster, and I run for the bathroom.

It's closed.

I knock on the door. "Mom, are you in there?" She has to be. The door is locked, and it only locks from the inside.

No answer. When I put my ear to the door, I hear the trickle of running water. It's not loud enough to muffle my voice the way a shower might.

"Mom," I say again and bang on the door in earnest. Even if she had music on and was showering, the noise I'm making would be impossible to ignore. When I still don't get an answer, I kick the bottom of the door. "Mom, let me in, or I'm breaking down this door!"

Still no response.

I don't actually break down the door as I threatened, as doing that might just injure her or me. Instead, I run back into the office and grab the letter opener from the desk. Using the blunt top of the knife-like device, I manage to unscrew the bathroom's door handle. Taking the thing apart, I push open the door.

The first thing that registers is that the bathtub is full of water—but something's wrong with this water.

It's red.

There's also a razor covered in something red, lying on the white tiles of the bathroom floor.

Then I take in the figure in the water.

It's Lucy. Dressed in her robe, she's submerged in the tub. The right sleeve of the robe is rolled up, and there's a red line on her exposed wrist. The water is redder around that line.

In stunned incomprehension, I notice the water faucet sound is gone. The water is frozen on its way into the bathtub. I must've phased into the Quiet without even realizing it.

My brain is still struggling with what my eyes are seeing.

It looks as if Lucy cut her wrist . . . which would make the strange note I found in the office a suicide note. Only that doesn't compute—Lucy would never kill herself.

The key question is whether she's still alive. Judging by the color of the water, she's lost a significant amount of blood.

I approach her, and without hesitation, place my palm on Mom's forehead. Getting into the state of Coherence is the longest, most difficult mental effort of my life. As I slow my breathing in an effort to relax, I have to constantly remind myself that while I'm in the Quiet, no time is passing for Lucy. The situation, though dire, isn't getting any worse as I'm doing this.

After what feels like an eternity, the familiar state overcomes me, and I'm in Lucy's mind.

* * *

*I'm sorry,* we write.

I, Darren, instantly disassociate. She wrote the note herself, which I knew was likely from the handwriting, but since writing can be faked, it's still a revelation.

Feeling sick, I fast-forward the memory.

We're standing next to the bathtub, checking the water. It's nice and warm. We get in, pick up the razor, and wait until our body adjusts to the temperature.

I, Darren, can't watch the rest. I know she's going to cut her wrist. I know, without doubt, this isn't a staged suicide.

I jump forward to the moment I entered this room.

We're floating in a river of relaxation. The earlier nausea is gone. Bright white lights dance in our vision. Our eyes feel like they do after we get our picture taken by Sara's damned overzealous camera with the super-bright flash. It also reminds us of the days when we used to stare up at the sun as a little girl. Memories of being that little girl in a village in China appear in vivid details in our mind. But then these memories dissipate, taking with them all the cares of the world. Only a sense of contentment remains.

I, Darren, disassociate with a slight sense of relief. She's alive, though I have no idea for how long.

When I first saw her in the tub, surrounded by her own blood, my initial instincts told me that mobsters had staged this 'suicide' as payback. But I was wrong. My mom committed this act herself. She wrote the letter herself. She cut her own wrist. And she's letting herself bleed to death. But this doesn't make sense. Could she have been Pushed? That's the only explanation that makes sense. Perhaps, as a small mercy, the Pusher had blocked her from feeling any of the horror of what she did. But this 'mercy' is also causing her to let go of life that much quicker.

That's not going to fucking happen. Not on my watch.

Laser focus overcomes my mind, and I begin Guiding my mom.

*You will fight for your life.*

*No matter what it takes, you will hold on.*

*If pain helps you stay conscious, allow yourself to feel pain. If pain will make you go into shock and lose your grip on life, then it will flow out of you as though it were never there.*

*Live. Survive. You have people who love you. You have people who need you. You can't fucking give up . . .*

After what feels like hours of pouring jumbled instructions into Lucy's struggling mind, I get out.

* * *

I walk up to my frozen body and don't even recognize my face. My expression isn't mere horror; it's something that makes my face look aged and deformed. I didn't think grief could do that. And I didn't even fully understand the enormity of what was happening then, not like I do now.

I reach out, and ignoring the insanity of the gesture, I give my frozen self a hug. As soon as my hand touches his neck, I phase out.

As soon as the sound of running water is back, I spring into action.

I run up to the tub, the razor crunching underfoot, and reach for Mom.

A moment later, she's in my arms, her bathrobe a wet, bloody mess. Her body is tiny, and for the first time in my life, she seems fragile.

As I lift her, she takes in a ragged breath, looks at me incomprehensibly, and tries to speak.

I walk as fast as I can. I can't drop my precious cargo, so I make sure my steps are even. With all this adrenaline running through my veins, she feels weightless.

I enter the bedroom, leaving streaks of blood on the carpet. When I place her on the bed, the white sheets instantly turn pink. I take one of the sheets and rip it into strips. I then tie off the makeshift bandage around her wrist, creating a sort of tourniquet to staunch the blood flow as best as I can.

She opens her eyes and focuses on me for a moment. Then she whimpers, saying something unintelligible, and her eyes lose focus.

"Hang in there, Mom." When I speak, I realize I'm crying. "Just hang on."

She feels cold, so I wrap her in blankets. Carefully but swiftly, I carry her down the stairs.

I have to lay her on the ground to open the car door. Thank God for those blankets.

The car is locked, so I have to waste valuable seconds running back into the house to get the keys. I'm now grateful for Lucy's obsessive neatness. As always, the keys are on the little hook by the front door.

I lay her in the back of the car and enter her mind. I don't let myself experience her trauma, not because I'm gutlessly avoiding feeling her pain, but because I don't trust myself to not take it away. Taking away her pain might cause her to give up, and I need her to fight.

That's what my Guiding reinforces: *Fight. Survive.*

When I phase out, Lucy moans.

"I'm sorry," I say softly. "Please stay with me, Mom."

My voice seems to soothe her, or maybe she only had the strength for that one outcry.

I get behind the wheel. Part of me knows I need to get myself together. Driving while in this severely distraught state might cause an accident, and if the accident doesn't kill her, the delay surely will.

I take a calming breath, but then I hear some mumbled whimpers from the backseat.

Fuck calm. I floor the gas pedal.

My heart is pounding in my ears and the streets are all a blur as the car is pushed to its very limits. My foot doesn't move off the gas pedal. If Mom's little Toyota could speak, it would be begging for mercy.

I'm not completely reckless. I use an approach that won't slow us down, not even for a moment.

At regular intervals, I phase into the Quiet, and while time stands still, I clear the road ahead of us.

I make a jaywalking teenager change his leisurely gait into a mad dash for his life. I make every car up to a block ahead of us pull over. When someone is about to cross the road, I change that person's mind.

I'm halfway to my destination when I hear a siren.

Shit. Not that.

I know I can tell the police officer that I have an injured detective in the back, which should resolve the situation fairly quickly, but I have an even better idea.

I phase into the Quiet and enter the cop's mind.

I Read him first. He clocked me driving at 120 miles per hour and was planning on giving me a Breathalyzer test—to start. I Guide him to forget about the speeding and forget about me too. What he will do is rush to check out reports of gunshots near the crossing of Seaview Avenue and Hylan Boulevard, which is next to the hospital.

When I phase out, I let the cruiser pass me and tail him. He'll clear the way for us. This works like a charm. The rest of the way to the hospital is even quicker, thanks to our escort. In less than ten minutes, I'm running into the Staten Island University Hospital ER with Lucy in my arms.

"I need help!" I yell.

No one responds.

I look around and make eye contact with a nurse or a clerk who's sitting behind a desk. She clearly heard me. I run over and stare her down.

Her face is stern and she looks at me unsympathetically. "Can I help you?"

"Do you need to fucking ask?" I say. "I'm holding a person, in my arms, who's clearly injured."

"I need you to calm down, sir," she says with attitude.

I'm overcome with so much anger that I phase into the Quiet. Entering her mind, I frantically Read her for any useful information.

Dr. Jaint is the best surgeon in this hospital. Great. He's going to help us today, even if he doesn't know it yet.

Next, I pilfer her mind to learn the codes and procedures regarding this type of situation. Then I begin Guiding her.

*Officer down,* I mentally tell the disgruntled nurse. As I Push this into her brain, I realize it isn't even false information. My mom *is* a detective.

Just in case, I continue: *The fucking governor's daughter is hurt. If you fuck this up, you will never work again. Hell, the governor will hire a hit man to kill you if this woman dies. Dr. Jaint has to be the one to save her, and it has to be this hospital's quickest rescue in history.*

I add a few more crazy details along those lines. I don't care if the story adds up. I don't care if she has amnesia afterward. All I need is swift and immediate action.

I finish with one last instruction: *When this is all over, you will look for a different job. Try something in the janitorial industry.*

Then I get out of her head and leave the Quiet.

I see an expression of genuine concern on a face that seemed to have lost this ability. Good. She makes phone calls, announces codes and names over the intercom, and even pulls out a walky-talky. I hear something about a 'code ten' and something along the lines of 'Dr. Jaint, please prepare for surgery.'

In less than a minute, a nurse shows up with a stretcher. Unlike the woman whose mind I just violated, this one looks extremely competent. Still, I'm not willing to rely on the presumption of competence. I give this one a Push too. *Help her like your life depends on it.*

I follow the stretcher and clear our path from people the way I did with the cars.

*Yes, I'm allowed to be in here,* I make everyone believe as we enter the operating room. *You'll answer my questions as though I own this hospital.*

"Where's the doctor?" I ask.

"I saw him in the cafeteria," a nurse answers, looking confused.

I transition into the Quiet and run to the cafeteria. I'm moving so fast that I trip and fall twice. This is the Quiet, I remind myself. Time is standing still.

I recognize Dr. Jaint by his nametag. I get inside his head and sear a list of simple but potent Guiding instructions into his brain:

*Run to the operating room.*

*Everything you hold dear—your family, your life— depends on saving this woman's life.*

I phase out and watch as the nurses prep the OR. Lucy is hooked up to a bunch of wires and machines.

I have to Read someone because, in my current mental state, I don't understand the medical jargon they're spewing at each other.

*She's in critical condition,* one nurse's mind reveals. *She'll need a blood transfusion.*

From another nurse's mind, I learn they have the blood they'll need. Good. For a moment, I wondered whether my blood type is a match for Lucy. If it weren't, there would have been a record number of volunteers lining up to donate. I make a mental oath to learn what my blood type actually is, as well as the blood types of the people closest to me.

This is when the doctor slams through the doors. Concern edging toward terror is evident on his face.

I'm clearly getting better and better at this Guiding thing. Maybe too good.

I get inside the doctor's mind to calm him.

*Take a breath*, I Guide him. *And do your thing.*

# CHAPTER SIXTEEN

I watch them work their magic.

I've always been squeamish. When I'd see surgery on TV, I'd look away, cringing. That's *not* how this goes. I watch every bloody detail, unable to look away. I'm afraid that if I look away, or even so much as blink, something irreversible will happen. Irrationally, I feel as if my gaze alone is keeping Lucy alive.

The clock tells me the whole thing takes twenty minutes, but I feel as though I've been watching this macabre dance for days.

"She'll be fine," Dr. Jaint tells me when he's done. "She just needs to rest. Let's take her to Room 3 in

Intensive Care. We need this room for other patients." He sounds apologetic.

"No problem," I say, my voice hoarse. "Take her there, and I'll follow."

On our way, I make the first phone call. "Mom, drop whatever you're doing, and come to the Staten Island University Hospital," I say and placate her as best as I can, ignoring her million questions. I finish with: "Everything is okay—she's fine—but you need to get here *now*."

The dreaded conversation with Sara over with, I call Mira. I couldn't go into freak-out mode with my 'easy to give a heart attack to' mom. I had to be strong for her. With Mira, I can let some of my tension out. But to my disappointment, my call goes to her voicemail. She must be in the air.

"Mira, call me as soon as you can," I say. "This is urgent."

As a poor alternative to speaking with Mira, I sit down in Room 3 next to Mom's bed and focus on my breathing, trying to calm my overactive nerves.

I look at Lucy as I breathe. She's still deathly pale, but her breathing seems more even.

After a minute, I start thinking more rationally. How could this have happened? There's no way Lucy would ever commit suicide. I recall my earlier thought about potential Pusher interference, and I know that I need to find out for sure.

If someone attempted to murder my mom, that person will pay dearly.

I phase in. The hum of the hospital is gone. I walk up to Lucy and place my hand on her forehead. It's easier to calm my mental turmoil now that I know she's going to be okay.

When I get inside her head, I make sure my Reading begins with what happened an hour ago . . .

# CHAPTER SEVENTEEN

"Sorry to leave you with this messy kitchen to clean up," Sara says to us, smiling. "I'll clean up after dinner."

"No worries, hon," we say. "You have to run. I understand."

"You're the best." She gives us a peck on the cheek and noisily descends the stairs to the first floor.

We feel one of those quiet moments of joy and contemplation, moments when we marvel at how lucky we are when it comes to familial bliss.

We hear the door bang shut but don't hear Sara lock it. The little happy moment almost fades. She forgot to lock the door—again. Our wife, the absentminded professor. Stoically, we climb down and lock the door.

With that done, it takes us a few minutes to clean up the kitchen. Then we take out the files from the nearby cardboard box and spread them out on the kitchen table.

The now-dead Russian mobster, Arkady, fucked up when he killed the Tsiolkovsky family. The explosives he used were traceable, which is how we solved the case. Granted, we looked up the explosives data in a newer database than the one that existed when the crime was originally committed. But still. The case wasn't worked properly because of the false impression that this was a mob-on-mob hit. Who provided the misinformation? And why? The only explanation that fits is that someone on the inside was covering something up.

It was a form of torture to put this aside when Darren requested it yesterday. Now that he's about to stop by and explain whatever the problem is, there's no harm in being ready to resume the investigation, seeing how we're itching to do so. So far, we just hinted at our discoveries to Kyle, the only person in Organized Crime we know we can trust.

We're distracted from our thoughts by the sound of a car pulling into the driveway. We get up and look out the window. *Think of the devil.*

"Hi, Kyle," we say, opening the door. "What brings you here?"

"Hi, Lucy," he says. "Sorry. I couldn't wait till later to learn about that case you mentioned."

"That's funny. I was just reviewing my notes on it."

We make our way to the second floor. Kyle sits down at the table and looks at the printouts we made and the papers covered with notes.

"Want some coffee?" We turn the coffeemaker on without waiting for an answer. Kyle is clearly preoccupied with the file.

"Please, take a seat," Kyle says in a strange voice.

We sit down across from him at the table.

And then I, Darren, disassociate when I feel *someone else* entering Lucy's mind.

It can't be. It just can't. The Pusher is inside Lucy's mind, but that would mean . . .

Stunned, I let the memory unfold.

*Relax,* comes the first instruction. *Forget what you're doing. You will sit still until I leave. You can't move, given your shock. Given your grief. When I talk to you, just listen, but don't remember any of the words. Instead, I want you to realize how shitty life has gotten lately. How depressed you've been. How senseless everything is and how pointless. Let yourself*

*remember what happened to Mark. Remember what
happened to the baby. The guilt, the depression—it's
so overwhelming, and you can't take it anymore.
When you get the urge to slit your wrist, don't fight it.
Fill up a warm bath and do it there. Warm water
improves blood flow. You will not feel any pain.
Instead, you'll relax and float like you're riding a
cloud.*

I, Darren, let these horrendous instructions ring
in my mind.

A few things the Pusher said don't make sense,
like the mention of my father, Mark. What does he
have to do with anything? What did the Pusher mean
by 'let yourself remember'?

But that's not what's overwhelming me the most.

It's the tone of voice in Lucy's mind. It's familiar
to me. The instructions in Lucy's head sound like the
ones I heard inside the heads of the mobsters who'd
kidnapped Mira. And also like the ones inside the
head of the murderous nurse, the one who gave me a
near-fatal overdose of morphine and tried to
smother me with a pillow. All these Pushing
instructions came from the same person.

A person whose real-life voice I know well
because I've heard it throughout my life.

It's Kyle—the closest person to a father I've ever
had.

I still can't accept it, so with masochistic determination, I allow the memory to continue.

In a stupor, we watch Kyle. We can't move for some reason, but we don't want to move either. We're relaxed.

"I really am sorry about this," Kyle says as he gathers our notes. "It's such a shame." He walks over to the fireplace, takes out a lighter, and burns the papers.

We don't understand what he's doing, but the relaxation we're feeling is pleasant.

"I really wish you hadn't dug into this Arkady business. It's ancient history." We look at Kyle and see an expression of deep sorrow on his face, like at the captain's funeral. "Now that I know the little bastard I helped you raise is a fucking Leacher, I can't just make you forget the way I usually would. Your mind isn't safe anymore. Not when Darren can just Leach the information straight out of it."

None of it, except for the name of the mobster, makes sense to us. Through our haze of relaxation, we realize Kyle could be the one behind the cover-up. Then we promptly forget this thought.

"So if you need anyone to blame for me having to do this," Kyle continues, "blame *him*. Blame Darren. But don't worry. Your sacrifice won't be in vain.

He'll come to your funeral, where I'll finally rid the world of that blight."

I, Darren, disassociate.

Kyle is right in more ways than he realizes. Back at the Coney Island Hospital, it was me who set my mom on the path to investigating the Arkady case by telling her about Mira's parents. I also see how my Reading ability is what forced Kyle's hand. It's a horrible thought, one that nearly paralyzes me with guilt. With effort, I overcome it and instead focus on what really matters.

Kyle is *the* Pusher.

I have no doubt now. He was the one controlling Arkady and the one working with Jacob. He erased the memory of Jacob from Arkady's mind. But that could also mean . . .

I decide to dig deeper in Lucy's head. Much deeper.

"Lucy," Mark says. "How are you still standing?"

"Seriously," Kyle adds. "Five shots for someone your size is like ten for me or Mark."

"What?" we say incredulously. "I can drink both of you pussies under the table."

I, Darren, realize I've gone too far into the past. Given how young Kyle looks, this must be before Lucy even met Sara, back in the crazy days when the three of them—Mark, Kyle, and Lucy—kicked ass and took names in Organized Crime. Young Mark looks achingly familiar, like the reflection I see in the mirror every day. I try not to dwell on this. He's my biological father, so it's not that big of a surprise.

I should move toward the present in Lucy's memories, but I can't stop experiencing this. This is probably as close as I'll ever get to having a drink with my father, the father I never knew. So I let the memory play out, watching them drink and joke without a care in the world.

"I'll walk you home," Kyle says to us eventually.

"I can do it," Mark offers.

"You've been eyeing that blonde," Kyle reminds him. "Why don't you go say hi? I got this."

Mark looks at the blonde, burps, and then shakily makes his way over to her table.

"I don't need to be walked," we argue. "I'm not drunk."

We know we're lying. We are extremely buzzed. But so are our asshole partners.

"Fine," Kyle says stubbornly. "You go, but I'll be right behind you. It's a free country."

"Whatever," we concede with annoyance. "Let's just get this over with."

The walk is oddly silent. We can't help but notice how tipsy Kyle's walk is. *Who needs to walk whom home?* we think but don't say it out loud. We're not in the mood to start an argument.

"This is me," we say when we get to our door. "Thanks for the walk."

"No problem," he says. "Can I come in?"

"Sure," we say.

When Kyle walks in, we stare at him expectantly. "The bathroom is down the hall."

"That's not why I asked to come in," he says. "I wanted to be alone with you for a second. I wanted to talk."

Shit. Not this. Our heart sinks. We were dreading this day. We're no expert when it comes to men, but the looks Kyle has given us in the past always seemed odd—longing and lustful.

"I love you, Lucy," Kyle says, his speech slurred. "It's not the drink talking. I fucking love you."

We take a deep breath and organize our drunken thoughts.

"I'm sorry, Kyle," we begin. We don't want to break our best friend's heart, but he hasn't given us much of a choice. "It's not you. It's me. I don't like men that way . . ."

His expression is hard to understand. "You're just going through a phase," he says softly. "Women belong with men."

"I don't think so," we say more forcefully. Kyle can be such a bigot sometimes. It drives us crazy. "Besides, even if I wanted dick, what makes you think I'd go for yours?" That's definitely the liquor talking, and we instantly regret the words.

Then there's a Pusher presence in our mind.

*You love me,* the instructions tell us. *You want me just as much as I want you . . .*

I, Darren, disassociate in horror, but not before I see a glimpse of Lucy meekly following Kyle into the bedroom, murmuring sweet nothings to him.

Dizzy with dread, I jump ahead a couple of months in Lucy's memories.

"I'm sick again," we tell Kyle over the siren. "Nauseous for the third morning in a row."

Kyle stops the car.

"What are you doing? They're getting away," we say.

A Pusher presence enters our mind.

*Forget the pursuit. We're taking a trip to the doctor's.*

I, Darren, follow the rest of this thread, completely stunned.

"How can this be? How can I be pregnant?" we ask in a brief moment of clarity from the Pusher's influence.

The Pusher presence re-enters our mind. *Forget the test results for now. You're just having a rare condition called pseudocyesis—a false pregnancy.*

I, Darren, can't watch in detail—it's just too crazy—so I skim Lucy's memories, trying my best not to go too deep into the turbulent emotions of her pregnancy. When she begins showing, Kyle Pushes her to take a six-month vacation. Everyone at the department thinks she's visiting China. But in reality, she spends those months in a dingy apartment Kyle rented for her in Queens. He messes with her mind at regular intervals. The whole horrid affair culminates in a birth. Then he Pushes her to give up the baby. The agony Lucy feels, even despite the Push, is terrifying. It's so deep that, though I'm skimming, the intensity of it hits me like a physical punch.

Then, even after Kyle makes her forget the whole thing, she intuitively knows something is wrong with the world. Something is missing. This might be what led her to be so obsessive-compulsive sometimes, in her work and at home. Maybe she's looking for that something that's on the tip of her awareness—a splinter in her mind.

I fast-forward through more of her memories. Two weeks later, she almost remembers the birth, but not before Kyle Pushes her to forget everything all over again. And then he repeats the mind wipe fourteen days later.

This tells me that Kyle's Reach must be about two weeks. After that, it wears off, and Lucy starts remembering the events concerning her baby.

Something else clicks for me. This is why he's been hanging around Lucy all these years. He was making her forget. It had nothing to do with him providing me with a male role model.

I wonder why he didn't kill her back then. Maybe he did love her, in his own loathsome way. His infatuation with her must've faded with time, though, because it didn't stop him from trying to kill her today. In a similar vein, I wonder why he hadn't Pushed her to get an abortion. And then I remember all the fights we had on this very subject. Of course. Kyle is Mr. Pro-Life all the way, even when it came to the product of his own rape.

*This* was the baby he allowed her to remember before she attempted to kill herself. But he said he'd allow her to remember something about Mark too.

With a heavy heart, I seek another memory. I already have an idea of what I'll find, but I have to see it. Otherwise, I won't believe it's true.

We're walking up to Mark's house. We don't recall the drive over. Strange how these things sometimes happen—you drive someplace but do so almost by instinct.

Mark opens the door.

"Welcome," he says, smiling. After he gives us a kiss on the cheek, he looks thoughtful. "Why didn't Kyle come with you? I thought this was like a little department reunion."

"He had something else going on," we say.

"What about Sara?" Mark asks. "We could've made this into a double date instead."

"Darren is very cranky today," we say. "He has an ear infection."

"Margie will be so disappointed that he couldn't make it. Looks like it's just us again."

"Looks like," we say.

After a moment's hesitation, he says, "Look, Lucy. I haven't seen Kyle at all since I left the department. He wasn't at my wedding. He never returns my calls. Do you know what happened? Did I do something?"

"I don't know," we say honestly. And then something triggers a directive in our mind. "Let's talk about this later," we say, the words predetermined. "Can I use the restroom?"

"Sure," Mark says, looking confused. "It's through the kitchen."

At this point, it's more correct to say that only I, Darren, am experiencing this. Lucy isn't present in her own mind. Not in the regular sense of the word. She's more like a robot in a Lucy shell.

We enter the kitchen, with Mark walking a few feet ahead of us. We see Margret, Mark's wife. Her back is to us, and the smell of fried garlic combined with the sizzle of oil tells us that she's cooking.

Before Margret can turn to say hello, we take out the gun with a quick, practiced motion and fire at the back of her head, watching as it explodes and her body falls to the floor.

Mark spins around to face us. There's no trace of confusion or surprise on his face, only horror. Somehow he knows what's happening.

As we fire the next shot, he starts twisting to the side, as though he has some supernatural insight into the bullet's path. But he's not fast enough.

His limp body falls on the floor a few feet from his wife's.

We methodically approach and wipe Mark's lips. He kissed our cheek after saying hello and might've left some DNA. Then we carefully back away. We were instructed to make sure no blood gets on our shoes or clothes.

Still on autopilot, we leave the house, drive to the bridge, and dispose of the gun. Then we drive back. As soon as we park in Mark's driveway, our mind goes clear, and Lucy is back.

We ring the doorbell. No one responds. We notice the door is unlocked. We open the door a sliver and yell, "Mark! Your door is open."

No one answers.

We let ourselves in.

*Something isn't right,* our inner detective screams.

That's when we smell it: the familiar, metallic stench of death. We're beyond horrified.

And then we see the bodies.

Our friends—the parents of our child—are dead.

Rage and grief mingle together in a poisonous cocktail as the enormity of the loss begins to dawn on us. Yet some cool part of our mind reminds us that this is a crime scene.

Pushing aside our emotions, we examine everything as thoroughly as humanly possible.

No break-in. No evidence of any kind.

How did the shooter do this?

We call it in. We use an 'officer down' code, which always gets the EMTs and the police to the scene faster.

"This will be the most important case of your career," we tell the coroner on the phone in a shaking voice. "I want some answers, and I want them yesterday."

I, Darren, disassociate.

So this is why Lucy had such a hard time solving my parents' murder. She went about it the usual way, looking for a regular suspect. How could she fathom a crime where she was the killer? A crime Kyle committed with Lucy as the murder weapon?

She never stood a chance. And neither did my biological parents.

And then it hits me.

I saw my parents get shot. Margret was clearly caught off-guard, but Mark must've phased into the Quiet at the sound of the gunshot. That's why he looked like he knew what was happening. He might've even Read Lucy's mind and learned that she was being controlled by a Pusher. Of course, that knowledge wouldn't have helped him. It was too late by then. Margret was already dead, and Lucy was aiming the gun at my dad and pulling the trigger. He tried to twist to the side to save himself, but even a Reader is not fast enough to avoid a bullet at close range.

My dad had to know that—which means that he had to know he was also about to die.

I think I'm too emotionally numb at this point to fully comprehend the horror of it. Either that, or something else is distracting me at the moment, an emotion that doesn't leave room for grief.

An emotion that's overtaking my mind like a hurricane.

Rage.

Kyle messed with Lucy's mind. He raped her. Then he made her give up her baby. He had her kill my parents, and he made Lucy try to kill herself.

The fury that fills me is indescribable.

Kyle will die.

I will kill him.

I will *enjoy* killing him.

I never knew I was capable of wanting to kill someone so much. Even if he'd tried to kill me, I wouldn't have wanted to hurt him this badly. I'd want to do *something* to protect myself, sure, but it wouldn't feel like this. Not even close.

For what Kyle did to my mom, I want to tear him into little pieces.

Even that day on the Brooklyn Bridge, the day I mistakenly thought Sam had killed Mira, my hate for that fucker wasn't *this* strong. It was a momentary rage, and what I'm feeling now is qualitatively different. It's something cold and calculating.

Something dark. I feel it becoming a need, like the need to breathe or eat. This rage must be coming from a more savage part of my brain, a part I hadn't realized I possess. But I don't care where it's coming from. All I care about is feeding it what it wants—a sacrifice of Kyle's blood.

I need to get out of Mom's head. I need to start planning my revenge.

First, though, I have a decision to make. What do I let Lucy remember? It's clear she had genuine amnesia about killing my parents, as most people do when they're Guided to do something so out of character. She may never remember the rape for similar reasons. But when it comes to her baby, Kyle fucked up. She'll likely remember something, now or in the near future, without Kyle's regular memory wipes.

On top of that, what should she think of her suicide attempt? She won't remember it either, but she's a detective. One look at their house, combined with the injury to her wrist, and she'll put it all together. Then, for the rest of her life, she'll think she went crazy. I don't want her to live with that.

*You will forget about your baby,* I instruct. *Forget him or her until I'm ready to tell you everything. You were cutting open a package, slipped, and cut your wrist. You will not question the stupidity of this explanation. Not until I'm ready to explain this too.*

Will she buy it? I believe so. Bert believed worse bullshit after Hillary's treatment.

I exit my mom's head with just one thought, one soothing mantra.

Kyle will die.

# CHAPTER EIGHTEEN

As I wait for Sara to arrive, I step out into the hallway and make another phone call.

"Bert, buddy. I'm going to be in your debt forever," I say instead of hello.

"What's up, dude?" Bert says. I hear worry in his voice. "You sound strange."

I don't blame Bert for thinking I don't sound like myself, since I don't feel like myself either.

"It's my mom," I say, trying to normalize my voice. "It's Lucy. She's in the hospital."

"Oh my God, Darren. What happened?"

"It's not a conversation for over the phone," I say. "We're at the Staten Island University Hospital."

"Okay. My cab just got out of traffic on Belt Parkway. We're still driving through Brooklyn. I can have him go to Staten Island."

"Do it. Thanks, man."

"See you soon," my friend says and hangs up.

I've never needed my friends so much in my life— especially Mira—but they're all stuck midair between New York and Miami. If Kyle learns that his attempt failed, he'll come here to finish the job, or send someone else to do it. That means I need the help of someone who knows how to protect people.

Someone who works in security.

For a second, I consider calling Caleb and making a deal where I agree to fuck anyone my grandparents wish me to in exchange for Caleb helping me out. But seeing as Caleb's under arrest in Miami, he couldn't help me even if he wanted to. Maybe he knows other people in his line of work in New York?

No. Before I resort to something like that, I need to weigh all my options. As I think, I get the epiphany I should've had right away. I know someone who might be even better suited for this than Caleb.

I browse through the contacts on my phone, press call, and wait.

"Hello," Thomas answers.

"Thomas. I'm so glad I reached you."

"Darren? What a pleasant surprise."

"Are you in town?" I ask. When we last spoke, he was planning on taking a vacation too.

"Got back two days ago," he says. "Unlike you, I didn't have a good reason to stay away."

"In that case, I could really use your help. My mom is in the hospital and needs protection. It's related to that matter we spoke about when we first met . . ."

"You mean that unfinished business with one of *us*?"

"Right."

"Where are you?"

"Staten Island University Hospital," I tell him.

"I'll have a few Secret Service agents there shortly, and someone to Guide the operation, if you know what I mean."

"I do." I try not to sob with relief. "Thank you. You have no idea how grateful I am."

"I'll see you soon," Thomas says and hangs up.

Feeling more hopeful, I go back into the room to check on Lucy.

Disregarding the oxygen tube, the monitors, and all the other scary hospital equipment, she looks good. At this point, she has some of her color back in her cheeks, as much as her pale Asian complexion allows for, anyway. Her breathing is even smoother now. All her vitals on the monitors look good. She's basically sleeping, and sleeping pretty peacefully at that.

I step outside the room again, phase in, catch a nurse, and Guide her to get me a sandwich from the cafeteria. I'm starved, but I don't want to risk leaving Mom alone for even a few minutes.

In a weird way, I'm grateful to my Enlightened grandparents for asking Caleb to abduct me. It led to me meeting Mimir—the demigod-like being I spoke with during the Joining with the Enlightened. Thanks to that incident, my mom is alive. If Mimir hadn't warned me, I'd probably still be figuring out how to deal with the Julia situation. Without the threat of something happening to Lucy, I never would've left the Enlightened compound so boldly. Worse, if they hadn't kidnapped me at all, I'd be on the beach in Miami, oblivious to everything I now know. Lucy would be dead, and I'd never know it was Kyle who was responsible.

How *did* Mimir know Lucy was in trouble? He said he knew because *I* knew. But I didn't know. Or did I? Did I have all the information necessary to suspect Kyle without realizing that I did?

As I think, things fall into place.

Like the fact that the Pusher is a Traditionalist—a fact everyone has mentioned, more than once. Whether part of the Orthodoxy conspiracy my grandparents mentioned or acting as a solo agent, everyone agrees that whoever was after me was likely a Traditionalist, because only a Traditionalist would see my parents' union as a horrible crime against the old ways.

And what are Traditionalists like? According to what I was told, they are very . . . well, traditional . . . in their views.

And what is Kyle's most defining quality? Why did we have so many arguments while I was growing up? Because he's as traditional as can be.

This alone, however, doesn't make Kyle guilty. Nothing in isolation does. I recall the strange phone call Kyle got while he was visiting me at the hospital the day I got shot in the head. After the call, he bailed on Lucy, whom he'd brought to see me.

Now it occurs to me that the call was probably from Jacob, who told Kyle about my heritage—the reason Jacob had the Russian mob make an attempt on my life that morning. After the call, on his way out, Kyle must've Pushed that nurse to try to kill me. Given how willing Kyle was to kill me once he learned the truth, I feel very lucky that my biological mom had Guided Lucy and Sara to go to Israel and pretend that Sara was artificially inseminated with me. I was so mad when I learned about that lie, but Sara pretending to be my biological mother probably saved my life. Thanks to that story, Kyle never suspected I might be anything but an ordinary kid. A kid he'd never tried Guiding, thanks to the taboo on touching children that Liz told me about.

As I think about it, I realize Kyle probably didn't even know Margret was ever pregnant. In Lucy's memories, he began to avoid Mark at some point, likely due to his relationship with Margret. Besides, Mark and Margret seemed to have hidden her pregnancy from most of the world, their OB-GYN being the unfortunate exception. It was that doctor's records that must've given Jacob—Kyle's Reader partner—that extra certainty that I was Mark's son, though Jacob might well have tried to have me killed based solely on my resemblance to my dad. How stupid did Kyle feel, with a 'hybrid abomination' being under his nose this whole time? Since he'd seen me grow up, it probably never occurred to him to look for any kind of a resemblance to anyone.

Speaking of resemblance... Kyle also has the same facial features as most Guides. Facial features I also have. I never would've realized it without thinking of him in this context, but now, those subtle clues are obvious. This explains why, on some occasions, folks thought Kyle and I were blood relatives. Those people were misled, to a small degree, by these ethnic-like similarities between Guides.

Then a major realization hits me. The Russian mob. They're the big clue once you know who the suspect is. Kyle has worked in Organized Crime for decades. That's how he picked the scariest guys to use as his weapons. He has files on them. Taxpayers have been financing Kyle's private assassin research for years.

And finally, my parents' unsolvable murder leads back to Kyle, or to someone who was similarly close to my parents. I should've realized this sooner. According to Hillary, her sister Margret was a very powerful Guide. If a regular Joe Schmoe had tried to kill her, she would've made him kill himself instead—or reversed any Push that person had received.

The only way to kill her was to catch her off-guard, so the killer had to be someone neither of my parents would perceive as a threat. Someone who was close to them. Someone they loved like family. That was the only way someone could've shot Margret in the back in her own house—which leaves Lucy and Kyle at the top of the suspects list. And as it turns out, they were both responsible in a weird way.

Coward that he is, Kyle decided to use Lucy to do his dirty work. He Pushed her to kill Margret first because she was the more dangerous of the two; she could've reversed Kyle's compulsion in Lucy's mind, so Kyle had Lucy use the element of surprise.

If I can come up with this many clues just off the top of my head, I understand how the combined intelligence of the fourteen people who made up Mimir figured out that Kyle was the threat. From there, it must've been a small leap to conclude that Lucy was in trouble. Mimir knew Lucy was investigating Mira's parents' murder—the murder that was ordered by Jacob, Kyle's ally. The murder Kyle manipulated the rest of his department into dismissing as mob-on-mob violence.

Mimir saw the danger the way *I* should have, but failed to.

As I chew the tasteless sandwich the nurse brought, I realize that if Lucy had died, I never would've forgiven myself for not figuring all this out sooner, for being the one who, thanks to his big mouth, put her in danger in the first place.

My phone rings.

"I'm downstairs," Bert says.

"Meet me in Room 3 in Intensive Care," I say. "Say you're here to visit my mom."

He arrives after I finish my food.

"How is she?" he asks right away. "What happened?"

"Let's step out into the hallway," I say, and as soon as we're away from any prying ears, I tell him everything.

"Shit," Bert says. "I've never liked that uncle of yours, but I'm still flabbergasted. To just up and try to kill you as soon as he learned you're half-Reader, half-Guide? What about all the years he's known you?"

"Well, we have one thing in common," I say darkly. "When I get my hands around his neck, I'll also forget about all the years we've known each other."

"And this person, Thomas, he's a Guide, like Hillary?" Bert looks uncomfortable with my newfound bloodlust.

"Yes, and about that." I shift from one foot to another. "Let's not tell him you know as much as you do. I trust him and all, but just in case, it's best he doesn't find out. For your sake."

"Oh, right. Unlike you and Mira, they can't read my mind," he says excitedly. "So I can lie."

"That's right. My cover story is that I Guided you to do my bidding."

"Yes, Master," Bert says in his best Dracula's-worshipful-servant voice.

My phone rings. It's Sara. She's here, so I explain where to meet us.

"I'm so glad she's okay," Sara says when Bert and I enter Lucy's room. Sara's face is nearly as pale as Lucy's, and I see that her hands are trembling. "Can you please explain to me what happened?"

I phase into the Quiet.

Hesitantly, I walk over to Sara and enter her mind. The level of anxiety my mom is capable of is insane. If I were this worried, I'd be phasing into the Quiet every few seconds and be barely functional. I debate Guiding her to make her relax, but decide against it. I limit my Guiding to making sure Sara believes the same story as the one I concocted in Lucy's mind.

I get out of Sara's head and Read Lucy. She's content in her sleep. I don't experience pain or discomfort, but then again, a sleeping mind isn't very helpful in gauging someone's health.

I phase out.

"The knife slipped," I say and tell Sara the story.

Bert is making eyes at me from behind Sara's back. Eyes that say, "I can't believe she's buying it."

When I'm done with the story, Sara launches into her interrogation. "How did you get here so fast? How was Florida? Where's Mira—"

"She just opened her eyes," Bert says, interrupting her barrage of questions.

Sara goes to Lucy and sits on the edge of her bed, lightly resting her hand on her shoulder. Lucy's eyes focus on her wife. She looks surprisingly sharp, considering her ordeal.

"Hi," she says hoarsely. "Where the hell am I?"

I explain what she's already primed to believe. "When I told them 'officer down,' they went out of their way to help you," I conclude.

"To think of all the ways I could've gotten hurt, and this happens on a day I'm *off* the job," Lucy says humorlessly.

"Excuse me," says a familiar voice through the crack in the door. "May we come in?"

"Please," I say, trying to hide my surprise. "Mom, you remember my therapist, Dr. Jackson."

"Please, call me Liz," Liz says predictably. She hates it when I call her anything but that.

I still can't believe she's here. It looks as if Thomas brought her in as reinforcements. Or she might be here to hang with him; they are dating, after all.

"Hello, Liz," Sara says, blinking. "What are you doing here?"

"Darren called me when your wife got hurt," Liz says. "He was so distraught I thought I'd check in on things. He's been a patient for years."

"Of course," Sara says. "Thank you so much for coming."

"This is my boyfriend, Thomas," Liz says, pulling Thomas inside the room.

Both Sara and Bert look at Thomas with fascination. Even Lucy looks over, though her expression is harder to read.

I wonder if they find the couple's age difference odd. Liz looks like a hot teacher and Thomas like a student she seduced—only ten years later. I wonder what Sara would think if she knew that on top of everything else, Liz is Thomas's shrink. Maybe she's picturing me in Thomas's shoes. That might be it. Maybe she's wondering whether my therapist made moves on me when I was a teen. Which would've been awesome, by the way.

My thoughts are interrupted when Thomas pulls me into the Quiet.

"Are we bringing her in?" I nod toward Liz. "If so, we should probably use my Quiet session, since I have a long story for you."

"You decide whom to trust," Thomas says. "And I appreciate you thinking about my Reach."

"It's okay to bring her. Especially since I now know who the mystery Pusher is. And it's not Liz."

Thomas phases out, and I phase in and bring him in with me.

Thomas gives Liz a chaste peck on the neck to pull her into the Quiet.

I proceed to tell them a version of my story, leaving only one thing out—Kyle's identity.

"Your poor mom," Thomas says, looking at Lucy. His usually stern face is a shade warmer. "To be forced to kill her own partner? There's nothing worse for a cop."

"At least she doesn't remember that," Liz says. "You were right in that regard. Your other mother looks like she might lose it, by the way. I'd be happy to do a subtle relaxation session on her."

"That's how she always looks," I say. "But will it make her feel better?" The idea sounds promising, though I feel guilty manipulating my mom's emotions.

"What I do puts Xanax to shame," Liz says with confidence. "And I've been testing it on live human subjects for many years. They always come back for more."

"In that case, please," I say. "And in the long term, do you think you can help with Lucy's baby situation? It'll probably be a painful shock to just remember she gave up her child like that . . ."

Liz nods. "I'll make sure the doctor advises her to see me after she checks out. And I'll also make sure she's receptive to the idea of getting therapy."

"You can make her believe it's for her OCD," I suggest. "Thank you for this. I really appreciate it."

"Don't mention it." Liz walks over to Sara and starts doing her Xanax thing.

"And one more thing," I say, realizing I can no longer tell Lucy everything. "Can you make her forget to ask me for the explanation I promised her earlier on the phone?"

"What explanation?" Liz asks.

"Do you need to know?" I ask. "To make her forget safely and all?"

"I can do it without knowing, but curiosity is a weakness of mine. You know that."

"Then I'd rather not explain," I say. I'm glad Liz didn't lie by saying she needed to know, but I still don't want to admit that I was about to bring my mom completely up to speed, not when I don't know Liz's feelings on the matter.

Liz gives me an analytical look, but doesn't push the issue. She knows not to bother.

"So are you going to tell us who did this to her?" Thomas asks.

If he was trying to defuse the tension in the air, he couldn't have asked a worse question.

"Depends," I say. "What will happen to this person? What's the plan?"

"I honestly don't know," Thomas says. "Liz?"

She shrugs. "I'm not sure either. But given that he attacked one of us, I'd say it's a matter for the Elders to deal with."

"What about my mom? What's the punishment for what he did to her?"

"If you're talking about her"—Thomas points at Lucy—"they might not see it the same way as you and I do. She isn't one of us, so our laws don't extend to her. If you're talking about your biological mother, then absolutely, he will have to answer for that murder."

"What. Will. Happen?" I ask through clenched teeth, too angry to confront him on the fact that his Elders wouldn't see what Kyle did to my mom—the rape and the other fucking atrocities he did to her mind—as a violation of their laws.

"The Elders' justice is shrouded in mystery," Liz says. "So we honestly don't know."

"That's not good enough."

"What does it have to do with telling us who the Pusher is?" Thomas asks. "Surely you can tell us that?"

"I plan to kill him," I say evenly. "And don't you try to shrink-talk me out of it."

Liz gives me a thorough look. "Actually, I think this is a very rare case where I believe action will help you achieve *catharsis. So I won't stop you.* "

*"Whatever you're planning, I won't rat you out,"* Thomas adds.

"In that case, his name is Kyle," I say bitterly. "Liz, you might've heard me refer to him as *Uncle* Kyle."

# CHAPTER NINETEEN

"You have an uncle who's one of us?" Liz asks, her eyes round with surprise. "I didn't know this."

"Neither did I," I say.

"There's only one Guide named Kyle in the city," Liz says thoughtfully. "Grant."

"That's him. Kyle fucking Grant," I say through gritted teeth.

"Wait," Thomas says. "He's in law enforcement."

"You know him?" I ask.

"Somewhat. Though he never hangs out at the club."

"I know him a little better," Liz says. "And I could easily see him as a Traditionalist. I always knew he had issues, but I never suspected such deep-seated—"

"He's a dead man," I interrupt. "So you don't need to analyze him."

Liz sighs. "I'm sorry," she says, "but I'm going to have to go back on one thing I said. I don't think killing him is a good idea."

"Why the fuck not?" I snap. Great, now I'm yelling at my shrink.

"He's been around you your whole life. He's been like a father figure to you. Do I need to draw you a diagram?"

"He stuck around so he could wipe Lucy's mind at regular intervals," I explain, my voice tight with anger.

"That may be true," Liz says quietly, "but it doesn't change what you feel about him."

"What I feel is that he and I can't breathe the same air," I say sharply. "If you want to help, tell me something useful about him."

"We didn't hang with the same crowd," she says. "I only knew of him because he was a Guide."

"Oh shit," I say as something dawns on me. "That explains it."

"What?" Thomas asks.

"In Lucy's memory, Mark asks why Kyle disappeared from his life. And now I think I know why. Mark married Margret, who's a Guide, which means she would've recognized him had they met."

"That's true," Liz says. "She would have known him, though probably only as much as I do. She was obviously—"

"Wait. It just occurred to me." I stare at Liz. "You knew my biological mother?"

"Yes," she answers. "I knew her. I know everyone."

"You'll have to tell me about her one day," I say. "But right now, I have some important business to take care of."

"I really don't think—"

"Liz, I'm sorry to interrupt," Thomas says, "but I think Darren should do what feels right."

"Men," Liz says derisively. "All this macho bullshit. If you go through with it, don't come begging *me* for therapy."

"Fine," I say. "I'm sure I won't have trouble finding another therapist. Maybe even one who won't lie to me for over a decade."

"That's classic projection—"

"Seriously, Liz. That's enough," Thomas says sternly.

To my huge surprise, Liz stops whatever psychobabble she was about to spew at me. I never realized Thomas had the power in this strange relationship. Interesting.

"I'm sorry, Liz," I say. "I didn't mean to snap at you."

"No, I was out of line," Liz says, shaking her head. "Just think before you do anything irreversible. That's all I'm suggesting."

"I'll take your words under advisement." I'm lying through my teeth. "Either way, we need to find out where he is. He's still a threat to Lucy."

"So what's the plan?" Thomas asks.

"You, Bert, and I will go run an errand," I tell him before turning to my shrink. "Liz, would you mind keeping an eye on things here?"

"Sure," she says.

"Sounds good to me," Thomas says.

Giving them both a grateful look, I phase us out of the Quiet.

"Mom," I say ambiguously, a trick I developed as a kid.

"Yes?" Sara and Lucy say in unison, and I can't help but smile. Works every time.

"Since you're feeling better, Bert and I need to swing by our work," I say, looking at Lucy. "There's this big move in the portfolio, and they can't deal without—"

"It's not a problem," Lucy interrupts. "Thank you for saving me."

"I'll be back soon," I say. "You won't even notice I'm gone."

Sara gives me a hug, and I kiss Lucy goodbye on the cheek. Then I walk out with Bert following on my heels.

Behind me, I hear Thomas make an excuse and Liz give some weird explanation as to why she'll stay with my moms. She must've greased their mental wheels through Guiding, because they act like Liz's story makes sense. I really hope that stuff doesn't cause permanent brain damage.

"Your men aren't exactly inconspicuous," I say to Thomas as we pass five big dudes wearing black suits and earpieces in the hospital hallway.

"No, they're not. But they're effective," Thomas says curtly. "Liz will make sure no one pays them any heed."

Bert is about to comment on something, but I shake my head. Then I phase into the Quiet and pull Thomas in.

"Please don't talk too much about the Guiding stuff in front of my minion," I say. "I don't want to make him forget more than I have to."

"Why do we need this guy at all?"

"He's part of my contingency plan."

"I don't even know what the primary plan is, let alone the contingency," Thomas says.

"We're going to the police department, to start," I say. "Is that good enough?"

"It'll do for now. Let's take my car."

I phase out, and we exit the hospital.

Thomas's car is the same one he used in the big standoff on the Brooklyn Bridge. Though he crashed it, the car looks as good as new again. I hoped this would be his ride since this car has a cache of weapons in the back. I'll need those, but I don't mention this to Thomas.

Before we leave Staten Island, we swing by my moms' house. We clean up the scene to make it fit my 'clumsy mom' story. The good news is that my moms have so many extra bed sheets and blankets that they won't even notice the ones they had on the bed are missing and have been replaced.

Next, I change out of my bloodstained clothes and into a pair of old jeans and a T-shirt that I keep at my moms'. The clothes are a little stiff, but they'll do.

"Okay," I say when we get back into the car. "Our next stop is the police department."

Thomas puts the Manhattan address I provide into his GPS and begins driving.

Our trip starts off silently. I don't want to talk too much since Thomas thinks Bert isn't supposed to know stuff, plus I'm not in a very talkative mood.

"Here's what I'm wondering," Thomas says, breaking the silence after a couple of minutes. "Why didn't Kyle attack you in Miami?"

"I bet he couldn't find us," I say. "As a precaution, none of us told anyone the specifics of where in Florida we were vacationing."

"But there should've been an electronic trail—your phones, credit cards, that sort of thing," Thomas says. "With so many people involved, someone could've slipped."

"We had Mira, the queen of paranoia, and a ton of cash. Plus we had Bert, the god of making electronic trails disappear and a paranoiac in his own right."

In the rearview mirror, I see Bert puff up like a peacock.

"But Caleb found you," Thomas points out. "So you slipped up somewhere."

"True," I admit. "I have no idea how Caleb found me, but I wouldn't be surprised if it involved one of the Enlightened using their boundless Depth to Read a massive amount of people all over Florida—something Kyle couldn't do. On his own, he can't Read at all."

"Right. That man who died, Jacob, he was his Reader partner. But where he had one, he could have others."

"Maybe. My crazy grandparents did mention a whole organization called the Orthodoxy."

"Right, the mysterious organization that combines Leacher Purists and our craziest Traditionalists," Thomas says skeptically. "I don't see those groups uniting so easily."

"It doesn't matter. Kyle probably didn't even bother looking for us since he had a surefire way of smoking me out. He was planning on getting to me at my mom's funeral."

My friends digest that morbid scenario for a few blocks in silence.

"I have an idea about the Orthodoxy," Bert says. He's always hated uncomfortable silences, and I hope he hasn't forgotten how little he's supposed to officially know. Not that I know how much someone in this pretend position would be allowed to know to begin with.

"What's your idea, minion?" I say in a commanding tone, hoping that ridiculous term convinces Thomas that I'm Guiding Bert.

"This Orthodoxy is probably behind the 'suicides' of the prominent scientists I've been telling you about. Don't you see that what happened with your mom has the exact same MO? When combined with the USB drive results—"

"Darren," Thomas says, his voice even. "Is *this* the expert you gave the USB drive to? The USB drive my people couldn't crack?"

"That's because the encryption was strong, but not—"

"Yes, that's him," I say, stopping Bert from going into a post-graduate-level lecture on cryptography.

"I'm impressed," Thomas says, looking in the rearview mirror. "I can see why you brought him up to speed."

"What? No," I say defensively. "I just let him know things because he's pretty bright and can usually give me wise counsel—"

"I didn't buy it at the hospital, and I'm not buying it now," Thomas says. "But Liz did, so I didn't contradict you. When it comes to matters of exposure, she's a lot more cautious than you and me, having grown up a Guide and all, so I didn't want her to put her brainwashing sights on your friend."

"Thanks," Bert says. "So you don't mind?"

"No," Thomas says. "Especially since, in my line of work, I might need your help."

"Blackmail," Bert says sadly. "At least Darren will stop calling me his minion now."

"Nothing like that." Thomas smiles. "I'll keep your secret regardless. Just please consider helping me."

"I don't think I want to stop calling you my minion," I say.

"I can make your Harvard diploma disappear." Bert crosses his arms. "For starters."

"Oh yeah, *minion*? Surely you forget that I can use my superpowers to make you eat your own—"

"Your destination is on the left," Thomas's GPS chimes in.

"Okay, pull up there," I say, humor forgotten. I point to a 'no parking under any circumstances' spot across the street from the police building. With Thomas's nifty Secret Service plates, no one should bat an eye at this.

He pulls over. "So, what's your—"

I don't hear Thomas finish the rest of his question because the world goes silent as I phase into the Quiet.

Thomas is stuck with his mouth open mid-sentence.

My plan is simple.

Walk in. Find Kyle. Then come back, take a gun out of Thomas's arsenal, and bring Thomas into the Quiet with me. Together, we'll go to Kyle. I'll bring Kyle into the Quiet with us and shoot him. Then, once he's Inert, we'll figure out step two.

Approaching the police station, I walk through the revolving door. The station looks eerie, like some kind of police-themed wax museum.

I make my way to the second floor where Kyle's department is located.

When I reach his desk, I find it empty.

I look inside the nearest bathroom, stop by the copy room and water cooler, and in general, search the floor for the man.

No luck.

Shit. I really wanted him to be here. Then again, maybe it's best we don't recreate the bridge debacle in the middle of a police station. But if Kyle is not here, I need to figure out where he is.

I find a few detectives at their desks in the Organized Crime section and Read them. They don't have much for me. Kyle came in this morning, but left shortly thereafter. He didn't tell anyone where he was going.

I look around Kyle's desk for any clues about where he could be, but don't find anything. I wonder whether he kept his desk clear of any evidence because he planned for this eventuality—a Reader or Guide snooping around in the Quiet. I doubt it. He was always neat, a trait he shares with Lucy. This thought reinvigorates my anger. The scope of his betrayal is mind-numbing.

I refocus on figuring out where he is. Even if he thought someone might snoop in the Quiet, would he take the extra step of protecting his computer? Those things don't work in the Quiet, plus most people think their computers are safe, especially detectives who have government-issued security. Luckily for me, whatever security they have is unlikely to be Bert-proof. This is the contingency plan, which has now become my primary plan, though it has tricky elements of its own.

I look around. For my backup plan to work, I need to do what my aunt likes to do.

I need to Guide a whole bunch of people.

I consider this. If she can do it, so can I, as my Reach is probably greater than hers. That aside, what exactly would I get everyone to do? One thing I can try is Guiding the whole precinct to fall asleep and stay that way for half an hour. That would give Bert enough time to do his thing. But this idea has a few flaws. Like what happens if a 911 call comes in? I don't want people getting hurt because of me. Well, no one except Kyle, that is.

Another option is to make them all forget they saw us. But a whole bunch of police officers and staff simultaneously getting amnesia is less than ideal, especially if someone is in the middle of responding to a life-or-death emergency when they see us. Whatever I do, it has to be subtle.

What if I make it so they don't see us at all? Yes, that could work.

I begin Guiding the nearby officers.

My idea is simple.

I start by painting my and Bert's exact descriptions in the targets' minds. Then I highlight the critical moment, which is when they see us. At that point, the directive is to let their attention wander onto something else—something more important than us—instead of registering our presence in their conscious minds.

We'll be the equivalent of that little stain on people's glasses that they never see.

Guiding every person this way is tedious and gives me a new appreciation for what Hillary did for us. It takes me what feels like hours to set everything up, though the number of people I have to deal with is a fraction of what Hillary dealt with at the airport. Even worse for her, she couldn't occasionally entertain herself by Reading random bystanders, the way I'm doing. Funny tidbits—such as the bald lieutenant's fetish for his coworker's mustache—definitely break up the monotony.

Finished with the interior of the building, I make my way back to the car. As I do, I Guide the handful of officers who are hanging around outside the building. Once I reach the car, I phase out.

"–plan?" Thomas says, finishing his question.

"The plan is simple," I say. "Bert and I walk in, go to Kyle's computer, and Bert will poke around in it."

"Are you going to brainwash me to do that?" Bert asks caustically. "Cause that's what it will take for me to waltz into a police department and hack into a detective's computer."

"I will if I have to," I say. "But I already made it so no one will say boo to us. Don't you trust me?"

"I don't trust you with my freedom from jail, no," Bert says. "But I do trust that you'd brainwash me to get your way. So I'd rather go on my own than get mind-controlled again."

"Good thinking," I say. "Because who knows what else I might've made you do while inside your head."

"Okay then. Let's go," Thomas says.

"I was actually hoping you'd stay in the car," I say. "In case something goes wrong, it'll be good to have an ally on the outside."

"You're not leaving me behind so you can kill Kyle by yourself, are you?" Thomas asks.

"If I were, why would I bring Bert?"

Thomas looks thoughtful for a moment. I wonder whether he phased into the Quiet to walk around the police department and verify what I told him. He doesn't know where Kyle's desk is, but he knows what the fucker looks like, so it's plausible.

When his face looks alert again, he says, "I'll wait in the car."

Bert and I head for the precinct.

After observing the officers outside, it's clear my Guiding is in effect. One officer sits down to tie his shoes at just the right moment, his gaze completely missing us. The other one stares intently at a nearby girl in a short skirt. Another looks into the distance, lost in thought. No one will remember seeing us because they pretty much didn't. Not consciously, anyway.

When we enter the building, things get even spookier. The woman at the front desk looks at her phone at the exact moment her eyes should've been turning toward us. Instead of greeting us, she starts dialing.

"Dude," Bert whispers, "they're ignoring us."

"Don't talk," I whisper back. "They're blind to us, but if they hear us, they might have amnesia about it later since their brain won't be able to reconcile my Guiding with reality."

Just to be safe, I phase in and check on the desk clerk. As I suspected, she has no amnesia, but doesn't have any memories of seeing us either. She was that absorbed in the phone call.

I phase out and follow Bert, who walks quietly the rest of the way. It's like we're invisible, but not just invisible. It's as though we're eye repellents. The funniest side effect happens when two rather rotund detectives almost plow through us. That's how absorbed they were in their conversation.

As we walk, a look of awe appears on Bert's face. I can't blame him. If asked, these people will say they never saw us, despite us walking through the precinct in plain sight.

When we reach Kyle's desk, I point it out to Bert.

Without a word, he sits down and touches the keyboard to wake up the PC. The monitor shows the login screen. The password page would deter most people, but Bert's fingers dance around the keyboard for only a few minutes before he's in. He rapidly opens and closes windows, and I'm not sure what he's doing. It's fine, though. I trust him. Eventually, he locks Kyle's machine and walks over to the printer to pick up some printouts.

"Let's go," he mouths.

Our path back to Thomas's car matches our way in; no one pays us any heed.

"They won't even see us on video," Bert says as he opens the door. "I poked around the system and deleted all relevant footage."

"Damn, Bert, that—"

"That was some impressive Guiding," Thomas interrupts. "At least from what I could tell from their reactions, or lack thereof."

"You checked the place out in the Quiet?" I ask.

"I couldn't help myself," Thomas says. Then he looks at Bert. "What did you find?"

"This," Bert says triumphantly and hands me a few of the printouts.

I look them over. "It's a list of names, Bert."

"It's *the* list," Bert says. "Don't you get it?"

"I don't," Thomas says. "I have no clue."

"He knows we don't understand," I say, sighing. "He just wants to build anticipation."

"Fine, be like that," Bert says, crossing his arms over his chest. "These are the same names as the ones

I got off the USB drive you gave me in Miami. The one I cracked for you."

"The names Jacob was going to give to his and Kyle's pet Russian mobsters to assassinate?" Thomas is on full alert now.

"The very same list," Bert says.

"If I had any doubt that these two were working together, they're gone now," I say as I digest that information.

"Right. Only it looks like your uncle—I mean, Kyle—is going to deal with them himself using his favorite tool: the Russian mob," Bert says, his elation growing. After enjoying our stunned silence for a few beats, he hands us each a few more printouts.

I look at mine. The pictures are of normal-looking people.

"That"—Bert points at the one I'm holding—"is a nanotechnology expert. Yours"—he points at Thomas's—"is a guy in robotics." He gives us more printouts and goes over the master list. We learn there are in fact two guys in the field of robotics, one in genetics, three in informatics, and one in nanotechnology.

All the targets are scientists, it appears.

"This really vindicates some of your theories," I say. I know this is what Bert wants to hear most, plus, in this case, it's the truth and my friend deserves the credit. "Though you never explained who this weirdo is." I show him the picture of a strange-looking guy with wild eyes.

"My guess is that he's the patsy," Bert says. "But before we talk about him, have a look at these."

This next set of pictures is different. These men look hardened and dangerous. A few of the pictures are mug shots.

"I take it these are the mobsters," I say.

"Yes." Bert nods. "The guy whose picture you're holding is worse than that Arkady character you had me look up. The cops are building a case against him for running illegal gambling clubs, but they haven't made a move on him because they're hoping to catch him doing something worse. They have him linked to several high-ranking mobsters who showed up headless in a New Jersey dumpster, as well as a few other atrocities."

I look at the picture. Victor Sokolov. In addition to what Bert mentioned, the file also says this man has military training and is famous in the criminal underworld as a marksman. In other words, he's the perfect weapon for Kyle. The name, Victor, sounds vaguely familiar, but I can't place it. I feel like I've come across a dangerous mobster named Victor during a Read before—

"This is all very interesting," Thomas says. "But it doesn't tell us where Kyle is."

"I still haven't shown you this." Bert hands us the last printout.

"A conference?" Thomas says. "You think—"

"*The* conference on transformative technologies," Bert says. "Which, of course, means most of the scientists on that list will be in attendance."

"You think Kyle will make these mobsters kill the scientists on the list?" Thomas asks, frowning.

"I think Kyle is planning to make it look like a mass shooting to cover up the fact that it's an assassination," Bert says. "A person going postal at a science convention raises less questions than a mafia hit, at least in this case. Now that I know about Guides and all that, I suspect some other crazy shootings can be attributed to—"

"Wait," I say. "No conspiracy theories for the moment. What makes you think that's what Kyle is planning to do?"

"Well, his usual way of operating is subtle—suicides and the like," Bert explains. "Kyle makes these deaths look like no Pusher was involved. So he comes up with this plan. That man with the wacky eyes you asked about? He's what made me suspect this course of action."

Thomas looks at the paper with the weird-looking guy again. "He was a gym teacher who got fired after being accused of having a relationship with a student. Has a long history of mental illness. Recently purchased a lot of guns. I think Bert is right. Kyle chose this man for a reason."

"Fine," I concede. "Maybe there's something to it. Do you think Kyle would personally supervise this plan? Do you think he's going to be there?"

"He's not *going* to be there," Bert says. "According to his car's anti-theft GPS system, he's *already* there. His car was in the Columbia University parking lot when I last tracked him. That's where the event is taking place.

I look at the conference printout more closely. Then I look at the clock on the dashboard. "Shit. This thing starts in twenty minutes."

"I'm on it," Thomas says and starts the car.

"Wait," I say. "Bert, you've outdone yourself."

"Oh yeah?" My friend grins. "I did owe you for introducing me to Hillary."

"We're almost even." And that's being generous. "Unless you two get married. In that case, I get your firstborn."

"Wait," Thomas says. "Him and Hillary?"

"Yep. Happy couple and all that. Which brings me to my point. I don't need you for this next part, Bert." I look at my friend. "My aunt wouldn't be too happy with me if something happened to you."

Bert gives a small sigh of relief, but then he says, "Are you sure, dude? You know I got your back."

I fight the impulse to chuckle. The image of my small-framed friend taking on a giant mobster is just too much. But I don't laugh. Bert probably would go with me if I asked, and that means a lot.

"I'm sure," I tell him instead. "If you're there, Kyle might take control of your mind and use you against us."

"You're right," Bert says thoughtfully. "I'm still getting used to thinking that way."

"I know," I say. "But keep in mind, you're our insurance in case something very unfortunate happens."

"I am?" Bert looks surprised.

"Of course," I say. "If something happens to us, tell Hillary about Kyle. She and Liz—the woman from the hospital—they'll deal with him."

"Though it shouldn't come to that," Thomas says after seeing Bert's worried expression.

"Yeah," I say. "But in case it does, I need another favor. Promise you'll help my moms relocate somewhere with an electronic trail so invisible that even the witness protection people would envy it."

"Of course," Bert says solemnly. "Call me as soon as this thing is over," he adds with uncharacteristic seriousness and gets out of the car.

"I will," I say as my friend slams the door shut.

As soon as Bert is on the sidewalk, Thomas slams the gas pedal, and we're off.

# CHAPTER TWENTY

"I doubt it'll work, but I figured I'd at least try to talk you out of this," Thomas says as he expertly navigates the busy streets of Manhattan. He's driving fast, but he seems so in control that his driving doesn't freak me out like Mira's and Caleb's. "You know we can get Kyle another day—a day when we have Guide reinforcements."

"You'd let him murder all those people?" I ask.

"You have a good point," Thomas says. "But there are other things we can do, like call the police about a bomb threat. Kyle would then have to reconsider his plan. And if he leaves any evidence of what he was planning behind, that would create a strong case against him for the Elders."

"You still insist we hand him over to these Elders? Even though you don't know what they'll do with him?"

"I'm sure they wouldn't just slap him on the wrist for—"

"No," I interrupt. "I'm not interested in that. I'm not taking any chances. Kyle will die. Nice and simple."

Thomas gives me a glance that probably means 'you're cold.'

"So what's the plan?" he asks as he turns onto the highway. "You do have one, right?"

"Not really. At least not an elaborate one," I admit. "But I'm thinking this: I scout the conference once we get there. Find Kyle in the Quiet. Bring him into the Quiet. Kill him there to make him Inert. Then kill him in the real world."

"I bet that was also your plan for the police department," Thomas says, and I shrug.

"It's a good strategy when dealing with people like us."

"It is, but the devil's in the details," he says as he takes an exit off the highway. "Do you have experience securing a public place such as a conference? Are you sure you can manage to kill a seasoned cop?"

"I don't have experience in securing anything," I admit. "Though I can fight, thanks to my training with Caleb."

"Still, you must see the wisdom in working with someone who has experience in securing—"

"Someone from the Secret Service, perhaps?" I see where he's going with this from a mile away. "You don't need to sell me on you joining this operation. It's why I called you in the first place."

"Ah," he says. "I thought you were so overcome with revenge that you wanted to carry out this mission on your own."

"No," I say. "As tempting as it is, I'm not crazy. I'm more interested in the practicality of getting this done."

"Good. Because if you were to pull a 'Mira' on me—"

"I won't be a liability," I say grimly.

"Then this has a good chance of succeeding," Thomas says, turning onto Broadway.

During the rest of the way to Columbia University, Thomas gives me the bare bones of how he'd go about doing what we need to do. As he speaks, I understand how lucky I am to have him with me.

"Do we do the disguise thing first, or the reconnaissance?" I ask once he's parked the car.

"Recon," he says. "Pull me in."

I phase in and bring Thomas in with me. We walk briskly, and I only vaguely register the surrounding campus. I conclude we had much nicer trees at Harvard.

"This could get messy," Thomas says when we enter our destination, a giant conference hall. "I was hoping there'd be fewer people since the conference hasn't started yet."

"The conference keynote speaker must be someone famous."

"Some guy named Craig Venter, according to your friend's printout."

"Some guy?" I say. "That's *the* synthetic genome guy. No wonder the place is packed."

"We'll just have to deal with it," Thomas says, confidently making his way through the crowd of mannequin-like scientists gathered at the hall's entrance.

"The two pathways are bad," he says as he looks around. "We'll have to cover both of them." He's referring to the fact that this hall has three sections of seats broken up by two walkthroughs, like a movie theater. Both paths lead all the way to the large stage.

Both have frozen people on their way to their seats and can be used as a way out of the room.

"We'll have to split up," I say. "I'll take the left pathway."

"Yes, but before we decide which one you'll take, let's see where Kyle is. You should take whichever path he's least likely to use."

I can't tell whether Thomas is testing me to see if I'll go 'Mira' on his ass. If I say what I really feel—that Kyle is mine and that I want to choke him with my bare hands—I have a feeling Thomas will pull out of the mission. So I force myself to nod in agreement, mumbling, "That's logical, Thomas, sure."

I follow him as he starts combing through the crowd. As I look at all the innocent people, I'm glad I'm here to stop the slaughter. I was so focused on my revenge that I didn't think about any other aspect of Kyle's plan, such as Kyle deciding to cover his tracks with mass murder. I wonder how many shootings in the past were the byproducts of Pushers like Kyle. When we spoke earlier, Bert was about to spout that as his latest conspiracy theory. I should probably listen to my friend's theories more carefully in the future, since he might well be right about this one. I had never been able to imagine how someone could wake up one day and decide to shoot a group of strangers. It's just unfathomable to me. Now I'm wondering whether those shooters might've been compelled by someone with Guiding powers and a more rational—in a psychopathic kind of way— purpose.

"I located all our suspects and targets—everyone but Kyle," Thomas says, interrupting my musings. What he says is so incomprehensible that I just stare at him for a second. Could he really be joking at a time like this? He looks completely serious.

"You know where all those people are?" I clarify. "The mafia, the crazy guy who's going to take the fall, and all the scientists?"

"Yes," he says and jumps onto the stage. "There, there, and there."

Even as he points, I have a hard time locating them in the crowd. I've never been as impressed with Secret Service training as I am now. Maybe I should do a stint in some elite force, like Thomas and Caleb have. For the first time in my life, such an idea doesn't sound completely crazy.

"We'll deal with them after we've located our primary target," Thomas says.

It takes Thomas a few more minutes to find said target.

The painfully familiar figure is standing furtively near the right backstage exit.

I look at Kyle as though it's the first time I've seen him. Here's a person I want to erase off the face of the planet. The person I've known for years, but didn't know at all. I step toward him.

"Darren, no," Thomas says. "Remember the plan."

As he says this, I realize my hands are clenched into fists so tightly that my palms hurt where my nails are digging into them.

Unclenching my hands, I audibly exhale. "Don't worry. I'll stick to the plan," I say, feigning matter-of-factness.

In truth, I'm grateful for Thomas's reminder. There's a chance I could've done something impulsive, like pull Kyle into the Quiet and start pounding on him. Punching Kyle is something I'm still itching to do, but now that I'm more centered, I resist it. Thomas is right. We need to position ourselves in the conference hall outside of the Quiet before we make Kyle Inert. We need to be close to him, as close as we can get, before we alert the fucker to our presence.

Thomas's exact quote was: "Our chances of neutralizing him from a close, physical proximity increase as the distance between us and the target decreases."

In normal-people speak, that means the closer we are to Kyle when he's Inert, the less chance he has of escaping. Even if we fail to kill him in the Quiet, the closer we are to him in the real world, the better our chances are of catching up with him. Once we pull Kyle in, the element of surprise will be gone, so it makes perfect sense for us to position ourselves as optimally as possible before crossing that line. Despite rationally understanding all of this, part of me still wants his blood *now*—

"The hallway behind him is a problem," Thomas says, interrupting my thoughts. "We need to close it off. It's the likeliest escape route."

I nod, and we walk along the hallway. It's narrow, twisty, and poorly lit. The path widens into a little alcove that has better lighting. I notice an old painting of wine bottles in a heavyset frame. The picture confirms my impression that this whole place feels more like an old, musty wine cellar than something that leads to the stage of a modern-day conference hall. The painting must've been left over from the early days when the hall was a theater, or maybe it was someone's strange idea for an interesting hallway design.

"There," Thomas says, pointing at the security guard at the end of the hall. "Guide him to exit through that door and lock it."

Before I Guide the man, I Read him and mentally thank all the stars for the job I have. Had I ended up working as a security guard, I probably would've shot myself out of sheer boredom. All the poor guy does is sit or stand in one place for hours.

"Let's go," Thomas says when he sees me take my hand away from the security guard.

We make our way past Kyle and back onto the stage. Thomas finds another path that leads to and from the stage on the opposite side from where Kyle is standing. This looks to be the side that the presenters will use. This side also has a winding hallway with another guard standing at the end of it. I block off the exit by Guiding the guard in the same fashion as the other one.

Got to hand it to Thomas. He's fully aware of his surroundings and always thinking a few steps ahead when it comes to executing the plan.

We return to the stage, and I look around.

"There." Thomas points to a man wearing a long trench coat. "Let's start with the patsy."

I make my way to him and touch the shifty little man on the back of his head. He has a bald spot there, which makes his noggin look like a bowling ball. Before I concentrate on getting inside his mind, I rub the spot in a circular motion.

"For luck," I say defensively when I catch Thomas's incredulous look. Then I concentrate and enter a state of Coherence.

\* \* \*

We enter the conference hall and look around. We're confused. We forget why we came here and even how we got here. This is bad. Lost time. This has never happened before. Maybe it's the new meds?

At this point, Kyle's telltale presence enters his mind.

*Rejoice. You did it. You made your place in history. You'll remember shooting many people. You'll take the guns when they are handed to you. They are your guns. You'll shoot each gun into the air to make sure your prints are on them, and then use the last one to shoot yourself in the head.*

Then the presence is gone.

*So I'm finally doing it,* we think. *I will be remembered forever. Everyone at school will wish they had paid me more attention.*

I, Darren, disassociate from the patsy's stream of megalomaniacal thoughts. The thoughts are partly his own and partly inspired by what Kyle made him believe.

Bert was spot-on with his theory. Kyle set this guy up to take the blame for the shooting. It's also clear this individual had fantasized about doing something like this long before Kyle got to him. That's what's so clever about what Kyle is doing. When this guy is later investigated as the shooter, nothing will look out of place because he fits the profile.

But I also see this guy wouldn't have acted on his fantasies, not without the right nudge—which Kyle provided.

It's interesting to observe someone in the midst of being Pushed. There's a certain *feel* to it. The Pushed mind has a certainty about its course of action that I've never seen in an unaltered mind. This is what the mind of a zealot must be like. The man has absolute conviction in the actions he's about to carry out. Distractions don't exist. All that exists is the Push that Kyle gave the man. When I'm done with my revenge, I think I might Guide some people and then Read them afterwards. It would be nice to better understand how the mind of the Guided works.

For now, though, I begin a Guiding session of my own.

*You're going to leave this place. You realize you want to turn your life around. Get therapy, and if that doesn't work, check yourself into a mental institution. Make sure you're not a danger to yourself or to others.*

I continue along those lines until I'm convinced the guy won't end up on the news one day, and then exit his head.

* * *

"Are you sure my Guiding will override Kyle's?" I ask as soon as I'm back in the Quiet.

"Yes," Thomas says. "Whoever has the longest Reach will override the other. And Kyle's doesn't even compare to yours."

"Good. Who's next?"

"That man. The big one."

Now that he points him out to me, I can't believe I didn't notice the guy myself. This dude is as close to a giant as I've seen and hard to miss, particularly here, in a room full of scientists. I'm shocked no one suspects him of being up to something. Then again, they might think he's with security. He does have that sort of look.

I Read the man and learn that his name is Igor and that he's indeed here to kill a few people. He's being Pushed, though killing is not against this guy's principles. I wonder whether he'll get the usual amnesia that people get when they're Guided to do something against their nature.

I Guide him: *Stand by the stage, pretend you're with college security, and enjoy the lectures. Try to remember as much as you can.*

This might be as unnatural for the brute as killing is to a normal person. Ironically, now that I've overridden Kyle's instructions, he might very well experience amnesia.

"Who's next?" I say when I'm done with Igor.

"That guy, their leader. His name's Victor," Thomas says. "Given his file, I suspect he'll be doing the bulk of the killing. The guy was a sniper back in the day."

I walk up to Victor. He's tall and muscular. Unlike his Neanderthal colleague, he exudes a type of cold intelligence. His demeanor reminds me of Caleb. He's one of those people who always look like they own the room. I grab his wrist and focus.

* * *

Two targets at our six o'clock, we think methodically, planning our shots. We'll take them out as soon as we see Igor reaching for his weapon. It'll be fun to practice our marksmanship like this. We haven't had practice outside of a shooting range in ages. Killing that scum Shkillet in the club a few weeks back doesn't count. Not from a practice perspective anyhow, since it was nearly a point-blank shot.

I disassociate. Boy, do I never want to make an enemy of *this* guy. The way he thinks about shooting someone is cold. Zero regret, zero remorse. He feels the same about killing as I do about making a sandwich—just something you do when you need to.

I begin my override session.

*You will not shoot anyone. You're here to expand your intellectual horizons. You will peacefully listen to the lectures, and you will be entertained. After all of this is over, as you lie in bed tonight, you will seriously rethink your life of crime.*

Happy with my Guiding, I exit Victor's head.

* * *

"Can I override my own instructions if I need to?" I ask Thomas when I'm back.

"Easily," Thomas says. "It's just a matter of using up more Reach."

"Every time I Guide someone, I use up some of my Reach?"

"I thought that was obvious. Those of us who actually run out of Reach learn this quickly."

"It isn't obvious," I say. "I thought Reach only controlled the duration of your influence. How far into the future you can *reach*."

"That's also the case," Thomas says, "but every Guiding you do is cumulative, as far as Reach is concerned. I can Guide one person to do what I need for half an hour, or thirty people to do what I want for a minute, depending on what I'm trying to accomplish."

"So controlling as many people as my aunt and I can is a difficult feat?"

"It would be impossible for those with my range of Reach, which is a good thing. You have no idea how much harm someone like Kyle could do if he had your kind of Reach. He wouldn't need the mob or the patsy. Anyway, we should get back to the task at hand. That guy there, the one with the shades, is the next person you should work on."

It takes what feels like an hour before I reprogram all the Russian gangsters in this place. When I'm done, they're no longer planning on shooting people and handing their weapons to the crazy fall guy. Instead, this conference will set a new record for the number of Russian mobsters paying close attention to a science lecture.

"This will be our mark," Thomas says as we make our way out of the hall, referring to the second phase of his plan. "Here, by Row 20."

As we walk back to the car and to our bodies, I think about what's to come. It feels infinitely more doable now than when Thomas first outlined his plan. As I reach for my body to phase out into the real world, I'm filled with dark anticipation.

It's really happening. Kyle is going to get what's coming to him.

# CHAPTER TWENTY-ONE

The noises of the world return, and I look around. A guy wearing shades and a baseball cap, probably a student, is walking toward us. I phase into the Quiet and Guide him to sell me those items. When I phase out and begin the transaction, the guy wants a hundred bucks for the stuff. I debate Guiding him to give me a better price, but decide it would be too much like stealing and hand him the hundred-dollar bill. It's bad enough he's selling me things he wouldn't have otherwise dreamed of selling.

"Great disguise," Thomas says after I put my new gear on. He pulls out his own shades, the kind you often see 'agents' wearing. "Let's take a look in the back."

As I'd hoped, the back of his car is an armory.

"Take this," he says, handing me a heavy revolver. I take it and tuck it behind my back, under my shirt. I'm getting used to concealing guns gangster-style.

Thomas straps on a holster under his suit jacket and puts his own gun in. It's a much fancier piece that has some initials on the handle and even a laser sight. I begin asking whether he has another fancy gun like that when, without a word, Thomas heads toward the building. I follow.

"Keep your head down," he says once we enter the conference hall.

Though the place is the same in the real world as it was in the Quiet, the noise and movements are a stark contrast to our previous excursion. Without much ado, we split up. I walk to my designated right-hand walkway. I'm making sure Kyle doesn't pass by me, and Thomas is doing the same on his side.

As I walk through the crowd, I keep track of the row numbers. I'm looking for Row 20—the position Thomas decided was the optimal distance to Kyle's hideout, and the marker for me to phase into the Quiet and retrieve Thomas.

My walk is uneventful until Row 25, where I notice a scientist looking at me strangely.

This guy resembles a tall, overweight version of Bert, but dressed carelessly, like Eugene. I can tell the hatred on his face is not his natural expression. That's all that registers before the man closes the distance between us and tries to punch me in the stomach.

Without willing myself to, I quickly move aside. His punch never connects with my midsection. The Bert/Eugene-hybrid dude stumbles. I spot a white-haired woman out of the corner of my eye a second before I feel a sharp pain as she grabs me by the hair, girl-fight style. I grab her wrist and squeeze, gently but firmly.

"I don't want to break your hand, lady," I say.

She lets go, but I feel another stab of pain, this time in my shoulder. Having had enough of this weirdness and pain, I phase into the Quiet.

The people around me all have one thing in common: they're frozen in the process of attacking me. The pain I felt a moment ago was from a guy who stabbed me with a pencil. I'm lucky he didn't have one of those high-end metal pens on hand, because that would've really hurt. As is, his pencil broke off without breaking the skin.

These random, peaceful-looking people attacking me can only mean one thing. But to confirm my suspicions, I Read the white-haired woman who grabbed my hair.

As I thought, Kyle Pushed her to attack me.

Which means he's spotted me.

Shit.

I take a second to change their minds about attacking me, and then run over to Thomas. No one is attacking him, which means Kyle hasn't noticed him, or else Kyle doesn't realize we're here together. If that's the case, then he might not realize how much trouble he's really in. Or maybe his Reach only allowed him to control the group that's attacking me, leaving none to spare on the folks around Thomas. More likely, though, Kyle just didn't see Thomas, which is great.

Thomas's frozen face is looking intently in my frozen self's direction, watching as I'm getting attacked.

I touch him on the neck.

"Darren, I was about to pull you in. I saw those people go at you."

"Yeah, it's Kyle. Guess he saw me."

"He must be Splitting and walking the perimeter," Thomas says. "I was hoping he wouldn't be this cautious, and if he was, that he'd fail to penetrate our disguises in this crowd."

"Doesn't seem like he knows you're here."

"We have to move *now*. We're close enough to where he's hiding—"

"Unless he moved," I interrupt.

"He wouldn't have had the time to get more than a few feet," Thomas says. "And if he doesn't know I'm here, he might decide to stay put."

I walk toward the stage, taking my gun out of the back of my pants. My heart rate increases when I reach the right stage exit where Kyle was hiding just minutes ago. Only Kyle isn't there. I run down the cavern-like path Thomas and I explored earlier until I get to the first turn of the corridor and almost bump into him.

Thomas was right. Kyle didn't get far.

"He decided to get out of here," Thomas says from behind me. "Cautious as ever."

"Are you ready to do this?" I ask. "Should we pull him in?"

"Wait." He walks farther down and positions himself in front of frozen Kyle.

"You're hoping he materializes in front of you?" I ask.

"Yes. But just in case he shows up behind *you*, I want you to face away. Take the safety off your gun."

I do as Thomas says, though it feels odd. If Kyle shows up behind me, I won't even see Thomas put a bullet in the guy, a sight I'd enjoy.

"On three," Thomas says and counts down. When he reaches three, my body tenses. By now, Thomas must've touched Kyle to bring him in.

No one appears in front of me.

For a second, everything is silent.

Then I hear a grunt from behind me.

I turn around and see Kyle holding Thomas in a headlock. Kyle must've materialized behind Thomas. I don't have time to wonder whether Kyle has mastered the 'show up in unexpected places in the Quiet' technique. Right now, I need to do one thing and one thing only.

Raise my gun.

As I take aim, I hesitate. Even after all the training I've received from Caleb, there's still a chance I might hit Thomas. It takes me only a moment to decide to throw caution to the wind. I should make the shot, and even if I hit Thomas, he'll just wake up Inert in the real world, which won't kill him.

So I take closer aim.

Kyle looks at me. He must see the determination in my eyes. With his free left hand, he reaches into his vest and pulls out a knife.

"Thomas, watch out," I shout, but it's too late. Even though Thomas bends, breaking out of the headlock, Kyle manages to plunge the knife into Thomas's thigh, halfway to the hilt.

Thomas screams.

Kyle rips the knife out and raises his hand to stab my friend again.

I shoot at Kyle, squeezing the trigger with a sudden jerk.

My bullet hits the wall about a foot higher than where Kyle's head is. Clearly, shooting under intense stress is not a skill I've mastered. Still, it wasn't a wasted bullet, as Kyle doesn't wait for my next one. He releases Thomas and runs down the corridor.

Thomas falls to the ground, clutching his thigh.

I approach him, trying not to look at all the blood.

"Go after him," Thomas says through gritted teeth. "Remember the guard you Guided? Kyle can't learn that he's blocking the way in the real world."

Without hesitating, I run after Kyle. Thomas is right. The best course of action is to get Kyle before he learns that this hallway is a dead end. Then, after we make him Inert, he'll take this same path and find himself trapped. This, of course, assumes it's us who'll make him Inert and not the other way around.

I hear a gunshot. Then another. And a third.

I feel no pain, and I'm still in the Quiet, so I assume Kyle missed me. My ears ring as if he shot the gun directly into them.

Without meaning to, I note the big holes in the wall in front of me. One is about a foot away from where my head was about to be.

A foot away from being Inert again, a possibility I don't even want to consider.

I shoot in Kyle's general direction and run faster. At least four shots answer mine, and like me, he isn't aiming, just shooting at random. I think he's doing this to slow me down. But despite more gunshots, I don't stop. In a berserker-like mode, I actually speed up.

As I turn the next corner, another blast sounds in my ears. This one much closer than the others. The bullet misses my shoulder by the width of a finger.

I return the shot, though Kyle is already behind a corner.

Then I push my legs to their limits.

As I sprint, I feel that strange sensation that I first experienced on the Brooklyn Bridge and a few times since—a feeling like I'm about to phase into the Quiet, but hit a mental wall that prevents it.

I shake my head to clear it and turn into the alcove area we scoped out during our recon. And that's when I hear the sound of a thousand thunderclaps. The pain in my ears is instantly followed by a blast of agony in my right arm, as if someone took a baseball bat to it. A baseball bat made of red-hot iron. The impact causes me to drop my gun.

He shot me, part of my brain screams. A wave of nausea hits me.

With great effort, I ignore the pain in my arm and look up to see Kyle reloading his weapon.

As I look at him, my anger rekindles and turns into a wave of pure hatred. The bloodlust hits me harder than the gunshot to my arm. The thin veil of civility is gone, and I want to claw and bite the object of my fury until he's ripped into shreds. Except I'm in no position to do anything but watch as he shoots me. I don't accept this, though. Acting without thought, I run up to the wall. With my left hand, I grab the heavy, framed painting of wine bottles and launch it at Kyle.

As the thing flies, I hear the click of Kyle's reloaded weapon.

I get lucky. The corner of the frame hits him right in the face. In the seconds of confusion that it buys me, I close the distance between us.

Still acting without deliberate thought, I execute a move that part of me knows is from Krav Maga. My left palm secures Kyle's wrist, and my right palm hits the gun, sending waves of pain to my brain as it connects.

My reward is Kyle's screams, and shortly thereafter, the metal clink of the gun hitting the floor.

I look at Kyle's hand. His finger is so unnaturally bent that I have to assume it's broken. It seems that the move I executed created a fulcrum point around the midsection of the gun. And that, combined with the fact that his finger was on the trigger and the physics of how fingers don't bend to the side, caused this rather favorable development. I hope it hurts even worse than it looks.

To my shock, the injury doesn't stop Kyle from forming a fist, an action that must hurt like a motherfucker. Like me, he must be running on pure adrenaline.

He throws a punch at my head, and I instinctively block it with my right elbow while using the left to hit Kyle in the jaw. My counter hit connects with his face, but I'm too overwhelmed with pain to rejoice. Having a shot-up right arm is not optimal for hand-to-hand combat.

Kyle recovers from my hit much too quickly and reaches for his vest. That's where the knife is, I remember in an instant.

Instead of hitting him, I use Kyle's momentary distraction to note the location of his fallen gun. The gun is right under my feet, but if Kyle gets that knife out, the gun may as well be a light year away.

It's time to do something reckless.

I consciously execute a move I've only experienced in someone's memories. I think it's called a round kick. It's a move kickboxers regularly execute, but financial analysts not so much. The biggest danger is that I'll lose my balance.

My execution is perfect.

My foot connects with the side of Kyle's head with a loud smack.

I don't even lose my balance, and mentally thank Caleb for all his training.

Kyle is stunned. I capitalize on this with an uppercut, choosing to strike out with my uninjured left arm this time.

The result reminds me of what boxers often look like after a knockout blow. Kyle looks like he's about to fall. His eyes glaze over, and he almost looks drunk.

It's now or never. I bend over, reaching for his gun, but as I do, I remember something.

Feigning a loss like this is Kyle's signature move. He would beat me with this trick at least six out of ten times when we used to play Mortal Kombat or other fighting games—back when I was a kid and thought he was my uncle.

If that's what he's doing, I know I'm fucked. But at this point, I'm committed to picking up that gun, so I just do it.

Once I have the gun in my hand, I straighten and see that my fear was justified. Just like in all those virtual matches of the past, I fell for his ploy, but this time, the fight is real. Kyle is holding the knife by the blade and has his hand positioned for a throw.

Only he's not releasing the knife for some reason.

Is the bastard toying with me? Is he waiting for me to raise my gun by an inch, giving me hope, before he offs me?

"Don't," Kyle says.

Is he trying to talk to me? This makes no sense.

Then I notice he's not looking at me, but at something beside me. This could be a trick to distract me, but I don't see the point.

Things begin to fall into place when I see a red laser pointer dot on his forehead. Holding my breath, I follow his gaze.

The relief I feel is overwhelming. It's Thomas. He has a gun pointed right at Kyle's head. My friend must've limped his way here while I was keeping Kyle busy. That trip must've hurt like hell.

"Don't do it, Thomas," Kyle says. "Don't shoot. There's something important I have to tell you."

The look of disdain on Thomas's usually inexpressive face is all the answer he needs to give. His right index finger tightens around the trigger.

"I'm your father, Thomas," Kyle shouts. "You're about to shoot your own father."

The look of disdain vanishes from Thomas's face. It's replaced by one of utter confusion, the same look that must be adorning my face as well.

I so badly need some extra time to think that I feel that near-phasing-out feeling again. I'm breathing so fast I wonder if I'm hyperventilating. It reminds me of the Bellows Breath exercise Hillary taught me, only I'm not doing it on purpose.

I need to digest what Kyle just said, but time is the one thing I don't have.

If Kyle is lying to confuse Thomas, he succeeded.

I begin raising my gun, but it's too late. Before it's raised even a foot, Kyle capitalizes on the confusion he created and throws the knife at me.

Instead of pain, though, something very strange happens—something I experienced a long time ago, back when I was a kid.

I'm in what my kid-self would think of as the about-to-die mode, though now I have a better term for it.

I'm about to phase in.

And, like all those years ago, the transition is not instant.

Given how close I am to Kyle, the knife should've reached me before I even had the chance to think, but instead, I have enough time to watch the knife as it flies toward me at a millimeter per second. It's going to rotate in the air, I realize with wonder. The whole thing reminds me of watching one of those high-speed-camera movie clips that show you things in slow motion.

I use this time to think.

About how Thomas is half-Asian and my mom Lucy is Asian. About how Thomas, like me, was adopted. About the rape I witnessed in Lucy's mind. About the baby she was forced to give up—Kyle's baby.

Can it be?

Now that I think about it, some of Thomas's mannerisms are a lot like Lucy's. They even share the same stony expression.

Could Thomas and I be related? Could we be stepbrothers of sorts?

As I watch the knife penetrate my shirt, I realize it could be true. Kyle might be telling the truth.

As the knife pierces the top layer of skin, I focus on the horror of what's about to happen. Once this thing reaches my heart, I'll die in the Quiet and become Inert again. I'll be vulnerable right when I need my power most. Not to mention that with my mom in the hospital as she is, I can't run away to another vacation spot and hide. Nor do I want to hide. I'm through with hiding.

And then, as the pain of the stab wound slowly registers, my world goes completely black.

# CHAPTER TWENTY-TWO

The world isn't just black. The world isn't here.

I can't hear anything. I can't smell anything. I don't have any awareness of my body, not even things like my face or the top of my head. Because of this lack of body sensation, I also can't tell where I am in relation to anything else, nor if I'm lying down or standing up. Nothing. I can best describe this feeling as a sort of floating sensation, though that's a crude approximation, since when you float, you know exactly where you are. You just feel weightless. Whereas the best way to describe my current state would be as nonexistent.

*Did the knife kill me?* What I feel is how a disembodied ghost might feel, if such a being existed.

But that's silly. I couldn't have died from the knife wound. That's not how getting killed in the Quiet works. After getting killed, I'm supposed to return to my body in the real world, albeit regrettably Inert.

This is not that. The knife didn't even get far enough into my body to kill me before whatever this is happened. This must have something to do with the world slowing down around me, and the near-panic attack I was having at the threat of becoming Inert again.

Getting progressively more anxious, I try to feel something physical again. I picture having eyes, ears, a nose, and the rest of it. Hell, I'll even settle for feeling my left big toe.

Suddenly, though I still don't possess any of my senses, I'm aware of lights.

Awareness is the best word for it, because I'm not really *seeing* those lights. The word 'seeing' is the only term I have for it. It's like if I could suddenly experience echolocation like a bat and wanted to explain it to, say, Bert, who doesn't have echolocation, I'd tell him, "Dude, it's as though I can *see* in the pitch dark." And this is similar. I'm aware of the lights, though definitely not via my vision.

I'm distracted from worrying about how to define my experience when the lights grow brighter. Or to be a stickler, when my awareness of the lights gets stronger.

Are these stars?

No, stars are always above you, and though I don't have any idea where up or down is, I have a contradictory certainty that these lights are not above me, but rather near me. I can't explain this nearness, though. It's mere intuition that if I needed to, I could reach the lights. And I can't reach the stars.

I exercise this 'seeing' sense by squinting my metaphysical eyes. The lights are actually broken into three largish clouds, like three galaxies, only as I said, I'm sure these aren't stars.

The lights are connected by spindly pathways comprised of fainter light. If I had to prove that these aren't stars, these connections would cinch the deal, since stars aren't connected by strings of fainter light. Or are they? One thing I'm not is an expert in astronomy.

These spherical clouds remind me of something. The thing they remind me of is almost there in my mind, as if it's on the tip of my tongue.

A sense of anxiety threatens to overwhelm me as a simple explanation about what's happening surfaces in my consciousness.

For the first time since I met Mira in Atlantic City, I wonder whether I'm crazy after all. Insanity would explain pretty much everything.

Worse than insanity are the other plausible explanations. What if I'm having some sort of medical episode? Something like an epileptic seizure or a brain aneurysm? What if I'm just a naked brain floating in a vat of chemicals, and the lights are electrodes they're about to hook up to my neurons?

"Nothing like that is happening to you," a foreign thought states. I don't know how, but I know with absolute certainty that this voice isn't mine.

The imaginary voice in my head garners support for the 'I'm crazy' theory.

"No, you're not," the foreign thought states. "You're not imagining this. You're not schizophrenic. And I am real."

These thoughts aren't spoken by a voice in my head at all. Strictly speaking, no words are being spoken. The meaning of these words is simply appearing to me in my consciousness.

"Right you are," the voice thinks into my mind. "These thoughts are mine, and I'm projecting them onto you." A slight sense of warmth and camaraderie arrives along with the thoughts, like an extra texture layered on top of the meaning of the words.

"Who are you?" I try to explicitly think back. To myself, I think, *Wouldn't an imaginary friend always say they're real?*

"I am Mimir," the thought comes. "We met yesterday. At that time, you thought I was imaginary also, but I assure you I am as real now as I was then."

"Oh," I think. "You're the manifestation of the mind merge between me and the Enlightened? The very good-looking guy who was floating in the air?"

To myself, I think, *He wasn't all that real when I 'saw' him last.* Yet, despite my skepticism, I still feel a sense of relief at having someone—or something—familiar in this strange place.

"That's how you perceived me, yes," the thought appears. "And you're also correct in how you describe the way I came to exist. It was as a result of the Joining. And I did state that I am as real as when we last met, not more. Your definition of my realness at that time is another matter."

"Thank you for your warning, by the way," I think at him. "My mom would be dead if it weren't for you."

"You're welcome. I'm truly glad you were able to save her."

"What is this place? Where are you? And what the hell is going on?"

"Oh, come on, Darren. You already know. I gave you the necessary clue the last time we communicated. If not that, then think of what your aunt told you."

I suppress my panic to reflect. And then it hits me.

"I remember now," I think in relief. "When I asked what would happen to you in the long term, after the Joining was over, you said you'd phase into the Quiet, to what I, after talking with Hillary, call Level 2. This is the other tier, a deeper version of the Mind Dimension."

If this revelation is true, the implications are truly unfathomable. It would mean that I did it. I am what my Enlightened grandparents wanted to breed—but a generation earlier than they had thought possible, thanks to my mom's super-long Reach. This is just as Hillary suspected. After a number of close calls that felt like I was hitting a brick wall, I finally phased into the Quiet—while already being in the Quiet.

"Correct," he thinks back. "My phasing in was a success, and so was yours after the threat of going Inert, as well as other stresses, finally allowed you to phase into this place as I knew you had the capacity to do. Though I must add that I loathe the term 'Level 2.' If nothing else, this is tier three of reality, as you began in the real world."

"Okay, but what exactly is this? Where is everything?"

"The short answer would be that everything is here. The longer answer would take longer and sadly, like the last time, we must keep our conversation brief."

"Why?" I think disappointedly.

"Because I have no idea how long you can stay here."

"Does Depth get used up quicker here?"

"Yes, or at least, we suspect it does," Mimir thinks at me. "Though since you're the first and only person I'm ever going to meet here, the theory is not testable."

"Why am I the only person you're ever going to meet? Aren't there Guide Elders who can phase into Level 2?"

"When someone is in a Mind Dimension, it's their own personal space, not a shared place—"

"But you're here," I interrupt. "So either I'm in your Level 2, or you're in mine."

"No. The situation is a little stranger in our case. I'm a part of you, remember? So where I am, you can be, and vice versa."

"So, in theory, if my grandparents could phase in from the Quiet, you would be in the same Level 2 as they are?"

"Yes, but it's only hypothetical, since they don't have the required Depth. Which is why I stated that you're the only person I'll ever interact with."

"And yet you don't think I have a lot of time here."

"Affirmative."

"How much time do I have?"

"That's hard to say. To start, we don't know how much Depth you're currently using up. Even if we did, we don't know the limit of your Depth, even in the regular, Level 1 version of the Quiet. The furthest you've ever Read someone was Lucy, and you went a couple of decades back—"

"Wait, how do you know—"

"What you know, I know," Mimir thinks. "I thought that was obvious by now."

"Right," I think. "You're part of me."

"The reverse. You're a part of *me*. Knowing what our subparts—you and the others—are experiencing is one of the rare forms of entertainment my kind and I have. Which reminds me, please protect your grandparents and their Enlightened friends. I know you hold a grudge—"

"Your kind?" I interrupt again. "You mean there are other beings like you, here on Level 2?"

"Time," he reminds me. "We don't know how much you have."

"You're just dodging the question," I counter. "I think every time the Enlightened do their Joining, one of you turns up, and you can probably all hang out here because you have parts in common, or rather, people that make you up in common."

"It's an interesting hypothesis."

"If I'm right, is there a version comprised of me and Caleb here someplace? Since I Joined with him?"

"There is. Every Joining produces one of us, but the resulting beings can only Split into this realm when the cumulative Depth of the Joining participants that make them up is strong enough. The other cases are rather cruel twists of fate for the thinking creations that—"

"Wait," I think. "What's this Caleb/Darren thing like?"

"The dumbest among us, but a good lesson in human nature," he thinks. "But seriously, we might not have too much time . . ."

"Can you at least briefly tell me what this place is? What's the nature of Level 2? Why is it this way?

How does it relate to the regular Quiet? And most importantly, what am I supposed to do?"

"You can be very amusing," he thinks. "You're treating me as though I'm omniscient."

"Meaning you don't know?"

"I can tell you my personal theory. But I'll have to simplify it so a lesser mind like yours has the chance to understand it."

"Did you get your sense of humor from me?" I think irritably. "It sure sounds like something I'd say if I were in your position."

"A tiny portion of my sense of humor came from you, sure. In any case, here's what I think. When you're in what you call the Quiet, your mind is in fact only partially there. That part clings to the comforts of your common, everyday reality and, using something like the mechanisms responsible for dreams, makes up that familiar 'time-stopped' world for you."

"If the Quiet is a dream, then what is the reality?"

"That I am less sure about, but whatever it is, it's a lot closer to what you're experiencing now. I think here, on Level 2, some of the false veneer the mind clings to is gone."

"But this place doesn't make sense," I think. "All I see are lights."

"Those lights are neural networks, but you already knew that. It was on the tip of your brain."

He's right. In hindsight, the 'galaxies' with interconnected lights are reminiscent of the pictures I've seen in textbooks and online of the electrical activity of the brain.

"You got it," he thinks. "And more specifically, that bright constellation closest to you *is* you. The one closest to that version of you is Thomas, and the slightly farther one is Kyle."

"So if I could see myself right now, I'd see one of those neural-network-looking things?"

"Only yours wouldn't be slowed in time the way theirs are," he thinks. "It would be a kaleidoscope of firings between the neurons via the synapses. At least, that's what I imagine you'd see, if you could see it."

"You make it sound as if that's not your experience. And what do you mean time would be slowed? It's stopped, isn't it?"

"What you see is not the same as what I experience, but mine would be impossible for you to comprehend. And I am not teasing in this case. My point of view would be as foreign to you as yours would be to, say, a guinea pig."

"Are you saying that time isn't stopped?" I think insistently, refusing to feel insulted.

"What you've always perceived as time stopping, both in the Quiet and here, is an illusion. The truth is that time passes much faster from the reference point on the inside of the Quiet."

"You mean to say that if I watched the world from inside the Quiet long enough, people would actually move?"

"You'd get bored waiting for it, and it would take a monumental amount of time, but yes, in theory, that's the case. The 'time-stopped' people are actually super-slow-moving people."

"Wait," I think. "You phased out a day ago. Doesn't that mean you've spent a lot of time in here?"

"In a way, yes. But the way I experience the passage of time is different from the way you do. And speaking of time, we don't have a lot, remember?"

"So you keep reminding me whenever I ask you something about yourself. Let me guess, we don't have time for you to show me what you look like either?"

"On the contrary. I would love to know what you would 'see.' So if you insist, why don't you try to become cognizant of me? A lot of things work by a matter of will around here."

I try to see him, to become aware of him, and as soon as I do, a cacophony of light appears.

Lights surround me from every angle. Then the lights move into the distance, and I see the whole entity. If the other networks—the ones that turned out to be Thomas, Kyle, and me—look like galaxies, then Mimir's looks like the image of the early universe, but a dozen times brighter and with dozens more interconnected clusters.

Then the lights surround me again and he thinks, "You flatter me when you compare me to the universe." The 'stars' comprising him fade. "We really ought to get you started. There's something you must do."

"And what would that be exactly?"

"Use your powers to your advantage and then figure out how to get out of here. That sort of thing. Unless you have a better idea?"

"Why should I learn how to get out of here when you keep saying that I'll exit on my own when I run out of Depth?"

"Because you don't want to become Inert, do you?"

"Of course I don't. But won't I be Inert regardless? The knife Kyle threw at me in the Quiet is going to enter my body when I return."

"Phasing out of here might take you straight back to reality," he thinks. "In one of my theories, anyhow. So that's an incentive to try."

"Fine. I guess I'm a lab rat."

"Guinea pig," he thinks, and as much as it's possible to think with a smile, he manages it.

"How can I use my powers then? And for that matter, how do I exit? I have no body and no senses. I don't know where to even start."

"Start with Reading," he thinks. "And do it the way everything else is done here. Will it. Desire to absorb Thomas's pattern. This is what I've been doing with yours and what works for me, so it should work for you."

So *that's* what the lights surrounding me represented. He was absorbing my pattern. Spooky.

"You got it," he thinks. "I'll disconnect from you and leave you on your own."

Something changes. The feeling of nothingness, of not being, becomes stronger. I didn't realize how much Mimir's presence was grounding me.

Through sheer will, I suppress my panic and focus on Thomas's pattern.

I picture surrounding it.

I imagine merging with it.

It's unclear how long it takes, but I eventually find myself closer to the pattern.

Yes, that's the most precise way to explain it. I'm instantly closer, without actually moving toward it, like an electron in quantum mechanics. I jump without traveling the intervening distance.

I decide I'm on the right track and focus on his pattern some more.

Something happens much sooner now.

I find myself surrounding his pattern.

As I observe the light of the neurons that are now inside me, a familiar feeling surfaces in my mind. I recognize it as the state of Coherence—the now-familiar state when my mind feels focused and relaxed right before I Read someone.

And as soon as I enter this state, I enter Thomas's mind.

# CHAPTER TWENTY-THREE

The pain from the knife entering our leg is overwhelming.

We rip a sleeve off our suit and improvise a quick tourniquet to stop the bleeding.

The smart thing would be to stay put, as movement increases blood flow and bleeding out would make us Inert, which is unacceptable. But Darren needs our help, so with all our remaining strength, we limp through the corridor, each step more agonizing than the next.

Multiple shots are fired close by.

Damn it. We need to hurry before Darren gets himself killed.

On the bright side, Darren is clearly still alive. If he weren't, we would've been thrown out of his Mind Dimension.

I, Darren, disassociate. Reading from Level 2 is the same as Reading in the Quiet, with one notable exception. I'm Reading a Guide, which was previously thought to be impossible.

It's a relief to feel grounded in a body again, even if that body belongs to someone else. Despite the excruciating pain in Thomas's leg, I find it preferable to the nothingness of Level 2. I fleetingly feel bad for Mimir. He has to live on Level 2 for eternity. Then again, I strongly suspect he doesn't mind. Thinking of Mimir reminds me that I might not have a lot of time. This interrupts my strong desire to Read deeper into Thomas's past. As much as I want to learn more about my friend, I can't risk becoming Inert. Not when I know exactly what I need to do. I let his present memory unfold, waiting for it to push me out of his mind.

We hear more shots. We walk faster, and as we do, we fight the lightheadedness that comes from severe blood loss.

We enter the alcove.

We see Darren reaching for a gun and Kyle going from loopy to alert. The bastard must've been faking. It's too late to warn Darren.

We see Kyle motion to throw the knife and raise our gun to stop him. The gun feels like it weighs a ton. The laser sight hits Kyle in the eyes, and we get his attention.

"Don't. Don't do it, Thomas," he says. "Don't shoot. There's something important I have to tell you."

We don't dignify his plea with a response. Instead, we allow our contempt to show on our face. After that quick indulgence, we focus all our remaining energy on pulling the trigger.

"I'm your father, Thomas," Kyle yells. The meaning of his words sinks in a nanosecond before we're about to pull the trigger. "You're about to shoot your own father."

Our finger slackens over the trigger.

A frantic chain of thoughts rushes through our mind.

This fits every clue we've uncovered about our roots. One of our parents is Asian, while the other is white—a fact we've verified through DNA testing, though it's something we've known with a high degree of certainty just by looking in the mirror. From the United States census data, we learned that it's more than twice as likely that our father was the white parent. When we looked it up, there were 529,000 *white male/Asian female* married couples as opposed to only 219,000 *Asian male/white female* ones. Furthermore, since we've only ever met white Guides, it stood to reason that our father was likely the one with powers.

We never investigated our parentage further than this for one simple reason: if our father didn't want to claim us as his son, why the fuck would we want to seek him out?

Then all of this takes a backseat to a whole new realization. If he isn't lying, and every instinct tells us he isn't, then we met our mother today. We met her at the hospital. And she was there because Kyle had tried to kill her.

Darren's story hits us in a new light. Kyle raped our mother and proceeded to erase our existence from her memory. It was because of Kyle that she gave us up . . .

Belatedly, we realize we've allowed the fucker to do exactly what he'd planned with that revelation. We've let our guard down. And now we see Kyle's knife flying toward Darren.

This is our last chance. We have less than a second to act, and we hope it's enough. Our finger squeezes the trigger.

* * *

I'm ejected from Thomas's mind and back into the netherworld of Level 2. Maybe I should have called it something like The Darkness? Or better yet, Limbo or The Abyss? Of course, that's a decision for another time.

At this moment, I have to come up with a plan. Here are the facts: If I run out of time in Level 2, I'll become Inert. Assuming that doesn't happen and I find a way to phase out of here—and if Mimir's theory is wrong—I might find myself back in the Quiet with a knife in my chest, leaving me Inert yet again. It's unclear whether Kyle will be Inert as well, as it's a tricky matter of timing between Thomas's bullet that's racing toward Kyle and the knife that's on its way into my heart.

My plan needs to work even if I'm Inert and Kyle is not—and I think I have just the idea. It hinges on one thing: getting inside Kyle's mind.

I focus on Kyle's light pattern in the distance. Just like before, I close half the distance auto-magically.

Focusing some more, I surround him.

This time, I'm repulsed by the idea of what's about to happen, but there's no helping it.

I repeat the actions that helped me tap into Thomas's mind. I focus on the lights, the neurons that are Kyle. As I do, the Coherence state takes over, and with it, Kyle's vile thoughts.

* * *

We're walking toward Igor to give him his instructions. Boy, is that Russian fucker big.

In the crowd, we see an Asian woman stopped in time in the middle of a conversation with her scientist colleague. The woman looks nothing like Lucy, but we feel a pang of regret nonetheless. By now, Lucy is dead. Of course, we rationally understand why it had to be done. There was no other way. Yet some irrational part of us wishes there had been some alternative course of action.

*We're here on an important mission,* we recall. At that, we forget all other nonsense. *We have a task to accomplish,* the thought comes again, and it has a cleansing effect. We get back in the zone and the world is simple again. Our laser focus brings all of our attention back to the task at hand. All that exists are the targets—targets whose actions we need to control—and nothing else. A sense of righteousness overwhelms us. With their hubris unchecked, these arrogant scientists will bring about the end of the world. It falls unto us to stop them . . .

I, Darren, disassociate with a mental shudder. I'm no stranger to unsavory minds. Just a few weeks ago, I witnessed the mind of the sociopath Arkady—the Russian mobster whom Jacob and Kyle had used as their own pet assassin. I thought Kyle's mind would be similar, but it isn't. Arkady didn't give a fuck about right or wrong. He just wasn't wired to empathize with, or care about, other people's pain. Kyle isn't wired that way. Instead of being a certifiable psycho, it's his worldviews that are warping his actions. The views are made worse by his zealot-like determination to achieve his goals at any cost.

The focus that came over him when he thought about his current task is frightening. He had no doubts, or more correctly, he suppressed his doubts. He didn't worry for a millisecond about the people that would get hurt. He didn't stop to consider the option of not killing anyone. No. In his mind, whatever needed to be done would be done. Black and white. The rest of the world completely disappeared. This strange mode of thinking is familiar, but I can't quite grasp what it reminds me of.

It's time to give Kyle a taste of his own medicine.

If I can Read, I can Guide. If I can Guide, I can execute my plan. I give my instructions to Kyle the same as I would with any other person.

*You will feel too calm and relaxed the next time you try to Split into the Mind Dimension. You will not even think about the Mind Dimension. You are here on a work mission for the Organized Crime Unit. You're at this conference to neutralize some Russian mobsters. Here's how . . .*

After I give Kyle the rest of my Guiding directives, I exit his head.

* * *

I want to shower, immediately, but that would require having a body, which I currently lack in this Level 2 nether-realm. I quickly distance myself from Kyle and approach the pattern representing my Level 1 self.

It's pretty obvious what I need to do to phase out.

Touching is what allows me to Read and Guide people, as well as what allows me to exit the Quiet. So to leave this place, I just need to do the equivalent of what is considered touching here. Which happens to be that thing I just did with Thomas's and Kyle's patterns.

"Goodbye, Mimir," I think into the emptiness of Level 2. "I hope we meet again."

Without waiting for my enigmatic new friend to respond, I focus on trying to surround the pattern that represents *me*. Again, without moving, I'm simply there.

This is it. I try to become one with my pattern.

Before I even register it, the transition happens, and I'm out.

# CHAPTER TWENTY-FOUR

Sounds are back. Sights are back. Smells are back. I'm aware of my body—every toe and every tooth—and aware of my body breathing.

It's amazing how much sensory data our mind absorbs on a second-by-second basis. It's usually ignored, but right now, I'm aware of it all.

All these senses are glorious.

The relief I feel is overwhelming.

But I have to recover quickly. Things are in motion that I can't miss.

I quickly take stock of my situation. I'm back in the conference hall. I'm standing near Row 25, surrounded by scientists who were attacking me just a moment ago (from their perspective). But they've stopped attacking me. They're just looking around, confused.

Looks like I bypassed Level 1, aka the regular Quiet. Otherwise, I'd be in the alcove with a knife in my chest. So Mimir's theory was right, which is awesome, because it means I shouldn't be Inert.

I try to phase in. The world stops. Except now I know that it isn't 'stopped' so much as slowed to a crawl. *Semantics*, I think as I run to where Kyle is hiding.

He's already walking onto the stage when I reach him.

There's only one reason why he would be walking toward Thomas and I rather than running into the pathway: my Guiding worked and he's following my instructions. At least, that's the likeliest explanation.

Can I phase into Level 2 and Read him to make sure?

I try. I do what I'd do in the real world to phase out.

Nothing happens.

I guess I need to work out how to phase into Level 2 at will. Doing it once hasn't made it easier, just like phasing into the Quiet when I was a kid. I eventually learned how to phase into the Quiet at will, but I hope I won't have to repeat all those near-death shenanigans this time around. I shudder to think that I might have to have people almost kill me every time I want to enter Level 2. It would make my new talent damn near unusable.

I get back to my body and phase out.

The sounds are back. Kyle runs across the stage and to the stairs that lead off it. In a flash, he's off the stage again.

When he walks up to Igor, the tallest and biggest of the Russian gangsters, I know without a shadow of doubt that Kyle is following my script. He tells the mobster something. Though I'm too far away to hear him, I know he said, "Don't move, bitch," because that's what *I* made him say.

He jams his gun into Igor's side for the same reason. I made him empty the gun of bullets back in his hideout, but Igor the Giant doesn't know that.

I make my way closer to the stage to see the rest of the scene unfold, but something is nagging at the back of my mind—something that's distracting me from enjoying my revenge.

Meanwhile, Kyle drags his hostage onto the stage—a place where Victor, great marksman that he is, can shoot him, which is the culmination of my plan.

I notice people looking at the stage in disbelief. I can't blame them. How often do you see someone be taken hostage? Especially during a science convention? And especially when the hostage taker is half the size of the 'victim'?

As I get closer to Kyle, I see Victor drilling the stage with his eyes. "Let my colleague go!" he yells. "I give you two seconds."

Victor has a gun aimed in the direction of the stage, just as I suspected he would. This is it. He's going to shoot.

Seconds pass, and Victor continues to just stand there with his gun aimed at Kyle. For some unfathomable reason, he's not pulling the trigger. Gasps begin to emanate from the audience as people start to notice.

I look back. Thomas is walking toward Victor. It's unclear what Thomas is thinking of doing, but I bet he's trying to make sure no one gets hurt. That's good, because it means Thomas won't open fire in a crowded room and shoot Victor before he has the chance to kill Kyle. Still, Thomas is getting close enough to tackle the guy.

Why the hell is Victor not doing his part?

And then the answer hits me, and I phase into the Quiet.

I run toward the gangster, cursing myself. I explicitly Guided the man not to shoot anyone. So predictably, he isn't shooting.

It's impressive he raised the gun at all.

I walk up to Victor and touch his outstretched hand.

\* \* \*

*We're not going to shoot anyone*, the thought repeats in our mind like a mantra. Nothing else exists, only the mantra.

I, Darren, disassociate. This strange focus that the Guided possess is a marvel. I took Ritalin—the drug rumored to help with concentration—once, just to try it out. The focus the drug gave me was okay, but nowhere close to the single-mindedness of the Guided. It's eerie.

Okay, I broke it, so I have to fix it.

*You can shoot the guy on the stage. In fact, as a good leader, you must. When he's dead, you will throw away your gun, because it's out of bullets.*

Happy with my instructions, I exit Victor's head.

\* \* \*

On my way back to my body, I reinforce my earlier control over Victor's cronies. They are to remain peaceful observers. I approach my body and linger before phasing out of the Quiet. I can't shake the feeling that I'm missing some variable.

Fuck it, I decide, and touch my frozen self's forehead.

When the sounds of the room return, I realize what's been bugging me.

I must stop Victor.

I'm not ready for Kyle to die.

And then, as though defying my thoughts, a shot is fired.

Or did I imagine the gunshot?

I'm not sure because I'm again surrounded by silence. The gunshot, or maybe it was my epiphany, made me phase into the Quiet for the millionth time today.

I run toward Victor, hoping it's the stress and not an actual gunshot that made me phase in. If it isn't too late, I'll Guide Victor to not pull the trigger.

Only when I get there, I see Victor's gun surrounded by a cloud of smoke.

Shit.

I didn't imagine it. He did it. He shot Kyle.

I run toward the stage.

Maybe the bullet hasn't hit Kyle yet. If I can Read him before the bullet does its job, all will be well. I don't actually care whether the fucker lives. Quite the contrary. I just need information from him, which I can only get if Kyle is still alive.

Getting closer, my heart sinks as I see that the irreversible has already happened.

Kyle's head is in the process of blowing up.

Victor has lived up to his reputation as a marksman. The bullet hit Kyle right between the eyes.

# CHAPTER TWENTY-FIVE

As I stand there, looking at my dead enemy, my feelings fluctuate between elation and defeat. Kyle got what he deserved, but I'm too late to get the last piece of information that I need from the bastard.

I sit down on the ground to absorb it all.

I finally understand where that nagging feeling was coming from. I recognize what was familiar about Kyle's intense focus. As he was thinking about getting rid of these scientists, his thought pattern was nearly identical to that of his victims'. He had the telltale signs of someone being Guided, signs I kept seeing inside the minds of the very people *he* had Pushed.

I didn't recognize it for what it was because I'd been running on my outdated assumptions about the world. Assumptions like 'you can't Push a Pusher.' Only, as evidenced by Kyle following my instructions and getting himself killed, that old adage no longer applies. You *can* Guide a Guide. You just have to do it from Level 2. If I did it, someone else could've done it too. I wanted to delay Kyle's death long enough for me to Read him and corroborate my suspicions, or better yet, prove myself paranoid, but now it's too late.

I forgot something else while in the heat of the moment. Even if Kyle were alive, it's not like I can reach Level 2 at will. This cheers me up a little, and I start walking back to my body.

As I walk, other questions pertaining to this strange new possibility swirl through my mind.

If someone *did* Push Kyle, who was it? And why? It's clear Kyle was acting like a bastard on his own most of the time. But something tells me that in this case, he might've been unwilling to carry out his mission in this manner. A big public shooting wasn't Kyle's usual MO, as Bert would put it. My 'uncle' was usually more careful. Prior to today, he'd made sure he was never at the actual scene of the crime and was always careful about concealing his identity when Pushing people.

Then something else dawns on me. If Kyle *was* influenced, did he deserve to be executed? Was he as guilty as the guy who stabbed me with a pencil? If he was someone's tool, then he might've been innocent.

The thought makes my heart sink.

No, I realize after a moment. This theory doesn't hold up. Kyle clearly tried to kill Lucy on his own. He didn't have the signature zealot-like thinking there. Quite the opposite. He felt regret, which he wouldn't have felt had he been Guided to kill her. Not to mention, when he committed all those other atrocities, he'd had very personal motives, such as love/lust. Motives that only benefitted him. Which means he was guilty enough to get exactly what he received. If anything, justice might've been too swift for my taste.

I put the theory of Kyle being Pushed out of my mind. So what if someone forced him to start this massacre? What business is it of mine? It's not like I've been chosen as the protector of the scientific community. Besides, I stopped the shooting, didn't I? But by stopping this mess, did I make a new enemy? Assuming someone was nudging Kyle to do his dirty work, am I already his enemy? Seems likely, but I have no way to know for sure.

My gaze falls onto my frozen self. There's a light of realization in his glazed eyes.

"I know, buddy," I say to myself. "But you were too late."

I touch my frozen self on the neck and return to the real world.

The dead silence of the Quiet is a stark contrast with the screams of frightened scientists.

Nothing energizes a crowd to move more than the sound of a gunshot.

Everyone scrambles for the exits.

I debate phasing in to calm the crowd, but the commotion will let Thomas and me leave without drawing any attention to ourselves.

I look his way. He abandoned his idea of tackling Victor and is walking along with the frightened stream of conference attendees. I follow his lead and let the wave of people carry me to the exit.

Eventually, I reach Thomas's car, and he joins me a few minutes later.

"Get in," he says. "We need to get out of here."

He doesn't need to ask me twice. I get in the car, and we pull out of the parking lot.

After we exit the campus, we drive in silence for a while.

"What the hell happened?" Thomas asks. "The knife never made it into your body."

"So you noticed that?"

"It was hard not to. Also, I don't think my bullet made Kyle Inert."

"I don't think it did either," I say.

I don't know how to proceed. I want to tell Thomas everything, but I'm not sure how much I can share about Kyle's demise. Thomas is his son, after all.

"So?" Thomas presses me. "Are you going to give me an explanation?"

"Yes," I say, making a quick decision. "I was able to Split, as you would put it, while I was already in the Mind Dimension."

I go on to tell him about waking up bodiless in the darkness of Level 2, and about my chat with Mimir. He stops me when I get to the part where I Read him.

"You Read me, like Leachers do?" Thomas gives me a wary look. "How far back did you go?"

"I didn't learn anything particularly private," I say. I probably should've dug a little deeper. Seems like he's hiding something juicy, because he looks relieved when I tell him I only saw his pained walk through the Quiet.

When I reach the part where I entered Kyle's mind, Thomas says, "I don't want to hear any more. Given his strange behavior, I can guess the rest, but I'd rather not know exactly."

"I'm grateful—"

"Don't mention it," he says, and the unspoken words are 'ever again.'

My phone rings. I look at it.

"Do you mind?" I ask.

"Take it," he says.

"Hello," I say.

"Darren, what the fuck?" says Mira's voice from the other end. She says it so loudly I'm sure Thomas heard her.

"Hello to you too. You sound tense."

"Tense? You leave me a 'call me urgently' voicemail, and then proceed to ignore my calls and texts. How the fuck should I sound?"

"I'm sorry," I say. "I called you from the hospital. My mom nearly died."

"Oh . . ." Mira sounds stunned. "I'm so sorry. Is she okay?"

"She's fine now, and the person responsible . . . well, this isn't a phone conversation."

"Of course." Mira sounds contrite now.

"Where are you?" I ask.

"Stuck in traffic on my way to Manhattan. I didn't know where you were, but that seemed like a safe start. Plus, that's where your aunt lives."

"Have your driver turn around and take you to the Staten Island Hospital. That's where I'll be shortly."

"I'll see you there," she says. "Hillary says she's going too."

"See you soon." I hang up.

"I guess you want me to take you to the hospital," Thomas says.

"Please. And do you mind if I make another phone call?"

"Of course not."

I click on one of my 'favorites' in my phone.

"Darren," Sara exclaims as soon as the call connects. "Thank God you called."

"Hi, Mom. How's she doing?"

"You need to get here as soon as possible and talk some sense into your mother," Sara says.

"Why? What's wrong?"

"She woke up after a nap and decided she wants to check out. I need you to remind that woman that she was just in critical condition."

"I'll see what I can do, Mom," I say, trying to suppress a grin. "I should be there shortly."

"Hurry, or else she might actually talk the doctor into it," Sara says. "Love you, bye."

"Same to you. Bye," I say and end the call.

"So, she—Lucy—is feeling better?" Thomas asks.

"Sounds like it. She wants to check out."

"She sounds like a fighter." Thomas's voice is unusually soft. I can hear him drawing in a breath, and then he says, "Darren, listen... there's something I wanted to ask you. Do you think you could introduce me to her?"

It takes me a second to understand his discomfort. Once it sinks in, I can't believe how dense I am.

"Of course," I say. "I should have offered, especially since you just found out she's your biological mother."

"You're sure it's true?" he asks. "That she's my mother?"

"Very. But I guess you can get a DNA test if you want to be one-hundred-percent certain."

"What do you think she'll think about this whole thing?" he asks.

"To be honest, I have no idea. You have to remember that Kyle prevented her from remembering you exist."

"I understand." Thomas's jaw hardens. "If I told her I'm her son, she wouldn't even believe me."

"Maybe not today, but I can't think of a more healing way to tell her she has a son than to say, 'You have a son, and here he is.' When she's allowed to remember, she'll want to know what happened to you. We just need to talk to Liz and figure out how to let Lucy remember as gently as possible. Once she remembers she had you, I know she'll want to meet you."

"You're right," he says. "I can be patient."

"For now, though, I'll tell her you're my new best friend, and we'll find every excuse for you guys to hang out. Her birthday is coming up . . ."

"Thank you, Darren. You don't know how much—"

"Please don't," I say. "Not after you had my back, twice now."

"Sure. I won't mention it."

"Plus, we're sort of related. Isn't that weird?"

"I think it's wonderful," he says. "I never had a sibling, but always wanted one."

"I wanted one too." I grin. "In fact, I could've used a tough older brother back in school."

My phone rings again. I look at Thomas apologetically.

"Take it," Thomas says.

"Dude, how'd it go?" Bert asks from the other end of the phone.

"Good," I say. "Meet me at the hospital. We'll talk about it."

"I'm already here. I suspected this was where you'd go afterwards."

"You know me so well. Stay put." I hang up.

"Darren," Thomas says. "Can you tell me about her?"

"Of course. As you said, she's a fighter." And for the remainder of the trip to the hospital, I tell Thomas about Lucy and about her side of the family. I retell her stories of what it was like to immigrate to the US from China as a kid. I tell him about her career as a cop. How much of a pain she was from my perspective when I was growing up. How thrilled my adoptive grandparents on Lucy's side will be to have another grandson. And how she and Sara met. Thomas absorbs it all with fascination.

In a way, I envy him. I would give anything to be on my way to meeting Margret, my biological mother. But more than that, I'm happy for him, and I'm happy for Lucy. You can't choose family, they say, but if I could, Thomas would be on the short list of people I wouldn't mind being related to.

As we park in the Staten Island University Hospital visitors' parking lot, I use the moment to check my phone. According to the texts I received on the way, the late Miami arrivals are already here. They're waiting for me in the cafeteria.

"Let's go check how she's doing," I say to Thomas as we get out of the car. "I'll introduce you."

# CHAPTER TWENTY-SIX

"Mom, this is Thomas," I say once we confirm she's feeling better. "He's a good friend of mine, and like you, he's also in law enforcement. Sort of."

"Nice to meet you, Thomas." Lucy gives him a smile. "Are you from the Third Precinct by any chance?"

"No, ma'am," he says.

"Maybe from the Fourth then? There's something familiar about you."

I say nothing, as tempting as it is. I need to consult Liz about the best course of action.

"I'm in the Secret Service," Thomas says without blinking an eye. "So work is probably not where you know me from."

I phase in and have Thomas and Liz join me in the Quiet.

"I'm going to tell you the craziest thing you've ever heard," I say to Liz. In the silence that follows, I tell her about Thomas's connection to Lucy, and how we need her help to reunite them. "Also, along the way, we'll need to shield her from the news that Kyle is dead. If you agree that she shouldn't be put under any extra stress, that is."

"She should indeed be kept in the dark about Kyle for now," Liz says and crosses her arms. The unspoken, 'You shouldn't have killed Kyle,' is clearly implied. Though I was vague as to how Kyle died, I have a feeling Liz connected the dots.

"Hiding his death from Lucy will be easy. We can apply a few nudges here and there," I say. "We can make Lucy lose her phone, and by the time she gets another one, she'll be in a better place, mentally, to get the news."

"That could work," Liz says. "As to her learning about Thomas, you're right on that count too. Slow and careful is the best approach. I'll think of the best way to give her the news and run it by both of you."

"Great. Now I need to chat with Mira and company in the cafeteria." With that, I walk up to my body and phase out.

"Can I get anyone some food?" I ask. "I'm heading to the cafeteria."

"I'd love a salad," Sara says. "Or a light sandwich of some kind."

"Nothing for me, thanks," Lucy says. "I want to check out before dinner. I loathe hospital food."

"Are you sure, Mom?" I ask. "Are you really feeling better?"

"I feel fine," Lucy says. "And I hate hospitals."

"Let me see what your doctor thinks about this," I say. "Please don't check out until I'm back."

Lucy rolls her eyes, and I exit the room as Sara jumps into her anti-check-out tirade.

I Read a nearby nurse to learn the location of Dr. Jaint.

As I promised, I Read the good doctor to find out what he thinks about Mom checking out. In his medical opinion, it's clear she's fine and checking out would be better than staying; statistically speaking, she has a greater chance of catching some disease here, since hospitals are worse than subway cars when it comes to germs.

That errand done, I find my way to the cafeteria.

As soon as Mira sees me, she runs up to me and rises up to her tiptoes to give me a huge hug. Her unreserved display of affection surprises me. She holds the hug for a few beats and then kisses me. Trying to dispel my confusion, I kiss her back.

"How's your arm?" I ask, pulling back after a moment.

"Much better," she says and punches the air to demonstrate. "Eugene's doing better also. Come say hello."

"Great to see you," Eugene says when we reach their table. The black eye Caleb gave him only got worse overnight, but he seems to be in good spirits.

"Bert told us half the story," Hillary says, her hand mussing Bert's hair.

"Here's what happened after he left," I say and tell them the whole story.

Mira's face shows a strange emotion at the mention of Victor, but I don't stop my story to ask her about it; there'll be time for that later. Since Thomas isn't here, I don't omit the role I played in Kyle's death. I tell them how I Guided Kyle to get in Victor's sights, and how I Guided Victor to pull the trigger. I even mention my suspicions about Kyle being under someone else's control, a theory that makes Hillary furrow her brows. Another conversation that'll have to wait.

"I need to get back," I say once I'm done. "Got to check on my moms."

"And then?" Mira asks.

"Then I'll know what's what."

I grab a salad for Sara and make my way to Lucy's room. The doctor's there and Lucy's already in the process of checking out. This development doesn't surprise me. Lucy always gets her way.

After a brief discussion, the next step is also decided.

We are all cordially invited to a big dinner at my moms' house.

\* \* \*

Everyone fits at my moms' dinner table—a remarkable feat.

Amazingly, Thomas's presence was never questioned. Nor was the fact that he wanted to help Sara with the cooking.

"This stir-fried lettuce is amazing," Lucy says. "Where did you learn to make it?"

"My adoptive mother taught me," Thomas says. For the first time since I've known the guy, a grin shows up on his stoic face. "She came from China as a teen. She taught me a lot of authentic recipes."

"It brings back memories," Lucy says.

I give Liz a look, and she shakes her head. My mom is obviously talking about her nostalgia for authentic Chinese cuisine. She isn't remembering that Thomas is her son. I'm just paranoid when it comes to the topic of memory.

I recall something I haven't shared with my moms yet, and say, "I have an announcement to make." I wait until I have their attention and continue, "When you met Hillary, I introduced her as Bert's awesome girlfriend. To save time, though, I didn't tell you the whole story about her." I then proceed to tell Lucy and Sara a fictional story about how Bert looked into my biological parents using his computer skills and he connected what he found out about my mom to Hillary. "What I didn't tell you," I say in conclusion, "is that Hillary is my aunt."

A barrage of questions follow, and everyone learns a little about Hillary's tumultuous upbringing. She doesn't call her parents Traditionalists when she's talking to my moms, but she does describe how she and my biological mom rebelled against their very 'religious' and overbearing parents. Her story of my idiotic grandparents is a slight downer to an otherwise happy dinner.

"Speaking of how people met," Sara says. "You've never told us where you met this wonderful woman." She smiles at Mira.

She's clearly trying to guide the conversation toward a more cheerful topic. I don't mind, so I say, "It happened—"

"Let me take that one," Mira says, surprising me. What follows is another fictional account that makes me sound very assertive and macho. In Mira's version of events, I approached her at a dance club, bought her a drink, told her a funny story, and all in all, swept her off her feet. Then she goes on to tell them how I took her on a trip to Atlantic City the next day, on the spur of the moment. Apparently, I'm very spontaneous too. By the end, she makes me sound like one of those millionaire boyfriends in romance novels. Then again, I *am* a millionaire. And I *am* her boyfriend. At least, I think that's what I am. In any case, my moms gobble up Mira's story with plenty of oohs and ahhs.

After a couple of drinks, Eugene stands up. He's solemnly holding a shot of vodka.

"It's a Russian tradition. If no one minds, I'd like to say a toast," he says, looking at Mira.

She hesitantly gives him a slight nod.

"Let's drink to having made great new friends," he says with aplomb. "Let's drink to the health of the hostesses. They, who raised such an awesome offspring." He winks at me. "Let us also drink to newly reunited families," he says more seriously, "as nothing is as important as family—"

"Za zdorovje," Mira says and clinks her wine glass to Eugene's shot glass.

Eugene beams at his sister.

"Zdarove," my moms mumble, trying to match Mira's perfect Russian. They clink their glasses with the siblings'.

"Za zdorovje," Thomas says, seemingly without an accent. He adds his own clink to the mix.

"Salute," Liz says, adding her glass to the growing crowd of drinks.

"Cheers," Bert and I say, joining the clicking with our beer bottles.

Everyone drinks and from there, dinner becomes progressively merrier, reminding me of Thanksgiving.

When it's over, Mira and I end up staying at my moms' house for the night, while it's somehow decided that Eugene will crash over at Bert's. There's even mention of coding and/or experiments, which I suspect Hillary finds disturbing, even if she doesn't show it. Thomas and Liz leave together, but of course, we don't discuss their sleeping arrangements, as it probably falls under strict doctor-patient confidentiality.

"You can take the bedroom on the first floor," Sara says after locking the door behind everyone. "I changed all the sheets in your room and put new soap and shampoo in the guest shower."

"Thanks, Mom," I say, trying to seem nonchalant. It's weird when you know that your parents know you're about to have sex under their roof.

"Don't mention it," she says. "I hope you two can join us for brunch tomorrow."

"I'd love that," Mira says before I can make up an excuse.

Today is just full of surprises.

\* \* \*

"Can you try not to be as loud as usual?" I say after getting Mira's pesky clothes off her.

"There's two floors between us," Mira says with a smirk. "Do you really think they'll hear me?"

"I have no idea, but it would be weird if they did."

"Well," she says, giving me a mischievous wink, "I guess you'll have to shut me up *somehow*. I'm feeling very noisy all of a sudden."

I know full well she's not kidding, so on a whim, I phase into the Quiet and kiss frozen Mira's naked flesh.

When a second Mira appears in the Quiet and sees where I kissed her body, her breathing gets heavier, and her mischievous look transforms into something far more sensual.

"I like the way you think," she says as she approaches me, and then our bodies intertwine on the bed with an urgency that reminds me of the very first time we had sex.

When it's over, I phase out, and then go right back into the Quiet.

After Mira materializes in the Quiet, she says, "Darren, what the—"

Then she stops talking when she sees me. It's not just injuries that get reset in the Quiet. I'm ready for another round.

"Oh my," she says. "This is the best idea you've *ever* had."

She jumps on me, and we make this second round more mindful than the last.

And then we repeat the whole experience a dozen times over, getting more and more creative as we go. We even make use of the frozen versions of ourselves. Yeah, don't ask.

Eventually, pure mental exhaustion overcomes us.

"One day, I want to spend a whole month in the Mind Dimension," Mira says sleepily, back in the real world. "Just you and me."

"You say the word, and I'll do it," I say. "It sounds romantic."

She raises an eyebrow, yawns, and says, "Okay. But definitely not right now."

"No, not right now," I agree. Scooping her into a spooning position, I hold her, reveling in the warmth of her skin against mine.

As we lie together, I think about the past and all the things that have happened in such a short time. It's really amazing how much my life has changed. I never would've dreamed I'd be where I am at this very moment.

As I drift off to sleep, I think about the future. The nebulous threat of the Enlightened and whoever was manipulating Kyle is still out there, but at this particular moment, I can't bring myself to care. Whatever comes, I'll deal with it. For now, in my pleasant drowsy haze with Mira in my arms, I can't picture a future that isn't awesome. The details of this future materialize, making me feel as though I can touch them . . . and then I'm fast asleep, and the momentary epiphany becomes a happy dream.

# SNEAK PEEKS

Thank you for reading! If you would consider leaving a review, it would be greatly appreciated.

Darren's story continues in *The Elders (Mind Dimensions: Book 4)*, which will be available at most major retailers in 2015. In the meantime, you can read about Mira in a short story called *The Time Stopper*.

Please sign up for my newsletter at www.dimazales.com to be notified when the next book comes out.

If you like audiobooks, please be sure to check out this series and our other books on Audible.com.

And now, please turn the page for sneak peeks into my other works.

# EXCERPT FROM *THE SORCERY CODE*

Once a respected member of the Sorcerer Council and now an outcast, Blaise has spent the last year of his life working on a special magical object. The goal is to allow anyone to do magic, not just the sorcerer elite. The outcome of his quest is unlike anything he could've ever imagined—because, instead of an object, he creates Her.

She is Gala, and she is anything but inanimate. Born in the Spell Realm, she is beautiful and highly intelligent—and nobody knows what she's capable of. She will do anything to experience the world . . . even leave the man she is beginning to fall for.

Augusta, a powerful sorceress and Blaise's former fiancée, sees Blaise's deed as the ultimate hubris and Gala as an abomination that must be destroyed. In her quest to save the human race, Augusta will forge new alliances, becoming tangled in a web of intrigue that stretches further than any of them suspect. She may even have to turn to her new lover Barson, a ruthless warrior who might have an agenda of his own . . .

* * *

There was a naked woman on the floor of Blaise's study.

A beautiful naked woman.

Stunned, Blaise stared at the gorgeous creature who just appeared out of thin air. She was looking around with a bewildered expression on her face, apparently as shocked to be there as he was to be seeing her. Her wavy blond hair streamed down her back, partially covering a body that appeared to be perfection itself. Blaise tried not to think about that body and to focus on the situation instead.

A woman. A *She*, not an *It*. Blaise could hardly believe it. Could it be? Could this girl be the object?

She was sitting with her legs folded underneath her, propping herself up with one slim arm. There was something awkward about that pose, as though she didn't know what to do with her own limbs. In general, despite the curves that marked her a fully grown woman, there was a child-like innocence in the way she sat there, completely unselfconscious and totally unaware of her own appeal.

Clearing his throat, Blaise tried to think of what to say. In his wildest dreams, he couldn't have imagined this kind of outcome to the project that had consumed his entire life for the past several months.

Hearing the sound, she turned her head to look at him, and Blaise found himself staring into a pair of unusually clear blue eyes.

She blinked, then cocked her head to the side, studying him with visible curiosity. Blaise wondered what she was seeing. He hadn't seen the light of day in weeks, and he wouldn't be surprised if he looked like a mad sorcerer at this point. There was probably a week's worth of stubble covering his face, and he knew his dark hair was unbrushed and sticking out in every direction. If he'd known he would be facing a beautiful woman today, he would've done a grooming spell in the morning.

"Who am I?" she asked, startling Blaise. Her voice was soft and feminine, as alluring as the rest of her. "What is this place?"

"You don't know?" Blaise was glad he finally managed to string together a semi-coherent sentence. "You don't know who you are or where you are?"

She shook her head. "No."

Blaise swallowed. "I see."

"What am I?" she asked again, staring at him with those incredible eyes.

"Well," Blaise said slowly, "if you're not some cruel prankster or a figment of my imagination, then it's somewhat difficult to explain . . ."

She was watching his mouth as he spoke, and when he stopped, she looked up again, meeting his gaze. "It's strange," she said, "hearing words this way. These are the first real words I've heard."

Blaise felt a chill go down his spine. Getting up from his chair, he began to pace, trying to keep his eyes off her nude body. He had been expecting something to appear. A magical object, a thing. He just hadn't known what form that thing would take. A mirror, perhaps, or a lamp. Maybe even something as unusual as the Life Capture Sphere that sat on his desk like a large round diamond.

But a person? A female person at that?

To be fair, he had been trying to make the object intelligent, to ensure it would have the ability to comprehend human language and convert it into the code. Maybe he shouldn't be so surprised that the intelligence he invoked took on a human shape.

A beautiful, feminine, sensual shape.

*Focus, Blaise, focus.*

"Why are you walking like that?" She slowly got to her feet, her movements uncertain and strangely clumsy. "Should I be walking too? Is that how people talk to each other?"

Blaise stopped in front of her, doing his best to keep his eyes above her neck. "I'm sorry. I'm not accustomed to naked women in my study."

She ran her hands down her body, as though trying to feel it for the first time. Whatever her intent, Blaise found the gesture extremely erotic.

"Is something wrong with the way I look?" she asked. It was such a typical feminine concern that Blaise had to stifle a smile.

"Quite the opposite," he assured her. "You look unimaginably good." So good, in fact, that he was having trouble concentrating on anything but her delicate curves. She was of medium height, and so perfectly proportioned that she could've been used as a sculptor's template.

"Why do I look this way?" A small frown creased her smooth forehead. "What am I?" That last part seemed to be puzzling her the most.

Blaise took a deep breath, trying to calm his racing pulse. "I think I can try to venture a guess, but before I do, I want to give you some clothing. Please wait here—I'll be right back."

And without waiting for her answer, he hurried out of the room.

\* \* \*

*The Sorcery Code* is currently available at most retailers. If you'd like to learn more, please visit my website at www.dimazales.com. You can also connect with me on Facebook, Twitter, and Goodreads.

# EXCERPT FROM *CLOSE LIAISONS*
# BY ANNA ZAIRES

**Note:** *Close Liaisons* is Dima Zales's collaboration
with Anna Zaires and is the first book in the
internationally bestselling erotic sci-fi romance
series, the Krinar Chronicles. It contains explicit
sexual content and is not intended for readers under
eighteen.

* * *

*A dark and edgy romance that will appeal to fans of
erotic and turbulent relationships . . .*

In the near future, the Krinar rule the Earth. An advanced race from another galaxy, they are still a mystery to us—and we are completely at their mercy.

Shy and innocent, Mia Stalis is a college student in New York City who has led a very normal life. Like most people, she's never had any interactions with the invaders—until one fateful day in the park changes everything. Having caught Korum's eye, she must now contend with a powerful, dangerously seductive Krinar who wants to possess her and will stop at nothing to make her his own.

How far would you go to regain your freedom? How much would you sacrifice to help your people? What choice will you make when you begin to fall for your enemy?

\* \* \*

The air was crisp and clear as Mia walked briskly down a winding path in Central Park. Signs of spring were everywhere, from tiny buds on still-bare trees to the proliferation of nannies out to enjoy the first warm day with their rambunctious charges.

It was strange how much everything had changed in the last few years, and yet how much remained the same. If anyone had asked Mia ten years ago how she thought life might be after an alien invasion, this would have been nowhere near her imaginings. *Independence Day, The War of the Worlds*—none of these were even close to the reality of encountering a more advanced civilization. There had been no fight, no resistance of any kind on government level—because *they* had not allowed it. In hindsight, it was clear how silly those movies had been. Nuclear weapons, satellites, fighter jets—these were little more than rocks and sticks to an ancient civilization that could cross the universe faster than the speed of light.

Spotting an empty bench near the lake, Mia gratefully headed for it, her shoulders feeling the strain of the backpack filled with her chunky twelve-year-old laptop and old-fashioned paper books. At twenty-one, she sometimes felt old, out of step with the fast-paced new world of razor-slim tablets and cell phones embedded in wristwatches. The pace of technological progress had not slowed since K-Day; if anything, many of the new gadgets had been influenced by what the Krinar had. Not that the Ks had shared any of their precious technology; as far as they were concerned, their little experiment had to continue uninterrupted.

Unzipping her bag, Mia took out her old Mac. The thing was heavy and slow, but it worked—and as a starving college student, Mia could not afford anything better. Logging on, she opened a blank Word document and prepared to start the torturous process of writing her Sociology paper.

Ten minutes and exactly zero words later, she stopped. Who was she kidding? If she really wanted to write the damn thing, she would've never come to the park. As tempting as it was to pretend that she could enjoy the fresh air and be productive at the same time, those two had never been compatible in her experience. A musty old library was a much better setting for anything requiring that kind of brainpower exertion.

Mentally kicking herself for her own laziness, Mia let out a sigh and started looking around instead. People-watching in New York never failed to amuse her.

The tableau was a familiar one, with the requisite homeless person occupying a nearby bench—thank God it wasn't the closest one to her, since he looked like he might smell very ripe—and two nannies chatting with each other in Spanish as they pushed their Bugaboos at a leisurely pace. A girl jogged on a path a little further ahead, her bright pink Reeboks contrasting nicely with her blue leggings. Mia's gaze followed the jogger as she rounded the corner, envying her athleticism. Her own hectic schedule allowed her little time to exercise, and she doubted she could keep up with the girl for even a mile at this point.

To the right, she could see the Bow Bridge over the lake. A man was leaning on the railing, looking out over the water. His face was turned away from Mia, so she could only see part of his profile. Nevertheless, something about him caught her attention.

She wasn't sure what it was. He was definitely tall and seemed well-built under the expensive-looking trench coat he was wearing, but that was only part of the story. Tall, good-looking men were common in model-infested New York City. No, it was something else. Perhaps it was the way he stood—very still, with no extra movements. His hair was dark and glossy under the bright afternoon sun, just long enough in the front to move slightly in the warm spring breeze.

He also stood alone.

That's it, Mia realized. The normally popular and picturesque bridge was completely deserted, except for the man who was standing on it. Everyone appeared to be giving it a wide berth for some unknown reason. In fact, with the exception of herself and her potentially aromatic homeless neighbor, the entire row of benches in the highly desirable waterfront location was empty.

As though sensing her gaze on him, the object of her attention slowly turned his head and looked directly at Mia. Before her conscious brain could even make the connection, she felt her blood turn to ice, leaving her paralyzed in place and helpless to do anything but stare at the predator who now seemed to be examining her with interest.

* * *

*Breathe, Mia, breathe.* Somewhere in the back of her mind, a small rational voice kept repeating those words. That same oddly objective part of her noted his symmetric face structure, with golden skin stretched tightly over high cheekbones and a firm jaw. Pictures and videos of Ks that she'd seen had hardly done them justice. Standing no more than thirty feet away, the creature was simply stunning.

As she continued staring at him, still frozen in place, he straightened and began walking toward her. Or rather stalking toward her, she thought stupidly, as his every movement reminded her of a jungle cat sinuously approaching a gazelle. All the while, his eyes never left hers. As he approached, she could make out individual yellow flecks in his light golden eyes and the thick long lashes surrounding them.

She watched in horrified disbelief as he sat down on her bench, less than two feet away from her, and smiled, showing white even teeth. No fangs, she noted with some functioning part of her brain. Not even a hint of them. That used to be another myth about them, like their supposed abhorrence of the sun.

"What's your name?" The creature practically purred the question at her. His voice was low and smooth, completely unaccented. His nostrils flared slightly, as though inhaling her scent.

"Um . . ." Mia swallowed nervously. "M-Mia."

"Mia," he repeated slowly, seemingly savoring her name. "Mia what?"

"Mia Stalis." Oh crap, why did he want to know her name? Why was he here, talking to her? In general, what was he doing in Central Park, so far away from any of the K Centers? *Breathe, Mia, breathe.*

"Relax, Mia Stalis." His smile got wider, exposing a dimple in his left cheek. A dimple? Ks had dimples? "Have you never encountered one of us before?"

"No, I haven't," Mia exhaled sharply, realizing that she was holding her breath. She was proud that her voice didn't sound as shaky as she felt. Should she ask? Did she want to know?

She gathered her courage. "What, um——" Another swallow. "What do you want from me?"

"For now, conversation." He looked like he was about to laugh at her, those gold eyes crinkling slightly at the corners.

Strangely, that pissed her off enough to take the edge off her fear. If there was anything Mia hated, it was being laughed at. With her short, skinny stature and a general lack of social skills that came from an awkward teenage phase involving every girl's nightmare of braces, frizzy hair, and glasses, Mia had more than enough experience being the butt of someone's joke.

She lifted her chin belligerently. "Okay, then, what is *your* name?"

"It's Korum."

"Just Korum?"

"We don't really have last names, not the way you do. My full name is much longer, but you wouldn't be able to pronounce it if I told you."

Okay, that was interesting. She now remembered reading something like that in *The New York Times*. So far, so good. Her legs had nearly stopped shaking, and her breathing was returning to normal. Maybe, just maybe, she would get out of this alive. This conversation business seemed safe enough, although the way he kept staring at her with those unblinking yellowish eyes was unnerving. She decided to keep him talking.

"What are you doing here, Korum?"

"I just told you, making conversation with you, Mia." His voice again held a hint of laughter.

Frustrated, Mia blew out her breath. "I meant, what are you doing here in Central Park? In New York City in general?"

He smiled again, cocking his head slightly to the side. "Maybe I'm hoping to meet a pretty curly-haired girl."

Okay, enough was enough. He was clearly toying with her. Now that she could think a little again, she realized that they were in the middle of Central Park, in full view of about a gazillion spectators. She surreptitiously glanced around to confirm that. Yep, sure enough, although people were obviously steering clear of her bench and its otherworldly occupant, there were a number of brave souls staring their way from further up the path. A couple were even cautiously filming them with their wristwatch cameras. If the K tried anything with her, it would be on YouTube in the blink of an eye, and he had to know it. Of course, he may or may not care about that.

Still, going on the assumption that since she'd never come across any videos of K assaults on college students in the middle of Central Park, she was relatively safe, Mia cautiously reached for her laptop and lifted it to stuff it back into her backpack.

"Let me help you with that, Mia—"

And before she could blink, she felt him take her heavy laptop from her suddenly boneless fingers, gently brushing against her knuckles in the process. A sensation similar to a mild electric shock shot through Mia at his touch, leaving her nerve endings tingling in its wake.

Reaching for her backpack, he carefully put away the laptop in a smooth, sinuous motion. "There you go, all better now."

Oh God, he had touched her. Maybe her theory about the safety of public locations was bogus. She felt her breathing speeding up again, and her heart rate was probably well into the anaerobic zone at this point.

"I have to go now . . . Bye!"

How she managed to squeeze out those words without hyperventilating, she would never know. Grabbing the strap of the backpack he'd just put down, she jumped to her feet, noting somewhere in the back of her mind that her earlier paralysis seemed to be gone.

"Bye, Mia. I will see you later." His softly mocking voice carried in the clear spring air as she took off, nearly running in her haste to get away.

* * *

If you'd like to find out more, please visit Anna's website at www.annazaires.com. *Close Liaisons* is currently available at most retailers.

# ABOUT THE AUTHOR

Dima Zales is a *USA Today* bestselling science fiction and fantasy author residing in Palm Coast, Florida. Prior to becoming a writer, he worked in the software development industry in New York as both a programmer and an executive. From high-frequency trading software for big banks to mobile apps for popular magazines, Dima has done it all. In 2013, he left the software industry in order to concentrate on his writing career.

Dima holds a Master's degree in Computer Science from NYU and a dual undergraduate degree in Computer Science / Psychology from Brooklyn College. He also has a number of hobbies and interests, the most unusual of which might be professional-level mentalism. He simulates mind reading on stage and close-up, and has done shows for corporations, wealthy individuals, and friends.

He is also into healthy eating and fitness, so he should live long enough to finish all the book projects he starts. In fact, he very much hopes to catch the technological advancements that might let him live forever (biologically or otherwise). Aside from that, he also enjoys learning about current and future technologies that might enhance our lives, including artificial intelligence, biofeedback, brain-to-computer interfaces, and brain-enhancing implants.

In addition to writing The Sorcery Code series and Mind Dimensions series, Dima has collaborated on a number of romance novels with his wife, Anna Zaires. The Krinar Chronicles, an erotic science fiction series, is an international bestseller and has been recognized by the likes of Marie Claire and Woman's Day. If you like erotic romance with a unique plot, please feel free to check it out. Keep in mind, though, Anna Zaires's books are going to be much more explicit.

Anna Zaires is the love of his life and a huge inspiration in every aspect of his writing. She definitely adds her magic touch to anything Dima creates, and the books would not be the same without her. Dima's fans are strongly encouraged to learn more about Anna and her work at www.annazaires.com.

CPSIA information can be obtained
at www.ICGtesting.com
Printed in the USA
LVOW01s2128271016
510551LV00012B/1415/P